AN UNEXPECTED SLEEPOVER

The kind of man Belle one day married didn't need to be rich in money, just love—oh, and he also had to be a full-blooded Fairy.

Sighing at the improbability of meeting such a model match, she rolled over, relishing the wide open spaces of the antique bed.

When that spot warmed, she rolled over again, only this time her path was blocked—by muscle.

Manly muscle.

After sliding a good couple feet to safety, she glanced that way to find a shadowy figure reclining against the headboard, long, tuxedo-clad legs crossed at the ankles.

"What the—" She sharply pulled back again, as if a rattler shared her bed.

"Leavin' so soon, *Princess?*" Sinewy strong arms pulled her back against the hot, hard length of Daniel "Boone" Wentworth.

"I think the better question is," Belle said, squirming toward freedom, but not making a whole lot of progress. "What the heck are you doing in my bed?"

LAURA MARIE ALTOM

Sleep Tight

LOVE SPELL   NEW YORK CITY

LOVE SPELL®

September 2004

Published by

Dorchester Publishing Co., Inc.
200 Madison Avenue
New York, NY 10016

ISBN 0-505-52569-0

Visit us on the web at www.dorchesterpub.com.

*For hunk and real-life angel, Cozumel dive master,
Jose Luis Xiu, who held my hand
through the most terrifying drift dive ever!*

*And to my favorite adventurer
and all-around cool kid, my son, Terry.
I love you, sweetie!*

Sleep Tight

Prologue

Darkness swallowed Boone whole.

Consumed him.

Crept into every pore of not just his body, but his soul.

I'm coming for you, it said.

Noooo . . . Boone fought back, his sweating, drugged limbs writhing between the sheets. He wasn't ready to die. Not like this.

He fought against the dark, but it seduced him, beckoning him into warm waters where there were no rights or wrongs—only his own desires. Powers beyond imagination entitling him to everything in this world and others that was rightfully his.

Come, my child . . . This is more than just your birthright, 'tis destiny.

It would be so easy.

Following the voice.

The swell of emotions dark hot sexy swirling through him on spokes of pleasure pain.

1

That's right. Come to me . . . Come to me . . .

No. He had to fight. To find his way back into the light. To life.

Ahhh, it said, *but for you, does light represent life, or perhaps death?*

The question was a trick.

Boone knew this, but at the same time, wondered if maybe what the voice said could be true.

Could everything he thought real be wrong?

Was the whole world upside down?

Or just him?

Chapter One

Tonight

The place was different.

Smelled different.

Like sex.

A sort of faintly sweet, pissy smell causing his nostrils to flare and his groin to tighten.

He was hungry. Always hungry.

Boone dragged in a deep breath. No. All of that before—it was just a dream. He wasn't giving in to it.

Not here.

Not now.

He had a longneck beer in one hand. With his free hand, he squeezed the marble newel post of his childhood home's entry-hall staircase and forced an *everything's normal* smile that he figured probably looked more like a panicked grimace.

Boone squeezed the post harder, absorbing the cool marble's strength.

He squared his shoulders.

3

Reminded himself he was Daniel Eli Freakin' Wentworth IV. Master of all he surveyed.

Granted, it might sound a little corny seeing as how all he currently surveyed was one of his ma's never-ending parties, but for the moment, it would have to do. In light of his apparently worsening mental state, affirmations of the man he'd once been were all he had left.

"Simmer down, everybody," Maude Wentworth—his mother—urged from the base of stairs that *Architectural Digest* had called architectural Botticelli. After reading that phrase, Boone's dad had snorted beer all over himself. Ma had just preened. She really got off on that kind of public stroke. Reputation didn't just matter to her—it was *everything*. Her innate need to be loved. And with his dad gone, that need was getting harder and harder to fulfill—hence the formality of tonight's shindig. The snobby nouveau riche of Clairemonte Falls, Texas, ate up this hoity-toity crap. "The princess isn't used to such rowdy crowds. We don't want her offended by her very first Texas function."

Boone cast his mom an affectionate grin.

After the pain she'd gone through in suddenly losing his father to a heart attack just six months earlier, it was good to see her smiling again—at least for the short time they still had together.

As hard as she'd taken his father's death, there was no telling what she'd do when she found out her son didn't have long on this earth.

Boone took another swig of his beer.

Damn this persistently dry throat.

And his eyes—they stung like someone shook 'em full of Tabasco. Even though he knew it wouldn't help, he released his death grip on the newel post to give 'em a good rub.

More beer.

He definitely needed more beer.

And for the screeching violinists his ma hired to stop.

Okay, so he didn't quite get the big deal about her having a genuine, fresh-off-the-boat-from-Europe royal co-hosting her latest soiree, but if being in the company of a princess brought the roses back to her cheeks, that was good enough reason for him. But the white roses stinkin' up the place like she was hosting some country-music queen's funeral—those, his newly heightened sense of smell could do without.

Maryvale Clawson, the most influential grande dame of Clairemonte Falls, leaned forward to ask Maude, "Do you know if the princess has anything planned for next Saturday night?"

"Shh!" Maude scolded, hand to the heaving bosom of her black-beaded gown. "Curtsy. Here she comes, everyone. Curtsy! *Curtsy!*"

A lazy smile tugged at Boone's lips.

Way to go, Mom, take that old Maryvale down a notch.

Five trumpeters blared a ceremonial fanfare, but while everyone else in the room made complete jackasses of themselves by bending and squatting in their too-tight clothes, Boone adopted a Rhett Butler pose, resting his elbow on one of the massive newel posts flanking the foot of the stairs. He'd place bets that the smirk on his face resembled Rhett's, too, only he wasn't going to get caught by some scrappy thing like Scarlett.

Nope.

His health issues aside, after what had happened to him the last time he'd fallen for a member of the fairer sex, he now knew he was destined to die lonely. A real kick in the pants seeing how much he'd looked forward to one day settling down with a wife and kids. Hell, he'd even been looking forward to one day getting a dog.

Judging by his current rate of decline, though, he wouldn't be around to see his next birthday. That being the case, he didn't much think it was fair to go getting a pup, only to leave the little fella homeless.

Easing the knot in his throat with one more sip of beer, Boone returned his attention to the matter at hand.

Damn.

Even if he was dying, maybe he'd been a bit hasty in swearing off *all* women.

He gazed up the stairs he used to slide down as a boy. The crazy beautiful creature poised at the top stole Boone's next breath.

The princess walked—no, floated—down those stairs, her champagne-colored, piled-high hair calling out to the bad boy in him.

Come and get me, you big stud. See this pin right here? The one right at the tip of your itchin' fingers? All you gotta do is tug right here, and all this luscious hair is gonna spill all over my juicy fruits, and then—

Boone took another swig of beer before discreetly readjusting his boys.

That smell of sex? It emanated from her.

She held her head high—regally. A good thing, seeing how she was a genuine princess. Dressed in that painted-on gold number, her pale skin looked delicate as a piece of his ma's pricey porcelain.

The one thing not delicate about this woman was her expression. Her unforgettable features showed as much determination and sheer will to succeed as he used to display while chairing corporate board meetings. But he'd given up life in the fast lane because . . . Well, with so much livin' to do, he wasn't going to think about dying anymore tonight. Unlike himself, she looked at the top of her game.

She wasn't any run-of-the-mill ordinary princess.

She was a female *warrior*.

Realizing this was the kind of woman who inspired poetry, Boone took a fortifying breath—just in case all the beer he'd downed left him needing to rhapsodize about how her blue eyes reminded him of a pair of Texas bluebonnets perched on a field of pale winter wheat.

She reached the bottom stair, nodded at him, then smiled with a slight show of perfect white teeth.

Okay, so it might not be romantic, but ever since he'd traded his penthouse for the privacy of the family farm, which was located smack dab in the middle of nowhere, he'd learned a whole new appreciation for good dental health.

While Boone continued his frank appraisal of the princess, beside him his mother abandoned her curtsy to stand upright. "Your Highness," she said. "It's an honor to have you in our humble home."

The angel nodded that gorgeous head of hers again, only this time she aimed her thousand-watt smile straight at Maude.

Thwang!

There went Cupid zinging an arrow straight through his mother's heart.

Not good. As fine as this princess was, there was no use in his ma gettin' her hopes up. Due to fate's latest kick in the pants, grandkids were out of the picture.

Still, for no other reason than stubborn pride, while the angel wasn't looking, Boone mussed up his hair and straightened his bow tie.

"P-princess." Maryvale's eyes glowed with admiration. "Y-you're just . . . breathtaking."

As if used to such high praise, the angel merely nodded, then curved her lips into a mysterious sliver of a smile as she glided her way down the receiving line Maude had insisted her partygoers form.

Boone was now in the much-enviable position of seeing the princess's backside, and that was even hotter than her healthy white teeth!

And her scent—sleepy sexy Saturday morning after a *looong* Friday night.

He swallowed hard.

Well, at least one thing was for certain: After this impressive event, his mother's social standing would skyrocket. He'd never given a flip about what other people thought, but lately Maude had cared more than ever. And since he loved her fiercely, that meant he'd give her one hundred percent of his support—up to a point.

While he couldn't give her what she really wanted by extending the family, he would box the ears off anyone who stood in the way of her social happiness.

Nod. Smile. Stand straighter. Think Grace Kelly. Ingrid Bergman.

Arabella Antoinette Moody, or Belle, as everyone called her, had spent two weeks training for this job, but after the hours it had taken to reach the end of the receiving line, then join the party already under way in the ballroom, her lips now felt frozen in a smile. That trick her pageant-loving friend Vicky had taught her about rubbing Vaseline on her teeth to help improve her smile had worked too well.

Her back hurt, her feet hurt—even the back of her head hurt, especially where that antique silver hairpin Aunt Lila bought for a quarter at a yard sale kept stabbing the nape of her neck.

Momentarily ignoring her physical discomforts, Belle straightened, adding an extra half inch to her already statuesque five-nine frame.

Maude Wentworth approaching at three o'clock.

"Princess Shubi-tr-twa-swis . . ."

Belle nodded and smiled at the way Maude butchered her name, all the while thanking her Uncle Philbert, a retired Easter Bunny, for coming up with that all-consonant idea. It was Philbert who'd pointed out that if no one could spell her name—let alone pronounce it—then they sure couldn't do any fancy background checking.

Not that anyone using a mortal directory would've had much luck anyway. But just in case.

Guilt again clogged Belle's throat.

Oh, what a tangled web we weave . . .

"No," Maude said with a frustrated furrowing of her penciled-on eyebrows. "I meant to say Shu-bwrattos—"

Warmly grasping the woman's pudgy, glove-covered hands, Belle said in her best halting European accent, "Pah-leeze, my *friendz* call me Princezz Arabella."

Maude blushed, put her splayed hand to her heaping bosom. "Oh my, you already think of me as your friend?"

"But of courze." *Smile. Nod.*

"Where is my . . . oh, Daniel, there you are." Using a grip that looked capable of roping an errant calf and dragging him to a branding fire, Maude yanked her son Belle's way.

If she hadn't known better, Belle would have sworn he smelled of beer. Imagine, drinking beer at a party attended by royalty! No wonder society columnists said the man who'd recently stunned the state by taking a mysterious sabbatical from his many corporate posts might never marry.

Who would have him?

He hadn't even shaved for the occasion.

Her cheeks flamed.

Boy oh boy, do I love a man with stubble.

"Princess Arabella," Maude said, sweeping her hand toward her son. "This is Daniel. My pride and—" *Oomph.* Presumably to wipe the smirk from his wicked-handsome, square-jawed face, she elbowed his gut. "What's the matter with you?"

Noticeably short of breath, he pasted on a polite smile and stepped forward. "Prin-cess." Mocking her much-practiced head nod, he took the liberty of grasping her right hand and bringing it to his teasing lips.

Even through gold satin gloves, Belle felt the man's heat.

Red-hot, Texas heat.

The kind that sneaked its way under a girl's skin, leaving her sweaty and bothered and wanting a taste of . . .

Gracious, she needed to remember why she was here or she'd ruin her cover.

But then she made the mistake of looking into his eyes.

He pierced her with a gaze so brazen that a blush crept up her too-exposed chest, rising all the way to her only-recently-recovered-from-her-last-blush cheeks.

Oomph.

There went Maude's elbow again, but to Boone's credit, he took the hit like a man, then released Belle's hand.

Maude said, "Please forgive him, Princess. Apparently, spending so much time playing in the dirt has affected my son's social graces."

Playing in the dirt?

Did that somehow relate to the mysterious course Boone had taken with his life?

Not that she cared, Belle thought, placing her still-tingling hand at the base of her throat. "But of courze," she said. "I have heard American men like to be . . . how do you say? Out of doors."

Boone laughed, but it wasn't a gentlemanly laugh. More like an amused snort.

The nerve!

Even if she was just a *pretend* princess, no man snorted around her without the benefit of an—

"If you'll both excuse me," he said with a thoroughly charming formal bow. "It's high time I turn in."

"So soon?" Maude complained. "But the princess only just arrived."

"Yeah." he glanced at his gold Rolex. "Three hours ago." After sending both women a cocky wave, Boone trudged up the stairs, giving Belle too good a view of his tight behind.

His clearly embarrassed mother took Belle by the arm. "I'm so sorry about that," she said, leaning conspiratorially close. "Ever since his dad died, Daniel's been a mess. He up and quit his life's work. Just left everything in the hands of our corporate board. He says he's on a mission to find himself. You know, all that mumbo jumbo about discovering the true meaning of life, but if you ask me, the only thing he's managed to find is trouble."

With her free hand, Belle patted the woman's forearm. "That iz quite all right. I shall forgive heem. Forgeevness iz my family way." *In a pig's eye*, she thought.

Men like him are trouble all right—trouble I'm only too well acquainted with.

An hour later, Belle's feet hurt to the point that she worried her practiced smile must look more like a wince.

She gazed past the crystal rim of her punch glass, wearily noting the party showed no signs of slowing down.

In fact, if anything, judging by the way the once-snooty crowd had loosened up, she suspected someone had spiked the punch.

Boone?

She didn't even try holding back a grin.

Such a stunt would not only be fun, but just like him. Not that she cared.

"Princess?" Maude Wentworth appeared at Belle's side. "Might I have a private word with you?"

"But of courze," Belle said, setting her glass on a white-linen tablecloth before entwining her left arm with the older woman's right.

Safely out of earshot in a dimly lit den, Maude released the princess to shut and lock the door. "Well, now," she said, beaming as if she'd won the Texas Lottery. "I'd say that was money well spent, wouldn't you? Those snobby old coots don't suspect a thing."

"You really think so?" Belle asked. "My accent isn't too thick?"

"Nope. Not a bit. And I really do appreciate you letting Maryvale Clawson try on your crown. What a perfect touch. She'll be talking about it for days."

"Good." Belle's shoulders drooped. "This is a lot tougher than it originally sounded."

"Well, granted it's been a while since I retired, but I do still like keeping up with Fairy news. When Philbert sent me your picture, I just knew you'd be perfect for this role." She cleared her throat. "Um, now that we've had time to get better acquainted, there's just one more thing I need you to do."

"What's that?" Though Belle had only known the woman a short time, through Maude's longtime friendship with her uncle, Belle already felt as if they were family.

"Let's sit down," Maude said. "Something tells me you're going to fight me on this, and I want you in a spot where, if need be, I can wrestle you to the floor."

"That sounds scary," Belle said, heading for a plush, rose-colored sofa. "What could be worse than the trick we've just pulled on all those good people?"

"Ha! I can tell you're still in the prime of your innocence. Those people aren't *good*. They're self-righteous snobs, every last one of 'em. Why, right now my Clem's up in heaven having himself one heck of a good laugh. Besides, the only person here who knows the truth about your identity is me, and"—the silver-haired woman's eyes mischievously twinkled—"I'm having way too much fun being in on the joke to ever tell—at least not until I'm ready to reel 'em all in."

"You're bad, Ms. Maude."

"I know. *Ain't* it grand?"

"So?" Belle asked, slipping off her gruesome high

13

heels. "Hurry up and ask your question before my feet swell too big to fit back into my shoes."

"Okay. Here goes." Maude took a deep breath before saying in a matter-of-fact tone, "You're not just here to play the part of a princess. You were auditioning for a much larger role."

"Oh?" Belle's heart nearly pounded out of her chest.

"I want you to marry my son."

"What?" Had Maude gone senile?

This was only a temporary gig.

Just as soon as she got things settled back on the farm, she was back to her normal job. She was a Tooth Fairy, for goodness sake. She'd had years of training. And while she was hardly immune to the many *interesting* qualities of the opposite sex, she'd taken a vow of celibacy!

Sure, because Aunt Lila had frittered every dime, quarter and nickel the Moody clan had ever saved in that stock-market scheme, they were all in this temporary bind, but note the word *temporary*.

"Don't look so surprised, sweetheart. Philbert has been singing your praises for years. And in the past few days, I've gotten to know you like I would've my own daughter had I been blessed with one. Not only that, but I've seen the way my boy stared at you tonight. He couldn't take his eyes off you. What with your spunk and his sass, you're a match made in Fairy Heaven."

Hand to her forehead, Belle said, "Maude, not only did I just sign a new ten-year contract, but your son is half *mortal*. You don't know what you're saying."

"Of course I do. I want you to marry Boone and that's that. Ever since his daddy died, my boy hasn't been himself. I knew from the moment I saw you that you're just the gal to bring him out of this spell. And come on, Belle, it's not as if you're not going through a rough patch yourself. Philbert told me how hard things have been for you. Maybe all you need is your own personal Prince Charming to sweep you off your feet?"

"He told you why I took this job? I—"

"Yes, and so what if he did, child? There's no shame in being broke." She gave Belle's knee an affectionate pat. "Let me tell you something. Back when I met Boone's daddy, I was an Orgasm Fairy. How's that for a job?"

An Orgasm Fairy?

The exotic breed didn't much mix with the other Fairies, so Belle had never actually met one, but she had heard of them, and, well . . . Suffice it to say she hadn't imagined them looking much like Maude.

Belle tried hiding her surprise, but knew she'd failed miserably when Maude said, "Pretty amazing, huh?"

"Um . . ."

"That's okay. I didn't tell you that to get a rise, just to make a point. Though my former position might have been a tad unorthodox for the likes of folks standin' around here tonight, it was a job. It paid the rent and put food on the table." She grinned, patted her ample stomach. " 'Course I ate a lot less back then, but you know what I mean. Anyway, all I'm trying to say is that I realize tonight was difficult for you, but you've done nothing wrong. Tooth Fairies are a pretty uptight breed, but you just proved that a strong woman does what she needs to do to stay afloat."

"Maude, I—"

"Shh. Let me finish. I know my Daniel might seem like a pistol, but inside, he's marshmallow soft. Were you to thaw that outside layer, I know you'd just eat him up. He doesn't know I know this, but he was hurt

15

pretty bad by the last mortal filly he hitched up with. From the start, I told him she was no good, but he didn't listen, and I'm certainly not one to rub his nose in his failures. What I will do, though, is give him a helping hand. What that boy needs is someone special. A Fairy. And you need a real man—not that Boone or his daddy ever had a clue that I was, um, different from other women. *Better*," she added with a sassy wink. "You come from decent, hardworking Fairy stock, Belle, and I want you not only for my son, but for me too. You know, as a sort of link to my past. Who knows—if I'm lucky, one of my grandbabies might even be a Valentine Fairy. So?" She flashed Belle a hopeful smile. "Whaddya say? Make an old woman happy and marry my son?"

Chapter Two

Ten minutes later, ensconced in her lavish suite, Belle slipped beneath gardenia-scented suds and closed her eyes.

Paradise.

Nothing ever soothed her more than a nice hot soak, and boy, did she need soothing!

Could her impromptu meeting with Maude have been any more humiliating?

What had the woman been thinking, to suggest that Belle marry her son? He might have more money than God and a mother who was a genuine Fairy angel, but despite his holy lineage, Daniel "Boone" Wentworth was an ornery half-mortal devil.

Just like Ray—only he'd been one hundred percent mortal. One hundred percent *bad*.

Nope, Belle had been down the long, hot trail with a mortal Texan before, and all she'd gotten from it was plenty of heartache and the taste of red dust in her mouth.

As for marrying Boone Wentworth so he could rescue her and her family from their monetary troubles, well, that was just plain nuts!

Deep down, Belle knew that the only person capable of rescuing her was herself. As long as she had two strong arms, and a mind to use them, she didn't even *want* a man, let alone *need* one. She'd managed this whole nasty blackmail business over her son just fine on her own for all these years, so why would she need any help now?

What she did need was to talk to her little boy. And Aunt Lila and Uncle Philbert.

Granted, her beloved son, Ewan, whom everyone—including him—in her family and circle of friends thought she'd adopted, cared more about his flock of crippled or orphaned pets than their monetary troubles. And Aunt Lila lived in some la-la land where there was no such thing as trouble, but that was okay. Just hearing their voices would calm Belle's frazzled nerves. As did the knowledge that her paycheck from Maude would more than cover that month's mortgage, utility and food bills, along with the blackmail payment that made sure she kept her *real* job—the one that meant *almost* as much to her as her son.

Belle reached for the phone hanging near the head of the tub, even as she rolled her eyes at the extravagance.

She punched in the farm's number. It started to ring. Belle swiped at the fat tears clinging to the corners of her eyes. Part of being a Tooth Fairy meant heightened emotions. Like the children she served, she laughed easily, but she also cried easily—whether out of sadness, anger, fear or downright frustration.

After five rings, her aunt picked up. "Hello?"

"Hi, Auntie. It's me."

"Belle. I'm so glad you called. You having fun? Did

they have any of those swan-shaped puff pastries filled with that to-die-for fluffy cream?"

See? Everything in Lila's life was fluff.

Which was why Belle was here in the first place: to ensure that the elderly great-aunt who'd raised her never knew anything but the fluffy contentment to which she was entitled.

"Yes, ma'am," Belle said with an indulgent grin. "They not only had swans, but little cactuses with mini chocolate chips as the thorns."

"Oh, how I wish I could've been there."

"Me, too, Auntie." Belle turned off the water.

"We haven't had a bad time here, though. Ewan made me and Philbert the most fabulous meal."

"Oh?" *With what?*

"Peanut butter and jelly served al fresco, with corn from the garden, and an apple pie made from apples off that old tree down by the pond. They were a tad tart, but sugar sweetened them right up. Overall, I'd say aside from your absence, the night was divine."

A homesick tear slipped down Belle's cheek. Count on her wonderfully nutty crew to make even hard times fun. She swiped the tear away. "Sounds nice. Is Ewan near the phone?"

"He's out like a light. Spent the afternoon with the Matthews boy trying to save a baby bunny they found down by the pond. Poor thing—bunny, that is—died little over an hour ago. That dear boy cried himself to sleep. You don't want me to wake him, do you?"

"No, that's all right. Please just give him a hug from me." Closing her eyes, Belle envisioned her sweet son tucked snugly in his bed, dried tears staining his cheeks. She saw her aunt seated at the oak kitchen table. The room's only light would be the one above the sink, and the air would still be flavored with the rich scent of an after-dinner pot of coffee—if they still had any coffee to make.

Belle swallowed hard.

If only she were there.

Most folks assumed that Fairies lived somewhere high amongst the clouds—that is, if they believed in them at all—but the reality was that aside from their jobs, Fairies were pretty much ordinary people living ordinary lives.

Aside from not knowing the joy of shouting from the rooftops that Ewan was indeed her biological son, Belle had thought her life pretty much perfect until Aunt Lila had gotten a bug up her big, blond beehive to install their happy family in a bigger house. Lila's friend Julep—a retired Leprechaun—had a son who'd made it big in wishing-well redemptions.

Well, Aunt Lila and Julep had been friendly rivals for the past sixty years, and no way was Lila about to let Julep live out the rest of her days in a house flashier than hers, so she'd secretly contacted an architect and had him design her an antebellum mansion fully loaded with every cliché of the Old South.

White columns, crystal chandeliers, red-carpeted winding staircases—even a whole balcony dedicated to fainting.

Lila failed to tell anyone that in order to pay for the lavish project, she'd invested decades' worth of savings in a risky stock venture until it was too late, and every dime, quarter and silver dollar was gone.

Now, they barely had enough cash left for food, let alone paying the boys and girls whose teeth they then sold by the pound to those hoity-toity wing-makers who ground them into a fine iridescent powder. The powder was part of a top-secret recipe for making organic strap-on wings. Without those wings, Fairies like herself wouldn't be able to fly.

Lila said, "I'd hoped that by now you'd have come to your senses and were on your way home."

Great. Did her aunt have to choose now to have one of her rare lucid spells?

"I'm sorry," Belle said, "but I really didn't see any other way. We need the money."

After her aunt's heavy sigh, the slight crackle of static was the only sound on the line.

"What?" Belle asked, trying to hide the hint of panic tinting her voice. "You think we have another option?"

"Belle," her aunt reasoned. "How many times do I have to tell you, no matter how bleak the future looks, there's always a rainbow somewhere on the horizon. No matter how much you think our situation justifies what you're doing, the Fairy Council would frown upon this act you've been playing. As a reigning Tooth Fairy, you are judged by a higher moral code than others, and—"

Belle took a deep breath. "I'm sorry you feel that way. I'll make my peace with the Council some other time." After all, it wasn't as if this *favor* she'd done for Maude was the biggest secret she was keeping from them!

She'd said all she could of any real significance to her aunt, so after a few more minutes of small talk, Belle hung up, then pushed herself out of the tub to towel dry.

Faint sounds of the orchestra still drifted up from downstairs, filling her with fresh guilt for ditching.

She checked her hair and makeup in the partially steam-covered mirror.

Rats.

Not half bad.

If she hurried to dress, she could be back to the party in under ten minutes, but the newly found actress in her said she was still too tense to play the princess role.

Wrapped in a thick pink towel, she stepped out of the bathroom and into her darkened bedroom.

When her eyes had adjusted to the gloom, she dropped her towel to the plush carpet, pulled a fresh pair of gold silk panties from the top dresser drawer.

After slipping them on, she yawned.

Eyed the enormous canopy bed.

Maybe a short nap would restore her royal demeanor?

As she luxuriated beneath cool silk sheets, Belle's eyes drifted shut to a dreamy Texas waltz floating up from the party.

Such romantic music only made Maude's marriage proposal that much more indecent.

It didn't matter how handsome Boone Wentworth was, and in Belle's eyes, his riches certainly didn't make him a prize.

In fact, just the opposite.

Men who only cared about making money missed out on the finer things in life. Like teaching sons to ride horses and daughters to fish. Taking wives to country church suppers and making slow, sweet love after their long night's work ended and the morning bus had ferried the kids off to school.

The kind of man Belle would one day marry didn't need to be rich in money, just love—oh, and he also had to be a full-blooded Fairy.

Sighing at the improbability of meeting such a

model match, she rolled over, relishing the wide-open spaces of the antique bed.

When that spot warmed, she rolled over again, only this time her path was blocked—by muscle.

Manly muscle!

After sliding a good couple of feet to safety, she glanced that way to find a shadowy figure leaning against the headboard, long, tuxedo-clad legs crossed at the ankles.

"What the—" She pulled back again, sharply as if a rattler shared her bed.

"Leavin' so soon, *Princess*?" Sinewy strong arms pulled her back against the hot, hard length of Daniel "Boone"Wentworth.

"I think the better question is," Belle said, squirming toward freedom but not making a whole lot of progress, "what the heck are you doing in my bed?"

"No," he said, cinching her bare torso even tighter against the wall of his chest. "The *best* question is, what the hell happened to your pretty little Bugoslavian accent?"

"Why, you . . ." Though she struggled against him, her actions were futile. His strapping arms had become steel bars. *Take a deep breath. Smile. Nod.* "You must be mizstaken. I know no other way to talk than my mother tongue—"

"Save it, *Princess*."

The faint, pleasurable scent of his breath only confused her further. He smelled of beer and pretzels and some other intangible something that was all male— all uniquely him.

As alternate waves of panic and treacherous pleasure raced through her, her senses reeled.

"I've been waiting for you for quite a while," he said. "I wanted to get to know you better. But, shoot, looks like I hit the information jackpot by overhearing that phone call."

"Oh?"

"Yeah, *oh*. Your gig is up. Though I have to admit, you almost had me going for a while."

"Let me go," she said through gritted teeth, struggling all the harder against him. Why hadn't Maude told him she was a pretend princess? Was there time to spill the whole story before he ruined his mother's fun? And if Maude's fun was ruined, would she withhold Belle's pay?

"Not on your life. This is just gettin' good."

"If you're planning something twisted, you can forget it." Belle crossed her fingers behind her back. "I'm a third-degree black belt in, um, Tae Bo."

His already dark eyes turned darker. "Lying like that is liable to get you in more trouble than you're already in."

"Why's that?"

" 'Cause I love a challenge. And believe me, I've never once had to take a woman against her will."

That did it.

This guy didn't deserve to know the truth about his mother having hired her, and if he wanted to think the worst, then so be it.

"Grrr." Belle shoved the creep off of her.

When he tried pulling her back, his legs got tangled in the sheets and he fell to the floor.

Unfortunately, he took her along for the ride.

Even with her kicking and screaming all the way, it was only seconds before he'd once again used those tree trunks he called arms to pin her to his chest.

24

"You big bully!" she cried. "Your mother paid me to be here. How dare you manhandle me! I'm a princess."

Sort of.

As a Tooth Fairy, she did wear a lot of pink tulle, a tiara and sequins.

"How dare *I*?" *Thwomp.* As if she weighed no more than a day-old calf, he reversed their positions. "Who's the one who gained access to my mother's home based upon lies? You wanna cry for help, darlin', go right ahead. I'm sure the police would be very entertained by your twisted tale."

"Didn't you hear me?" she said. "There's no need to call the police or anyone else. Your mother *paid* me to play the part of a princess. I'm not denying this was all just an act."

"Right," he said, pinning her to the carpet. "And I've got a nice piece of swamp land to sell." Sometime during the tussle her long hair had broken free of its restraints, and it now billowed about her face and shoulders.

His touch whisper-soft, Boone cleared her hair from her eyes.

An embarrassing silence hung between them, worsened by the fact that his weight had become less of an irritation and more of a turn-on.

Planting his hands beside her shoulders, he raised himself up, meeting her gaze.

Even though neither of them had exerted themselves since falling, their breaths came short and ragged.

"What have you done to me?" he asked, tone wary.

"Nothing, I . . ."

He came closer, closer, until his breath fanned her face in hot, delicious strokes. As much as she hated

25

what had become of her once mighty free will, she was powerless to break his lock on her gaze.

Closer, closer he came, until all that stood between them were infinite amounts of time and the slick heat of her tongue-moistened lips.

The beat of her heart had long since turned sporadic and her breaths came shallow, if at all.

Kiss me, kiss me, her body traitorously cried as she unconsciously arched her midsection, trying to satisfy urges she'd thought long forgotten.

Kiss me, love me, her body begged. *Make good on that wicked promise in your eyes.*

A cocky grin tugging the corners of his mouth, the creep pulled back an inch!

Grrr . . .

She wanted to smack the confidence right off of Boone's handsome face. As it was, she was unable to do anything but watch him watch her while her bare nipples puckered in protest at the sudden chill.

"You want me, don't you?" he had the nerve to ask.

"You're sick," she spat.

"Yeah, but admit it, you *do* want me."

"I don't even *know* you," she said, wrestling to get out from under him.

"You will."

"Will not."

"Then I suppose I'd better just call my good friend, Sheriff Walters."

Her eyes narrowed. "You call the law and you'll look like a bigger fool than you already do."

He laughed. "Funny, but that's what the last gal who tried conning me said." He touched his chin. "And seems to me, last I heard she was doing time in the state . . ." He touched his hand to his forehead and winced.

Think, Belle, think.

Without marching downstairs and ruining Maude's fun, how was she going to convince this bully that she was in his mother's employ?

She tried squirming out from beneath the man who was single-handedly ruining her plan to save her family farm—not to mention her job, which would surely be lost, too, if she missed even one of those blackmail payments to keep the Fairy Council from learning Ewan was her son!

Unfortunately, with Boone still straddling her waist, resistance was futile.

She was good and stuck.

"Get some clothes on," he said, stunning her with the sudden gift of freedom, once again touching his forehead before squeezing his eyes briefly closed.

"Excuse me?"

"Fine. You don't want to play by my rules, then I'll dress you myself."

Before Belle had even a moment to react, he whipped off his white tuxedo shirt and tugged it over her head, sliding it past her breasts, her tummy, her hips. While she was recovering from the shock of radiant heat seeping from his shirt to her skin, he pulled the long sleeves taut, binding them straightjacket-style before slinging her across his shoulder.

Halfway to the door, he scooped up her high heels.

"Put me down!" she shrieked. "What do you think you're—"

"Save it, *Princess.* No one's going to hear." He jerked the door open, then stormed into the hall.

She tried wrestling her arms free, but the shirtsleeves held tight.

Foul-tasting bile singed her throat.

What did this modern-day scoundrel plan to do?

Not wanting to find out, she yanked up the hem of his T-shirt and chomped.

"Ouch!" he roared. "That hurt."

Duh. Causing mind-numbing pain was the plan.

The plan backfired, though, when her surprise attack made him spin about, in the process almost conking her head on a marble pillar. "What'd you do that for?" he demanded.

"Because I don't take kindly to strange men hauling me off into the night—especially when I'm only wearing panties and their shirt!" She bit him again before hollering, "Help! Help!"

"That's it." In a powerful swoop that left her breathless, he set her on her feet, leaning her mummy-style against the brocade-covered wall. Aiming his long, pointed index finger at the tip of her nose, he said, "Listen and listen good. I don't care what you do to me, but I will *not* have you ruining my mother's night by making a scene."

"*I'm* making a scene? *You're* the one carrying a half-naked woman over your shoulder like a sack of potatoes! What? Are you like insane?"

He looked away and growled.

Growled?

Belle's stomach churned.

Maybe the guy truly was psycho.

And there he was again with the forehead-rubbing.

Definitely *not* a good sign.

"I wouldn't be carrying you anywhere if you hadn't made me," he said.

"Made you?"

"Hell, yes. If you'd just cooperate, we might—"

"You want *cooperation*?" she spat. "Then I suggest you let me go. For the last time, Maude paid me to be here. She even had some fool notion of you and me being made for each other. Now, I know that may sound a little far-fetched, but it's the truth."

"Woman, do you think I just fell off a pumpkin truck? Believe me, I know a scam when I hear one."

Belle sighed.

This was ridiculous.

No matter what she said, Boone didn't believe her.

To show she meant business about gaining her freedom, she screamed, "Help! Somebody, please heeeeel—"

Mid-scream, he covered her mouth with his hand. She should have been outraged, but there was the awareness again. The warm tinglies.

"Okay, Princess," he said. "How much to shut you up?"

"That depends," she said, words muffled behind his loosened fingers. "Where are you taking me?"

He removed his hand from her mouth. "Far enough away that none of those good people down there will have a clue as to what you've been up to."

"That might sound like a plan to you, but I have re-sponsibilities. I can't just—"

"What'll it take for you to go with me? No questions asked?"

"I—well. I don't know. Why do you even want me?"

"Believe me, I—I don't," he said, lightly shaking his head as if to clear it. "But considering how depressed Ma's been, I can't take a chance on her finding out who you really are."

"But I already told you, she hired me. Feel free to go

ask her yourself. And her mood seemed A-okay to me. In fact, if you ask my opinion, she seemed downright ornery."

"You're a con artist. Of course you'd say something like that. It makes you sound less treacherous. The only part of her you're interested in is her bank account."

"That's not—"

"Come on, out with it. How much cash will it take to convince you to quietly see this my way?"

Belle added the dire numbers she already knew by heart, then multiplied by four. Chin raised, eyes challenging, she gave him the outrageous sum.

"Done." Once again he swooped her over his shoulder, once again telling her she'd made the wrong choice.

That'd been too easy.

She hadn't even asked where he was taking her.

Did Texas scoundrels murder to hush women like her?

Not planning on waiting around to find out, she once again yanked up his T-shirt, sinking her teeth into his warm, sun-bronzed hip.

"Ouch! Dammit!" He swung her around again, barely missing another pillar.

"Put me down!" she screeched, wriggling the lower half of her body like a mermaid's tail. Belle had met one once while on vacation in Cozumel—a mermaid, that is. Sweet girl. Had the most gorgeous red hair and could outswim a jet ski!

Quickening his pace to a jog, her captor said, "Listen, Princess, however much I'd like to permanently seal your biting teeth, I have no intention of hurting you—only keeping you quiet. So either you quit tearing into me like I'm a piece of jerky or you can kiss that cash goodbye."

Belle briefly considered biting him again just for the heck of it, but then images of her son and aunt and uncle flashed before her.

Lila and Philbert were too old to be evicted from the only home they'd ever known, and she sure didn't plan on raising her son as a wild boy on the side of some road.

With that in mind, Belle figured that the money she stood to gain by going with this madman was worth any risk it might entail. Courage bolstered, she asked, "How long do I have to stay with you?"

He took so long to answer that if she hadn't known better, she'd have thought her question was causing him actual physical pain.

"Six weeks," he finally said, standing her back on her feet. "After that . . . Ma leaves for Europe."

Six weeks!

Belle could never be gone that long.

She had her tooth route to run. Lila had taken over temporarily, but the mere thought brought instant panic. Just before leaving for Maude's, Belle had held an emergency yard sale to raise enough cash to pay the children—for now. If Belle was still around in the morning, the money from Maude would go a long way toward getting the family back on solid financial footing.

"One week," she said, jutting out her chin. "Take it, or I'm outta here."

Oomph.

He was back to manhandling her, snarling as he hefted her down a short flight of stairs.

"Six weeks," he said, "and I'll give you a bonus now." The sum he named was even more ridiculous than the first.

31

Now she *knew* he was insane!

Insanely attached to his mother, that is.

Had there ever been a man more concerned with protecting his mom's feelings and reputation? If Boone hadn't been hauling Belle around like a sack of potatoes, she might have actually thought his actions touching.

"Instead of cash," she said, wincing with every jostling step, "can you wire that sum to my bank?"

"Sure."

Belle frowned. Again, too easy. "Oh—and I'll need proof of the deposit."

"Done."

Chapter Three

Boone kicked open the servants'-entrance screen door. The angels smiling on him must have left it unlocked. Thank God. Being this close to his mother's faithful flock of minions made him antsy for a quick getaway. The last thing he needed was to be spotted hauling off the guest of honor, let alone hauling her off when she wore only his tuxedo shirt and he wore nothing but the matching trousers.

He shuddered to think how much worse all of this might've turned out if he hadn't had the foresight to slip on a T-shirt under his tux.

Of course he had no intention of paying the royal pain one cent over her initial bonus, but she didn't have to know that. Unfortunately for her, she was the second woman in less than a year who'd tried to scam him for money.

Also unfortunate for the princess was the fact that he'd fancied himself in love with Olivia, which made the princess's deceit that much harder to stomach. He prided himself on being an honest and fair man, but when it came to conniving women, his patience had run out.

Taking long strides across the blacktop drive, he tried not to think of how the day's heat exploded like twin firecrackers behind his eyes. Or how, at the same time as he agonized over the heat, a deeper pain tugged at his groin every damned time the princess's flowery perfume drifted his way.

Only it wasn't just perfume.

He knew he was crazy for even thinking it, but he smelled *her*—all of her. Not just the way her mouth was going to taste, but—

No! He pulled himself up short. He was a born and bred gentleman. He didn't go for women who weren't one hundred percent attracted to him.

That's the old Boone talking, the voice said. *The old Boone didn't have your appetites. Your needs.*

Like always, Boone fought the voice.

No.

He was better than this.

Better than resorting to kidnapping a woman under the guise of protecting his mother just so that ultimately he could have his way with her.

And to prove it, he nearly turned around, wanting to take the princess right back to her room where she'd be safe from whatever monster he was about to become.

Ahh, the voice said. *You* want *to take her back, but you can't, can you? You can't ever go back, either of you. Because the game's already too far along.*

Worse than the voice—and harder to ignore—was the way with each step the princess's breasts rubbed against those things growing on his back.

It was enraging yet at the same time erotic.

Could she feel them? Did she wonder what they were?

Was she burning for him, the way he was burning for her?

He inched his hands lower on the silky backs of her thighs, gripping them tight, not wanting her to fall.

Not wanting himself to fall.

Boone knew that what he was doing with the princess was wrong. He should've just called the police. Let them handle the whole mess. But the sickness in his head had other plans.

The voice told him to do whatever he damn well pleased.

It overrode his usual logic by reminding him of his newfound strength.

It stole his free will by moving his limbs in directions he'd never before taken.

With his free hand, Boone touched his pounding forehead.

Help me, he cried deep inside. *Won't someone please help?*

Even as Boone cried the prayer in his head, he knew it was no use. No one could hear him, and even if they did, they wouldn't understand. No matter how many people surrounded him—a ballroom teeming with socialites, or just this one featherlight woman—he was alone.

With his insanity.

His impending death.

"Look, mister," his hostage said in an entirely too authoritative tone. "Wherever you're taking me, could you hurry it up? If the Immortals had intended for women to be folded up like billfolds, they would've put our intestines in a stay-fresh removable pouch."

"Thanks," he muttered, hoisting her higher, trying not to notice that he'd only made his situation worse by bringing her delectable butt to eye level. "I'll keep that in mind next time I rescue Ma by kidnapping one of her guests."

"Oh, so you kidnap women often?"

"Just the smart-mouthed ones."

Just to show him what a smart mouth she really had, Belle bit him again.

Hours later, after dozing off in the cab of Boone's ancient truck, Belle woke to find that her situation had gone from bad to worse. She'd been leaning against her kidnapper's warm shoulder, and her legs had been covered by a masculine-smelling, buttery-soft brown leather coat.

His?

She scowled before pushing herself upright.

Even if he was her new employer of sorts—before leaving the previous night, he'd given her faxed proof of a hefty deposit into her account as a down payment—he was still the enemy. She had no business sniffing his coat!

"Morning," he said, glancing her way before turning his attention back to the road—no, correction; make that field.

He was aiming his rust bucket of a truck straight across a windswept prairie, and judging by the reddish glow in the eastern sky, he'd been driving across said prairie all night!

"Where are you taking me?" she asked, yanking his jacket off her legs to wedge it onto the seat between them.

He had the nerve to grin. "Where all bad princesses go."

"Since I don't see any towers or dungeons, mind giving me a hint where that might be?"

He laughed, but the devilish sound wasn't exactly encouraging. "You'll find out soon enough."

The muggy breeze streaming through the truck's open windows caused her to shiver, or was that the impossible-to-read expression on Boone's face?

She irrationally wished for his jacket back; at least his covering her had been some small sign that he had a soft side. And who knew, maybe she could use that to her advantage.

Ha! her conscience said. *Isn't it usually you who gets her soft side worked over?*

She frowned.

Okay, so she was a notorious sucker for anyone or anything down on their luck, but this eccentric millionaire definitely did not apply. A hard time to him was probably running out of imported champagne and caviar.

Earlier, she hadn't felt any fear, just eagerness to get her money, then get the heck out of the Lone Star State; but now, she again had to wonder what Boone planned to do with her. Especially since none of what she thought she knew about him added up.

He topped the Ten Richest Men in Texas list, so what was he doing driving a rust bucket of a truck that had to be older than she was? And why had he aimed that truck across the dark, endless prairie like he knew exactly where he was headed?

Men like him didn't navigate by the stars.

They used American Express Gold Cards to pay people to find their way. Could she have somehow run across Daniel Wentworth's long-lost evil twin? Could this man have stolen the real Daniel the same way he'd stolen her?

The way her luck had been running, Belle couldn't entirely rule out the possibility.

Worse yet, she had to go to the bathroom really bad.

"Even prisoners get bathroom breaks," she said, wincing when the truck hit a particularly bad bump.

"Cross your conniving legs. We'll be there in two minutes."

Be where? Just when Belle feared her teeth would fall out from the bumpy ride, Boone stopped the truck and turned off the engine.

The sudden peace was at first deafening. Then came a goat's bellowing baa. The rustle of a faint breeze through tall grass. The creak of Boone opening the driver's–side door. Along with the faint smell of exhaust came an outdoorsy freshness of morning dew and livestock and maybe even a spring-fed pond. The kinds of comforting smells she hadn't experienced since . . .

Well, since being on her own farm.

Eyes closed, for just a second it was all too easy to imagine herself home.

"Okay, *Princess*," he said in a condescending tone. "We're home."

She cast him a squinty-eyed glare.

Belle twisted on her seat to grab her shoes, but one heel was stuck in a hole in the floorboard. Yanking and twisting, she fumed.

Yeah, right, we're home.

Not even close.

Home was a house—not the open range. Home was

a place where you coexisted with people you loved—
not with kidnapping, overly cocky Texans with inch-
long burrs under their saddles.

She finally wrenched her shoe free and sat up.

Home was—

Beautiful . . . in a rustic sort of way.

Indeed they were *home*—not hers, but the pictur-
esque adobe structure had clearly been important to
someone—someone who'd long ago abandoned the
place.

As the sun rose higher, the house's state of neglect
became more clear. The four arched windows lining
the porch were covered with grit and dust. The front
door stood half open while a rooster strutted onto the
porch, belting out his welcome to the day.

Weeds choked what once must've been a pretty
flower garden. Emphasis on the word *once*.

At the moment, the few early-spring blossoms that
had punched through thick ground cover were being
gobbled for breakfast by a straggly goat.

"Shoo!" Boone shouted, flapping at the poor beast
with a black felt cowboy hat as pitiful as the house.

The horned billy not only ignored his master's command but charged his private parts.

Belle couldn't help but laugh at the sight of the arro-
gant Texan pinned to the front-porch rail by a barely
three-foot-tall goat.

"You think this is funny?" he called out. "We'll see if
you're laughing when this demon-possessed beast
comes after *you*."

"He's just hungry," she said, opening her car door,
then swinging her legs out before slipping into her
high heels. "Don't you feed him?"

"Shoot, no, I don't feed him. He's supposed to be eating snakes and mowing my yard, not eating my great-grandmother's flowers."

"If you fixed the fence, he might stay out of the flowers, don't you think?"

"What I *think* is that you ought to mind your own business."

"I was before you so rudely made *my* business yours."

"And what was your business again? Oh yeah. How could I forget? Scamming my mother."

"I wasn't trying to scam your mother," Belle said. "I already told you, I was—"

"Wait, let me guess. You were really at my mother's house to scam a rich bachelor into marrying you."

Boone took the princess's brooding silence to mean yes. Her implied confession struck his already aching gut. Of course, that was what she was after.

Him.

And if she couldn't attract him, then she'd have shamelessly gone after one of his wealthy friends. Just like Olivia, she was a gold digger.

And what had he done?

Brought her to the secret place he held most dear.

At a time when he had the most to hide.

He glared in her direction, at the way early-morning sun shone on her long, golden hair. The way dust smudges on her cheeks made his fingers itch for a warm cloth to wipe them clean. Then fix her a cool drink to sip—

What was wrong with him?

The least she could do was look like she'd spent the night in a pickup instead of looking so damned cute.

She hopped down from the truck and teetered on

those ridiculous heels across the dirt and weeds posing as his front yard. "Before you so rudely cut me off," she said, "I was about to—"

He shook his head. "Save it for someone who cares."

Turning his back on the money-grubbing schemer, he headed inside, pausing only long enough to boot the rooster off the door's threshold.

He hated having his house double as a chicken coop, but as yet he hadn't had a spare minute to adjust the front door latch and it always managed to pop open when he wasn't around to fix it.

"You don't have to take your anger with me out on him," the princess said, leaving her spot beside the now benevolent goat to cradle the rooster.

"Who do you think you are?" he asked. "Snow Stinkin' White?"

"Just someone who loves animals and appreciates them for all their hard work. Isn't that right, sweetheart?" She kicked off her heels, then bent down and stroked the rooster's feathers. "There you go. Run play. Daddy will be in a better mood when you get back."

"I'm not that damned thing's daddy, and I'd appreciate you staying away from my animals. In fact, stay away from everything while you're here. Just find a spot and sit."

"And just how long am I going to be here . . . *sitting*?"

"Until it's time for me to return you to—to wherever it is you come from."

"Oklahoma."

"Figures."

"What's that supposed to mean?"

"You're a smart girl. Figure it out."

Damn Sam, Boone thought on his way into the house. How was he supposed to remain sane with *her* hovering about? Every time she stood near him, this inexplicable thing happened in his brain. Like an electrically charged fog that made it hard to think.

It wasn't entirely bad, but it sure wasn't all good.

He never should have brought her here.

He should have put her on a bus to Boise, a slow boat to Botswana—anywhere but here. A woman had no business being out on the range, trying to make a living from the land.

Though his conscience pointed out that his great-grandmother had played a vital role in the farm's long-ago success, there was no doubt in Boone's mind that he could run the whole place by himself—at least as long as his health held out. And the princess's mere presence made him more determined than ever to do just that.

She trailed after him into the kitchen. "You never did tell me where the bathroom is."

"Out back. I'm hoping to get some indoor plumbing rigged up but haven't yet had the chance."

"So what you're really saying is that you have an outhouse."

"Yeah. You got a problem with that?"

Oh, did she have problems.

Belle ran her index finger through thick dust coating the rectangular oak kitchen table. The outhouse was the least of her problems. Not only did Daniel The-Millionaire-Maddeningly-Conceited Wentworth live in a shack, he lived in a filthy shack.

A rustling in the corner near an old wood-powered stove caught her attention. A hen roosted in the flour bin of an antique hutch.

Eyebrows raised, she looked at Boone. "I've heard of

convenience foods, but don't you think letting your chicken lay eggs next to the frying pan is a bit much?"

"Notice I'm not laughing." He stormed across the room, waving his arms and shouting obscenities along the way. "Move it, you Kentucky Fried reject!" The chicken did move, but her short flight out of the hutch and onto the floor resulted in an egg plopping out after her.

Splat.

Struck with uncontrollable giggles, Belle looked at the ceiling. The floor. But eventually, curiosity got the better of her and she had to see how Boone reacted to his chicken's handiwork.

His deep scowl told her all she needed to know.

"I thought you had to go to the bathroom," he barked.

"I do, but watching you is much more fun."

"Look, Princess, you're supposed to be here as a punishment, not to be entertained. So just go on out to the *facilities* to take care of whatever it is you have to do, then leave me alone."

"I'd be happy to, but first you're gonna have to get me some clothes." She fingered the soiled white tuxedo shirt she currently wore. "I mean, this looked . . ." she stopped short of admitting just how drop-dead-gorgeous he'd looked in the thing. "The shirt looked *okay* on you, but this color, not to mention the cut, is all wrong for me."

"Great," he mumbled, heading off in the direction of what she assumed was the house's only bedroom. "Not only did I cart off a near-naked princess, but a fashion critic."

"Oh, so now I'm a fashion critic just because I happen to want clothes?" She rushed up from behind him, blocking his way. "I've had about all I can take of you. How about you just drive me to the nearest bus station, and I'll be on my way?"

In her ranting, she'd moved to within inches of him, but now that she'd thrown out what she had to say, she couldn't help but notice how small and stuffy the room had become.

How hot and tight and firm and . . .

Oh my, when had her thoughts turned from the room to the contours of Boone's chest? The way growing heat caused his white T-shirt to cling.

He'd be much cooler if he took it off, she thought. But then seeing him bare-chested would only make her hotter.

She licked her lips.

Yeah, he should definitely keep it on.

Belle took a deep breath, trying to ignore his manly smell. Sun and sweat. Confidence. Sex. All things Tooth Fairies who'd taken vows of chastity had no business identifying!

If it hadn't been for the last no-good Texan she'd gotten messed up with, she wouldn't recognize a single one of those smells—let alone crave the act that produced them!

"Well," she said, sharply looking away. "Are you going to get me some clothes? Or shall I whip up something from the curtains?"

Just for kicks, she turned to see what kind of fabric she'd be working with.

When she saw that Boone's gaze had settled on the same wafer-thin red gingham scraps that would barely cover her, ah, arms, let alone more personal spots, she cleared her throat. "Seeing how that idea's out, why don't you just bring me something to wear?"

"Yeah," he said in an odd, sort of breathless voice. "I'll do that. Wait here."

Yeah.

She'd do that.

Using the time alone to get a clue!

What was wrong with her? No matter how sinfully handsome Daniel was, bottom line, he'd kidnapped her. Well, technically, she'd willingly climbed into his truck, but that was only because he'd paid her. And that was what had gotten her into this whole mess in the first place—her desperate need for money.

The ache at the back of her throat reminded her only too well of what had happened the last time she'd ended up with a Texan.

Looking on the bright side, at least this Texan wasn't broke. And ever since she'd given birth to Ewan, she'd always looked upon her tow-headed boy as far more of a blessing than a burden.

Sighing, she sidestepped a suspicious glop on the floor to sit on a worn brown leather sofa.

On her landing, a dust cloud erupted, but she waved it away to study black-and-white photographs hanging above the mantel. The great-grandparents Boone had spoken of?

The fireplace was fieldstone, framed on both sides with crude, book-lined wood shelves. Current fiction best-sellers sat alongside leather-bound classics and fat educational tomes on topics ranging from cattle raising to gardening to pioneer cooking.

"Here, try these on." As he came out of the bedroom, Boone held out a pair of green plaid boxers and a

white T-shirt. "Sorry about hauling you out here without any clothes, but . . ."

As much as Belle hated her current predicament,
she couldn't blame Boone for her lack of a wardrobe.

He *had* told her to get dressed.

She'd ignored him.

"Thanks." Tugging at the hem of his tuxedo shirt, she
stood, nobly crossing the room to take the garments.
"Where should I, ah, put these on?"

"Yeah . . . There's, ah, just a curtain for the bedroom
door, so I'll be outside. Then I'll show you the outhouse."

"Great. That'd be nice."

Nice?

On her brush past him, she tried not to notice how,
despite her height, his size made her feel dwarfed.

True to his word, he stepped out onto the porch
while she entered the controlled chaos of his bedroom.

Contrary to the rest of the place, this was one room
that, though messy, at least looked lived in.

A brass bed wore a cheerfully rumpled yellow
wedding-ring quilt. An oak dresser stood with its bottom drawer gaping, T-shirts and boxers spilling onto the
floor. Besides the quilt, the only other feminine touch
was a mirrored dressing table. Had the last woman
who'd used it been Boone's great-grandmother?

Belle's heart reached out to the woman.

What a tough life she must've lived out here on the
prairie. Yet despite the obstacles, with the love of a
good man, her days must have been full and happy.

That kind of love-filled life was the kind Belle
dreamed of living on her farm when she retired, but by
the time she got back to Oklahoma would she even
have a farm?

She frowned.

Unbuttoning Boone's formal shirt, she slipped it over her shoulders to toss onto the bed, then pulled on his T-shirt. It smelled of hours spent drying in the sun, and the slightly rough cotton rubbing her bare breasts made her entirely too conscious of the last chest the shirt had rubbed.

Trying to think of the clothes as mere utilitarian objects, she stepped into the boxers and tugged the drawstring tight, tying it in a bow at her waist. She let the shirt hang loose, hoping Daniel wouldn't notice her peaked nipples.

"You decent in there?" he shouted.

Her body was decent.

Her mind was another matter entirely.

Yet as much as she tried stopping herself, she couldn't help but look at that great big bed and wonder what he would look like asleep. Vulnerable. Or even better—or worse, depending upon how one looked at it—was the image of him awake in that bed.

Aroused.

Naked.

Coming toward her to—

"Princess? You still in there? Not that I care, but . . ."

As his words trailed off, fire flamed her cheeks.

Her feelings exactly—not that she *cared* about him, but what? What was it about him that made her imagination wander to places better left unexplored?

Belle pushed her hair over her shoulders and took a slow, cleansing breath that did more for her lungs than her sweltering fantasy life.

"I'm dressed," she said, high heels clomping as she stepped into a bright slice of sunshine slanting across the living room.

In that hushed heartbeat, the place didn't seem so

lonely. Forgotten. In need of a helping hand. *Her* helping hand that had never turned away a lost soul. Could a house qualify as a lost soul? Or was the house lost because of Boone? Was he the one needing help?

She looked at Boone, *really* looked at him, and for a second glimpsed pain in the fine lines at the corners of his eyes. In the grim set of his lips.

Was there ever a soul more in need of saving?

But from what?

Outside, a cloud passed over the sun, immersing both the room and Boone's face in shadows, breaking the spell the light had woven between them.

Boone was no lost soul.

Just the Texas scoundrel who'd kidnapped her.

Chapter Four

Belle took a deep breath, straightened her shoulders.

It was high time she remembered where she was and who she was with. This wasn't some game she was playing, being out here in the middle of nowhere with a stranger. But on the other hand, she had to remember that to Daniel Wentworth IV, it probably was nothing more than a diversion.

He was driven. A man who had more money than time to spend it. What could he possibly need, other than the smarts to leave this downtrodden farm for greener pastures?

She was a fool to have felt sorry for him.

Past experience had taught her what a mistake dropping her guard around mortal men could be.

He cleared his throat. "Come on. I'll, ah, take you to the outhouse."

After visiting the pitiful excuse for a bathroom, Belle tried sneaking off—to do what, she wasn't sure, seeing that making a break for it might land her in even more trouble—but Boone called her over to where he sat on a rickety chair on the rickety back porch.

"What's next on the agenda?" she asked, hands on her hips.

He stood. Pointed to the chair. "Sit."

"I prefer standing, thank you."

"Suit yourself," he said, drawing a gasp from her when he knelt to lift her right foot.

Instantly off balance, she planted her hands on his shoulders. "W-what are you doing?" she sputtered, launching a tug-of-war for custody of her foot.

With his free hand on her hip, Boone pushed her into the chair. "If you'd have just sat nice like I asked, you'd know what I'm doing."

From beside the chair, he grabbed a pair of shiny new red leather cowboy boots. "Thought these might be more comfortable." He eyed her ridiculous heels. "They're mine—one of Ma's damn fool Christmas gifts. I put some socks in the toes to make 'em smaller. Here," he added, handing her a bonus pair of clean-smelling white socks. "You'll wanna put these on, too. Protect those pretty feet of yours from blisters."

For a long time Belle just sat there, not sure what to say. Here she'd made Boone out to be some kind of kidnapping monster, but he was worried about her getting blisters.

She narrowed her eyes. "You think I have pretty feet?"

She could swear she'd heard another of his growls, but he sharply looked away before she got a chance to check his expression. "Holler when you get those on, and I'll give you the tour."

Five minutes later, feet surprisingly comfy in the

spiffy boots she'd nicknamed her ruby slippers, Belle trailed after Boone while he showed her a dilapidated chicken coop, a rock well house that felt deliciously cool but had a serious case of the dank and musties, and a tool shed that leaned more than one of those fence row trees that had spent its whole life bracing against the wind.

"Well, what do you think?" her guide asked once they'd finished the grand tour to stand in front of the barn. He crossed his arms expectantly.

What? Was she supposed to break into a round of applause?

She'd seen healthier farms run by elderly Fairy widows. While she'd give the man brownie points for effort, his results were sadly lacking.

Never mind the forlorn state of his outbuildings; his vegetable garden was in dire need of weeding, separating and fertilizing. He didn't even have a decent flock of chickens. With only the one rooster and hen, it was no wonder Boone allowed Henny Penny to reside in the kitchen. That was the only way he'd be sure she'd still be there in the morning!

"Well?" he asked again. "Don't hold back. The place is pretty impressive, huh?"

She struggled to keep a straight face. "It has a, um, certain rustic charm."

For a split second she could have sworn Mr. Tough Guy was crestfallen over her lack of enthusiasm, but then his usual gruffness slid back into place. "Rustic charm," he eventually said. "That's good. I'll have to remember that next time Ma wants to lend me her landscape architect. Come on, you have to see the barn. That's the heart of my operation."

The heart? What about the body?

Scowling, Belle scuffled after him, carefully avoiding goat poo.

After pulling open a large swinging door, Boone stepped back, gesturing for her to go first. She was about to suggest he do the honors, but then caught a glimpse inside and was drawn to the barn like a child to a toy factory.

"It's beautiful," she said, surprise catching in her voice. The vast open space reminded her of a place of worship.

Softly polished leather harnesses hung from wooden pegs on the walls, while hay bales were stacked neatly in a far corner. A loft filled with still more hay towered above their heads. The air smelled sweetly of straw and dust and feed. Of horses and the not-entirely-unpleasant fecund scent that came along with them.

Hazy sun punched through knotholes in rough-hewn plank walls. The barn was so peaceful, so right in its utter simplicity, that even the occasional buzzing fly didn't seem obtrusive, just a natural part of the rhythm of life.

One of the horses softly neighed, and she walked the short distance to rub the Belgian's nose.

She'd always loved horses.

The day a couple of months back when she'd had to sell her own had been one of the hardest of her life. She'd had her Appaloosa, Bunny, for fifteen years. Even though he'd gone to a good home, a home where a little girl would gently ride him for the rest of his life, that didn't lessen the pain she felt every time she thought about the animal who hadn't been a mere farm hand, but a friend.

Rubbing behind the horse's ears, she asked, "Who

tends your animals for you when you're gone?"

"I don't have much need to be away for more than a night very often, but Ma's ranch foreman doesn't mind coming out to lend a hand when I do."

The horse closed his eyes and snorted.

She went back to rubbing the part of his nose that felt like warm velvet.

There was one more question she was dying to ask, but wasn't sure she had the nerve. Maybe it wasn't polite.

Polite?

Ha! Like it'd been polite of him to drag her all the way out to this farm?

Squaring her shoulders, she forced herself to casually ask, "Why do you take meticulous care of the barn but leave the house a mess?"

Boone looked up from forking manure out of a stall and into a wheelbarrow. "Before he died, my great-grandfather told me that back in his time, the only farmers who succeeded were those who built their barns first. I mean, yeah, it'd be nice to have the house a little more homey, but as long as I've got a place to sleep, it doesn't really matter what the house looks like."

"Not that they aren't beautiful plow horses," Belle said, looking away from Boone's wicked-handsome, sweat-sheened face to focus on the tips of her boots. "B-but why don't you use a tractor?"

"Don't need one. Not that someone like you would understand, but I'm trying to make a go of this place just like my great-grandfather did. You know, using nothing but my own two hands and wits to keep me alive."

Someone like you.

He didn't know the slightest thing about her, but as much as his words had stung, she swallowed the bitter taste. "You think in this day and age you stand a chance of living by your wits?"

"You disapprove?"

"I guess I just don't get it."

"You wouldn't."

"If you've got a problem with me," Belle said, "let's get it out. You're the one who invited me to this party, remember? If I'm going to be stuck here until you cough up my dough, then the least you could do is lay off the insults. I know you don't approve of what I was doing at your mother's, but I don't remember asking for your approval—just your cash."

"That's what I mean," he said. "That right there."

"What?"

"The way you constantly talk about money, like nothing else in your shallow world matters."

"What do you know about my world?"

"Plenty," he said in an all-out roar. When both horses whinnied in complaint, he lowered his voice. "I know you've probably never done an honest day's work. I know you'd rather stoop to stealing someone else's money than earn it yourself. And most of all, I know you thought nothing of taking advantage of an old woman's hospitality just so you could make a quick buck. In my book, that's despicable. Downright evil."

Stupid, unstoppable tears loomed in the back of Belle's throat, but she stoically held her ground. It wasn't her fault that as a Tooth Fairy she cried easily, any more than it was her fault that she'd been kidnapped.

Boone knew *nothing* about her.

His painful words only reinforced that fact.

How many hundreds—thousands—of nights had

she flown the world over, fighting snow, sleet and ex-
haustion just to make kids smile? Granted, before
Aunt Lila had lost everything, they'd been comfortably
well off, but never rich. People didn't train to be a
Tooth Fairy for money. They did it for one simple reason: They loved children. Loved making children
happy.

Leaning his shoulder against the stall, he said, "Don't
you have anything to say?"

She snapped back, "Don't you ever hush? You don't
even know my real name, let alone what kind of person I am." Sick of his accusatory attitude, she swept her
hair from her shoulders, then left the now-spoiled barn
to head for the house.

She had work to do.

If he didn't care enough about the memory of his
great-grandmother to tend to the home and belong-
ings she'd held dear, then out of the love Belle had for
her own family, she'd nurture *his* home by herself.

While Boone watched the princess flounce across
the overgrown yard, he fought a flash of regret for being so hard on her. But the truth hurt, and if she
couldn't stand a little heat, then she'd better find a
new profession.

Or maybe her whine-and-whimper routine was part
of her profession.

Even if that were the case, why did he care?

The way he saw it, she was worse than a common
thief. At least the average robber didn't pretend he or
she wasn't in the business of ripping you off.

No, the princess's methods were far more insidious.
Just like Olivia.

As he traded the sweaty T-shirt he'd spent the night

in for a clean black one out of the tack room, his mind wandered back to his conniving ex-girlfriend.

Olivia had told enough lies to make Boone believe their goals and dreams were the same. She'd carefully laid a trap, and he'd never suspected a thing—at least not until the night he'd come dangerously close to proposing.

They'd been at a swanky country-club dinner with plenty of wine and candles and gardenias, seeing as how the ladies of the club said roses were passé. A twelve-man band played big-band classics.

Last dance of the night, Boone was popping the question. The romantic speech had been memorized. The five-karat solitaire was snug in his pocket.

Minutes before the big moment, Olivia told him she needed a "potty break," so he'd wandered out onto the terrace for fresh air. Never had there been a more perfect night for a proposal, and he was psyched.

Beautiful, smart, wild in the sack—Olivia was the perfect woman all rolled into one helluva sexy dark-haired package.

Shoot, with tiny white lights sparkling high in the trees and candles floating in the glowing pool, crickets singing and the scent of freshly mown putting greens and flowerbeds making the place smell all nice, he'd been thinking of maybe even popping the question out there.

Then he'd seen *them*.

Olivia and the golf pro, kissing like a couple of horndog teens. Boone thought he must've been hallucinating, so he stepped closer for a better look, but sure enough, he was right. He'd even heard them talking.

Olivia said, *"Tonight's the night. He's going to ask me*

to marry him. I'll play nice through the big wedding, then bam. Weeks later, I'll file for divorce."

"Don't you think he'll want a pre-nup?" the golf pro asked.

"Are you kidding?" Olivia laughed. *"Boone still believes in Happily Ever After. Believe me, once I get through with him, fairy tales will have become his worst nightmare."*

Boone rubbed his stinging eyes.

No matter how many times he told himself to put the night—the woman—out of his mind, he couldn't help but wonder if he'd ever trust again. But then, what did it matter if he trusted?

It wasn't as if he had more than a couple of months left anyway.

Just the thought of his dicey health made those damned things on his back itch and burn. He leaned against the nearest rough cedar post to give his back a good, long scratch.

Back in the days of frontier justice, a woman like Olivia probably could've been hanged. And while in this day and age marrying for money was perfectly legal, to Boone's way of thinking, it shouldn't have been.

So why, if he was so firm in his opinions of right and wrong, did he feel so damned sorry for causing tears in the princess's big blue eyes? And why, when her lower lip started to tremble, had he had the craziest urge to pull her into his arms and kiss away her pain, even though he had a truckload of his own to contend with?

He stabbed his pitchfork into a pile of horse crap.

The answer was staring him right in the face.

He'd fallen for her whine-and-whimper routine because that was just what she wanted him to do.

She was a con artist.

A good one.

But from now on, he would take her line of bull as seriously as a pile of fresh manure.

In the house, Belle kicked off her boots at the door, then decided to get a snack before tackling the decades of filth on the windows.

But on her way through the musty, dusty living room that smelled more like a barn than the actual barn, her plans changed. Funny how coming perilously close to stepping on not one pile of chicken droppings, but three, had that effect.

Controlling the resident poultry population now topped her To Do list.

"Out, Henny Penny," she said to the Araucana who'd cozied back into her flour-bin nest. "New management has taken over, and chickens are no longer allowed."

The hen eyed Belle with a throaty gurgle.

"Okay," she said. "We could have done this the nice way, but if that's how you want it . . ." Scooping the clucking hen from her nest, Belle carried her outside, gently flinging her from the porch. Henny landed on both feet, cast an offended glance Belle's way, then turned to the weathered brick front walk, where she took out her frustrations on a long-dead worm.

Belle brushed her hands together.

There. That at least righted the natural pecking order for the house.

She tried closing the door, but a warped floorboard stopped its swing. Once she'd put her ruby slippers back on to stomp the board into place, she finally got the door at least in the correct position to close, but then saw that the latch was broken.

Just as she was figuring out what to do about that, both Henny Penny and the rooster scurried back into the house.

She tried cutting them off at the pass, but it was no use; those teeny-tiny legs could hustle. And just to show her who was boss, the rooster leapt to the center of the kitchen table and belted out a cockle-doodle-doo.

Belle gave him a weary, mean-eyed glare. "You just see how cocky you feel when I fry you for dinner." For the moment, she had no choice but to concede victory to the bird, but rest assured, his time was coming.

By digging through a few disastrously cluttered kitchen drawers, she managed to find two tools—a screwdriver and a steak knife.

Oh boy.

Back out on the porch, she knelt in front of the door to study the latch.

From across the yard came the creak of the big barn door.

Belle looked up.

Boone was leading one of the workhorses to the field.

"Hey!" she hollered so loud that it caused the goat in the side yard to look up from his dandelion breakfast. "Could you please spare a minute to help me fix this door?"

"What for?" he asked, not even looking her way.

She took a deep breath and stood, forcing back a stinging retort. "*What for?*" she repeated out of principle, hands on her hips. "Because chickens don't belong in the house. And the only way we're going to keep them out is by fixing the door."

"You want it fixed, Princess, do it yourself. I'm busy."

Grrr.

Belle had thought she couldn't have despised the man more, but now he'd proved to be an even bigger donkey's behind than the last time they'd talked.

Maybe from now on it was best they didn't talk at all.

Boone must have reached the same conclusion. Without a backward glance, he led his horse toward the field where five arrow-straight rows of freshly turned dirt begged to be planted. The rich smell of the earth drifted Belle's way, causing her to concede that however much she despised Boone as a companion, she'd never met anyone with his kind of work ethic.

Already at seven A.M., after driving all night and not eating breakfast, there he was, getting a jump on the day's chores. Why? Why would a man with so much money work so hard on a farm that, from the looks of it, barely supported itself, let alone earned a decent profit?

Was farming, like Maude had said, Boone's attempt to find himself? Or something more? And what was it about him that made Belle care?

She should have despised him, and make no mistake, she did still feel plenty of good, strong contempt for the man, but along with that contempt had come a certain understanding. Whatever he was trying to accomplish with his land was similar to the battle she fought trying to keep her farm.

Sighing, Belle headed back to the kitchen.

If she had an ounce of smarts, while Boone was busy in the field, she'd borrow his truck and head straight for Oklahoma.

Opening the nearest cabinet door, she found, nestled among at least twenty cans of pork & beans, a Zip-Loc baggy crammed with Oreos. Taking a couple out to munch on, she surmised that even if she found the keys to the truck, she didn't have a clue where in Texas she was.

She'd always had a pretty good sense of inner direction when flying, but pretty good wouldn't cut it when driving aimlessly across the prairie with a limited supply of gas. Too bad she didn't have her wings with her now.

But even if she could leave, she wouldn't get her cash, and wasn't that the reason she'd gone with Boone in the first place?

Savoring the rich taste of vanilla cream that she'd licked from the base of the cookie, she figured she might as well stay. After all, how long could he reasonably keep her there? A couple of days? A week? Surely by then he'd realize you can't just go around kidnapping princesses—even if they are just-pretend!

In the meantime, she'd consider this crazy turn of events to be a vacation of sorts. A well-deserved break from saving her own world to help someone else with theirs. And who knew, by the time her captor saw what a great job she did of cleaning his house, he just might give her a bonus.

"I swear, Dandy," Boone said to his favorite horse. "If that woman thinks she's getting one cent out of me beyond what I already gave her, then she's crazier than a goose flyin' north for winter."

The horse raised his head in response, telling Boone that if even a horse thought he was right, then he was right.

"Who does she think she is? Scamming my mom, then waltzing out of *my* house demanding I fix the door. Does that seem reasonable to you?"

The horse's labored breathing and occasional snorts

weren't exactly the answers Boone had been hoping for, but then, expecting a horse to answer in the first place proved how crazy he'd become.

What a year it'd been.

First his dad had died, then there had been that fiasco with Olivia. Going to doctor after doctor trying to figure out what the hell was growing on his back.

And now, there was the princess to contend with.

In an attempt to make some sense of his life, find some meaning before dying, Boone had to make changes. Sure, he'd amassed piles of money over the years, but now, with the end so near, he wanted something more.

Something tangible, like watching the seeds he'd soon be planting grow to fruition.

Hell, maybe his whole urge to get his fingers in the dirt was some misguided metaphor for the children he would never have.

He'd gradually been learning how to handle both this place and his limited time on it, but now that *she* was here, all bets were off.

Boone knew darned well that fixing the front door had topped his list of priorities from the moment he'd stepped out of the truck that morning, but the fact that *she'd* asked him to do it had him fuming.

How dare she ask him to do chores for her—and in such a condescending tone—almost as if she thought she was genuine royalty.

Ha.

It was only mid-May, but the sun beat on Boone's black T-shirt with relentless heat.

If she weren't there, he'd just take his shirt off.

An eerie stillness had settled upon the land, and aside from the occasional songbird's warble or the annoying buzz of a fly, not even nature seemed willing to provide adequate distraction from thoughts of her.

Golden hair.

Endless legs.

Impossible-to-read smiles. Frowns that confused him all the more.

After plowing a few more feet, Boone realized he was not only hot, but hungry. Maybe that was the reason his mind kept straying from his work? What he needed was a handful of those Oreos he'd stashed alongside the beans supply, and damn if he hadn't forgotten to buy more cookies while he was in town.

"Not only is that woman bad for my mood, Dandy, but my stomach."

The horse answered with a soft snort that Boone suspected had far more to do with the gnats buzzing his nose than with anything he'd had to say.

Tugging the horse to a stop in the middle of a row, Boone unhooked himself and the beast from the plow, then took Dandy by his lead to the barn. "We'll tackle the rest of this later. Right now I've got more important business."

Dandy nodded, mouthing his bit with a low grunt.

"Knew you'd agree."

Fifteen minutes later, Boone had brushed Dandy and fed him and his partner, Daffodil, a half bucket of feed. From there, he peeked around the side of the barn door to make sure the princess was nowhere in sight.

Coast clear, he headed for the tack room to pull his cell phone from its hiding place in the pocket of an old denim work coat. He punched in his mom's private number.

Four rings later, she picked up. "Boone," she said, sounding slightly out of breath. "I wondered where you'd run off to. Please tell me you're not back at that farm?"

"If that's what you want to hear, I'll tell you, but the farm is my home now, Ma. You know that."

A long silence was followed by, "That doesn't mean I have to like the situation. Listen, while I have you, I don't suppose you know where the princess wandered off to? I'm frantic with worry over the poor thing— what with her being a stranger and all to our country."

A stranger, my—"Yeah, I was just getting around to that."

"Oh?"

"You see, the princess and I, well, we kind of hooked up last night and, ah—"

"Don't tell me, let me guess." His mother's gleeful whoop told him exactly what station her stagecoach had pulled into. At all costs, that coach had to be not just diverted, but run off the trail with both axles busted.

"Whoa, Mom, it's not like that. I—"

"Nonsense, Daniel. I know how irresistible you are when you decide to be a gentleman. I knew the princess wouldn't stand a chance against your Wentworth charm." Just as Boone tried letting his mom down easy, she said, "I can't wait to tell Maryvale that my grandbabies are going to have royal blood runnin' through 'em. She'll be so jealous she'll sour milk just by lookin' at it. And then I'll . . ."

While his mom rambled on about what a coup he'd made for the family, Boone's heart sank. Now not only did he have a con-artist princess on his hands, but a bootie-knitting mother.

"Daniel? Answer me when I ask you a question. We have plans to make. I know this is a little sudden, but when are y'all setting the wedding date?"

"E-excuse me?" he asked, having a hard time not choking on his words. "*Wedding?*"

"Well, surely you're planning to marry the girl? No son of mine is going to spend the night with an un-chaperoned princess, then not make an honest woman of her."

Chapter Five

A satisfied smile playing about her lips, Belle folded her arms and surveyed her morning's work.

She still had a long way to go in turning the old house back into a home, but at least the door was fixed and floor scrubbed. That afternoon she'd get to the windows, but already the place smelled more like lemony cleaning solution than a chicken coop.

Her stomach growled, reminding her it'd been a long time since her last Oreo. After slinging her latest bucket of filthy water off the back-porch steps, she wrung out the holey T-shirt she'd used as a mop, then investigated what was available for lunch.

Unfortunately, five minutes of snooping only netted two more cases of pork & beans.

Did Boone have a problem with the other food groups?

Palms flat against the counter, she pushed herself up, squirreling to somewhat of a standing position to see if the higher shelves held any variations on the pork & bean theme. Tucked at the rear of the top shelf she found flour, sugar, salt and a handful of spices that could be useful. Useful, that is, assuming she found ingredients more substantial than beans to use them with.

"What are you doing?"

"Ouch!" The surprise of Boone's voice caused her to hit her head against the cabinet frame. "Do you have to be such a sneak?" she said. "I could have been seriously hurt up here."

"Oh, that's ripe coming from you—especially since you're helping yourself to my kitchen like you own the place. And what's this?" He picked up the half-eaten bag of Oreos. "I've been saving these for an emergency. How could you eat them like there's a Seven-Eleven just around the corner?"

Using the counter for leverage, she managed to not-too-gracefully shimmy down, then stand before him, chin raised. "What cookies?" she said in her most casual tone. "I didn't even know you had any."

"Oh yeah? Then what's that?" He brushed an unmistakable smattering of black Oreo crumbs from her chest, and while Belle knew his action was purely a spur-of-the-moment result of his anger, nothing could have prepared her for his shocking touch.

He'd scorched her thin cotton T-shirt, launching all new cravings that had little to do with scarfing another cookie and lots to do with kissing him! "I, ah, guess you caught me," she said, ducking her gaze.

Boone could have kicked himself all the way out to the barn. Why had he touched her like that? In a place like that? He almost apologized, then figured, what was the point? A woman who'd stoop so low as to steal a man's cookies didn't deserve an apology. "Damn straight,

I caught you," he said. "Is there no limit to the depths you'd sink to in trying to ruin my life?"

"Ruin *your* life? Excuse me, but might I remind you yet again that *you* kidnapped *me*? Yes, I ate your stupid cookies, but only because there wasn't a single other thing to eat."

"There're plenty of beans."

"I'm allergic."

"Prove it."

"I don't have to prove it."

"Well . . ." Damn if he couldn't think of a way for her to prove it even if it were true.

Rubbing his hand over his forehead, he winced.

Man, his head hurt.

All this fighting was just making his other symptoms worse.

And, Lord, he was tired of fighting.

For months, he'd fought this farm.

Fought the dirt to get his garden to grow. Fought the goat to keep him from eating what little did grow. He'd fought the front door to keep the chickens out of the house, coped with the lack of rain or sun, or too much rain or sun, and the longer he stood in the kitchen's stuffy heat, he realized how close he was to giving up.

To just finding himself a sunshine-flooded island hideaway where he could curl up and die.

What was he trying to prove?

He'd already more than succeeded in the business world. Why was making a go of this run-down farm all he could focus on? Except, of course, for the princess.

Just then, his gaze landed on the flour bin. Lucky, the egg-laying chicken, his sole means of protein other than beef jerky and beans, wasn't in her usual perch. "Hey," he complained. "What'd you do with my chicken?"

The princess followed his gaze to the hutch. "Henny? I packed up her straw mattress and moved her outside. You know, the place chickens are *supposed* to live?"

Swallowing his anger over her renaming his chicken, he asked, "How'd you get her to stay outside?"

"Fixed the door."

"How'd you do that?"

"Elbow grease and a steak knife."

He stormed to the front door.

Sure enough, as he opened, then shut it, he saw that it had been miraculously fixed. He looked up to see Belle leaning a curvaceous hip against the sofa.

A smile played about her too-full, too-luscious, too-damned-distracting lips. "Told ya so."

"Yeah, well, what business was it of yours to fix that door anyway? Did I give you permission to mess with it? I thought I told you to sit."

"Daniel, I—"

"Would you not call me that? Only my mother calls me that, and believe me, you're a far cry from her."

With her big blue eyes looking perilously close to tears, the princess sat in his great-grandmother's rocker. Boone wanted to yell at her for going anywhere near that sainted chair, let alone casually plopping her ripe little behind in it, but he couldn't.

Something about the picture of her sitting there, so at home, yet so near tears, cast her in a fragile light, one that made warning bells clang.

Was this another one of her tricks? Would he ever trust anything the woman said or did?

"What's the matter?" he guardedly asked.

"You hurt my feelings," she said, pushing herself up

from the chair. "I worked hard this morning trying to keep your stupid chicken out of the house, and here, after I not only did that but cleaned up after it, all you can say is that I'm a far cry from your mother? Well, let me tell you something about your mother, mister. I like her a lot, but when's the last time she got down on her hands and knees to scrape chicken poop off your floor?"

The very thought of such a thing was so preposterous that Boone couldn't help but bust out laughing.

"You think that's funny?" Taking her frustration with him out against his chest, she balled her fists and pounded. "Listen, you kidnapping creep, I'm tired, I'm hungry, and the least you could do would be to show me a little respect. I didn't ask to be in this situation."

"Me neither," he said, grasping her wrists. "Believe me, there's nothing I'd like better than to take you back to wherever in Oklahoma you came from, but that's just not—*argh!*"

He released her to double over in pain, clamping both hands over the fire behind his eyes. Cold swirls of nauseous black.

"Daniel? Daniel, are you okay? Is there anything I can—"

"Leave me alone," he ground from between clenched teeth, doing all in his power to tame the beast inside.

"But—"

He forced himself upright.

Leaning hard against the nearest wall, he felt as if he were stepping outside his body. All at once, he was himself, but not.

The old Boone couldn't feel the pop of each individual sweat bead leaching from his forehead.

He didn't smell her so keenly.

71

Her sex.

Sweat.

Innocence.

If he allowed himself, he could swallow her whole. He had the supreme right. The voice in the dark had long since given not just permission, but blessing.

Come on, it urged. *What's stopping you? Right now. Bury yourself in her slick, hot folds.*

Boone looked at her, and though he knew she stood only three feet away, in his mind's eye she appeared to be at the end of a long, dark tunnel.

She was light.

He, the dark.

"Daniel?" she said again, sounding far-off and small. "Do you have a phone somewhere? Let me call for help."

Help.

Yes. He needed help. What he was thinking was wrong. He was a good guy. A—

"Where are the keys, Daniel? Let me at least help you to the truck."

"No." Washing his face with his hands, groaning, he nodded, but then shook his head. "I'm fine."

"No, you're not. My God, I thought you were having a heart—"

"I'm fine." He clamped her wrists, but wasn't sure whether he'd done it to control her or himself.

"Daniel—"

"Stop calling me that. Most everyone I know calls me Boone. I know it's corny, but . . ." He realized he still had hold of her wrists and drew her hands slowly to her sides. "You mentioned a while ago that I didn't know your real name. Well? Let's hear it."

"Belle. Belle . . . Moody."

"*Belle.*" Though he couldn't say why, he tried the name on for size. It fit his lips just fine. Too fine. With a slight shake of his head, he cast her a wary glare. "Belle," he said again just because. "I can't let you go until Mom's safely out of the country, because I don't know you. I don't know what kind of hell you're capable of raising."

"But I promise I won't say a thing about this to anyone."

Hadn't Olivia promised the same thing?

"While I appreciate your sincerity," he said, touching his still-throbbing forehead, "you have to be stopped—especially since you all but admitted that your real purpose at my mother's home was to catch yourself a rich husband. What if you go after one of my friends?"

"That's crazy! I never said I was out to marry money, and since I can't stand you, what makes you think I'd go near one of your friends? And really, if I were as good a con artist as you say, why would keeping me out of circulation a mere six weeks slow me down? Geez, Boone, if you'd listen to what you're saying, you'd realize none of it makes sense."

"Okay, so you might not have admitted you're out to marry money in so many words, but you sure didn't deny it."

"I'm denying it right now!"

"Too late. I don't believe you. Besides, if you were in my place, would you trust someone like yourself? My mother's worked a long time to garner the respect she has, and I don't want a fraud like you taking all that away."

Fire flashed in her eyes. "I'm not . . ." Just as abruptly as she'd started, she clamped her lips shut. "Never mind."

Was he pushing her too hard? "Look," Boone said,

"My dad"—he paused when the next word stuck in his throat—"died not so long ago. Ever since, Ma's had a rough time. I don't know what it was about you, but having royalty in her house perked her up. I can't bear for her to hear that everything she believed about you was nothing but lies. After her trip, maybe she'll be stronger. Ready to deal with the blow."

"That's ridiculous. Not only does she know I'm not a princess, but by now she has to have figured out I'm missing. All my clothes are still at her house. She probably thinks I was abducted—not by her son, but someone with darker intentions. What if she called the police?"

"She didn't."

Again her eyes narrowed, and the blue of her irises turned to midnight. "How do you know?"

"I have a cell phone in the barn, so I called her. She thinks we're having a fling. If you promise to play nice, there's just enough juice in the phone for one more call. Interested? Come on, Princess, what do you have to lose?"

What did she have to lose by peaceably staying with Boone on this farm?

Belle suppressed a snort.

How about her entire life as she knew it!

What kind of a woman was Maude to let her son go on thinking the worst about her? Where was her sense of Fairy honor?

With a few words, Maude could have cleared this whole mess up, but instead she'd upped the stakes of the game. What was she trying to prove? Was she hoping that with time, Belle might feel something besides loathing for her cocky son?

Still, what other choice did Belle have than to stay on the farm? It wasn't as if, back in Oklahoma, the Fairy Council was falling all over themselves to give her a better-paying job—which was why she'd resorted to the princess gig in the first place. And it wasn't even that she didn't feel well enough paid for her current job, but that Aunt Lila had—no.

No more complaining.

Belle squared her shoulders.

She was a strong woman, capable of solving her own problems.

A long-standing Tooth Fairy motto was that when life gives you lemons, make lemonade. This whole mess was nothing more than a big bushel of lemons just waiting to be sweetened up.

"Okay." She took a deep breath, staring into Boone's unreadable silvery-gray eyes, hoping he wasn't trying to pull one over on her. "I won't give you any more trouble. Just promise that at the end of our six weeks you'll give me my money." Holding out her trembling hand for him to shake, she asked, "Deal?"

"Deal." Boone shook her hand, denying the power her touch had upon his heightened senses while at the same time wondering if on such a clear day God struck liars with lightning. For one thing was certain: As sure as he was lying about paying the princess, she was lying about being reformed.

"Good," she said, giving him a firm handshake. "Take me to that phone. I've got to make an important call."

The barn was hot. Hot like walking into a big, hay-scented oven, but that didn't stop Belle from hustling to the phone. She couldn't wait to talk to Ewan and to tell her great-aunt an edited version of what had happened since their last conversation.

The horses were out to pasture, and aside from chattering barn swallows and the faint buzzing of a couple of lazy flies, the barn was silent. Sure enough, just like Boone had told her, when she reached into the right pocket of the denim coat hanging in the tack room, she found an ultra-compact phone.

So, for a man who appeared to be destitute, Boone at least had money for fancy toys. The cost of this baby would have paid a month's mortgage on her farm.

"Hi, it's me," Belle said when her aunt picked up. "How are you?"

"I was just wonderin' about you. Headed home?"

"No. I, um, well, Maude asked me to stay on a while longer."

"How much longer? Teeth are piling up out there. And what does she want you to do?"

"Oh, you know, just help out around the house."

"I thought she has hired help."

"She does, but—"

"You're not still pretending to be a princess, are you?"

"No, ma'am."

"What are you going to do about your route?"

"Actually, I was hoping you'd keep helping me out." Tooth Fairies who'd retired with honors were granted permanent custody of their wings in the event of a Tooth Fairy crisis. So far, such an event had thankfully never happened—at least not until the weekend at Maude's. "I've had more money wired into our account, so just have Philbert pick you up some dollar bills to use to pay the children."

"That's something I wanted to talk to you about. This

76

business of paying whole dollars is outrageous. Back in my day, I gave nickels!"

"I know, Auntie, but—"

Her aunt giggled. "You know, though, running your route the last few days has been invigorating. And here Philbert didn't think I still had it in me. He didn't believe me, but I told him—"

The phone's low battery signal beeped.

"Lila, I hate cutting you off, but is Ewan around?"

"Nope. He's off in the barn, tending a baby bird he found under the front-yard maple. Good thing, too. Before that, your uncle gave him a real tongue lashing for dragging mud all into the house from the pond. Said he'd been trying to catch a hurt beaver. Ask me, it was probably a rat."

Belle fought tears. Even covered in mud, chasing beavers or rats, Ewan was such a sweet kid with a great big heart. How was she going to handle being without him for so long?

She raised her chin.

She'd handle it because she *had* to. Because in this case, short-run pain produced long-term security.

"Please tell him I love him," Belle said. "And that I'll be home soon, but probably won't be able to call."

"Why ever not? Maude's rich as Croesus. Can't she afford long-distance calls?"

Beep beep.

Thinking she should probably reserve whatever power was left in the phone for emergencies, Belle said, "I've got to go. I love you. Please give Ewan a big hug from me." Before she was tempted to stay on the line as long as the battery had juice, Belle pressed the end button.

Why, when she was a grown woman, did she feel as scared and insecure as a child leaving her parents for six weeks at camp?

Why couldn't she remember that being with Boone was a job?

Nothing more.

No matter what her personal cost, saving her aunt's past and son's future was worth it.

Swiping tears, she indulged in a few sniffles, then straightened her shoulders.

She was Belle Moody.

Tooth Fairy.

Direct descendant of a proud line of Fairies who never gave up. She'd never bellyached about hard times before and she sure wasn't about to start now.

In fact, maybe now was the time to launch a new plan.

One that involved earning Boone's trust.

Deciding to get started washing those windows right away, she stormed out of the tack room and right into the wall of Boone's chest.

"Whoa," he said. "Where are you off to in such a hurry?"

His nearness turned even the mammoth barn oppressive. "I, um, thought I'd get back to the housework. I, ah, don't want to be a burden while I'm here."

He nodded. Then, after a few moments of gawky silence, added, "I meant to thank you for fixing that door latch."

She shrugged. "Wasn't a big deal. The uncle who raised me didn't have kids, so he taught me a lot of things."

"Well, I just wanted to say thanks."

"Sure." For a drawn-out second, their gazes locked, then Belle raced out of the barn. Something about the heat of the day combined with the intensity of Boone's stare told her she needed fresh air—quick!

Chapter Six

" 'Bout time you got off the phone."

Philbert Moody, onetime lead Easter Bunny of the entire Gulf Coast, chuckled. "Maude. No one ever did say what was on her mind half as plainly as you."

"And no one ever did infuriate me half as much as you."

Still grinning, he said, "Got me on that one."

"So? Was that her on the phone?"

"It was," he said. "Belle told Lila she was with you. I take it she lied?"

"Oh, now, Phil, I wouldn't call it a lie so much as—"

"She's one of the most noble bred of all of us, Maude. I think you know as well as I that even one lie by her is cause for alarm, yet how many whoppers has she come up with over the past year?"

"Did it ever occur to you that in finagling all this, we're lying, too?"

He cleared his throat. "I'm trying to focus on the fact that they both need help."

"True, and with my son, Philbert, I truly believe she'll finally be safe. And vice versa."

"You say that with such conviction, but surely you realize that no one—not even you—could possibly know that for sure."

"Ahh . . . but I can hope. Boone's past thirty. Belle's nearly there. Surely some larger sign would've manifested by now if they had been chosen to follow that course. Besides which, I've been tellin' you my theory for years, that—"

"Yeah, yeah, like two magnets pushed wrong side together, the two of them are gonna repel the Dark." Philbert sighed. "It's all just theory, Maude. What we've done, on the other hand—"

"What?" she asked with a sharp laugh. "You think I could be wrong?"

"I don't know what I think," he said, scratching his head full of thick white hair. "I was just reading in the paper this morning about an earthquake in one of those faraway places. Panama? Pakistan? Yes— Pakistan. That was definitely it. Far away, but—"

"That's right, you old coot. *Far* away. Felt the earth shakin' under *your* boots lately?"

He stared at a crack in the worn blue linoleum floor. It didn't look any bigger, but you never could be too careful about these things. Everyone in the Fairy World knew what earthquakes were a sign of. Too many more and . . .

"This is a dangerous game, we're playing, Maude. You recognize that, don't you?"

She snorted. "The only thing I recognize is that my boy has a hole in his heart, and that long-legged beauty of yours is liable to be the only one who can fix it."

* * *

"Ah, ah, ah, ah . . . stayin' alive, stayin' alive. Ah, ah, ah, ah . . . stayin' aliiiiiii-hiiiiive . . ." Belle rubbed extra hard on the smudge that refused to come off the bottom right pane of the back-door window.

There, finally, perfection.

Still humming the beat to her favorite disco classic, she put her hands on her hips and surveyed the job she'd done. True, it was only one clean window out of probably ten, but at least it was a start, and at least she'd proven it could be done.

She did a tidy disco point-and-turn combo she'd learned at the Academy, then, rag still in hand, picked up her bucket of sudsy water and crossed the room to tackle the window above the sink.

She placed the bucket by the window, then climbed onto the counter, teetering on her knees with her butt sticking out at a less-than-flattering angle.

"Oh, yeah, now we're having fun," she grumbled. "Were I a *real* princess, I'd be in Monaco, laughing it up on some rich guy's yacht. Just my luck that the only water my hands are in stinks."

Having used the precious little lemon-scented Mr. Clean she'd found beneath the sink to sanitize the floor, Belle had mixed up a window-washing recipe her aunt had given her. The vinegar and ammonia solution wasn't fancy, but it got the job done, even if she did smell like a pickle-canning factory.

"What are you doing?"

Splash!

The unexpected treat of hearing Boone caused her to knock the bucket into the sink. Great. Now not only did her hands stink, but when the water sloshed all over the counter, quite a bit landed on her.

"Thanks," she said, her tone anything but apprecia-
tive of his mocking grin.

"No problem." So why was he staring at her? Did she
have dirt on the end of her nose? Dust bunnies in her
hair?

She followed his gaze to the front of her T-shirt.

The T-shirt that, thanks to him, was now sopping wet.

Hastily crossing her arms over the afternoon floor
show, she cleared her throat. "Are you in here for any
particular reason other than to annoy me?"

"Funny," he said, scratching his chin, "but I forgot
what I came in for."

"And this is my problem now?" The more he stared,
the crankier she got.

Honestly, why did he have to look at her as if he
hadn't seen a woman in ten years?

And why, when she professed to dislike him so
much, did she have the strangest yearning, tugging
sensation in her belly, reminding her just how long
she'd vowed not to be with a man?

"Problem," he said, drawing out one of the ladder-
backed kitchen chairs from beneath the table to strad-
dle it, then cross his arms atop the back. "That's it.
Thanks for reminding me. That singing you were doing? It's got to stop. You're upsetting the livestock."

"E-excuse me?" she spluttered. "That's the craziest
thing I've ever heard. Besides which, I happen to be an
excellent singer. I've been asked practically every year
since I could talk to sing in the church choir—not that
you've ever set foot in a church—which fully explains
why you didn't recognize the voice of an angel." She
jutted out her chin, daring him to argue with that.

"Angel, my horse's behind," he said with a snort.

"Those high notes sounded more like bat screeches."

"Bats don't make noise."

"That so?"

"Yeah."

"Yeah, well . . . Damn if you aren't the most cocky, self-centered woman I've ever had the misfortune to meet."

"Oh." Now it was Belle's turn to snort. "Like there's so many of us women out here to catch your fancy."

"See? There you go. I'll bet you spent your entire childhood with a bar of soap in your mouth for being sassy." Boone took great pleasure in watching the princess's cheeks flame pink.

He'd take that as a yes.

Finally, he'd gotten her.

Even if it was a small victory.

As an additional upside, the pretty blush in those cheeks distracted him from the curves teasing him just under the wet T-shirt she wore.

Hell, if he'd had to take a hostage, why couldn't he have found an ugly one?

"I'm not sassy," she spat. "Just *right*. And you, being the pigheaded stud who—"

"Whoa. Stop right there. I'm not pigheaded, I'm . . . hey, did you just call me a stud?" He couldn't help sitting a little straighter.

So the princess thought he was hot, did she?

"Yeah. Stud as in big, *dumb* stud."

"Hold it right there. Now you're getting personal."

"Oh, and you're not, with all those cracks about my singing?"

Lord help him, but once again it looked like she was close to tears.

What was it about this woman that she could be spitting nails one minute, then crying over broken ones the next?

Damned if he'd ever seen anything quite like her, and damned if once again he wasn't fighting an urge to pull her tight against him and say he was sorry until the sparkle came back to her eyes.

He cleared his throat. "Look, Princess, all this fighting isn't solving anything. I can't even remember what I came in here trying to do."

"Stop me from singing."

"Yeah, well, maybe your cackling wasn't so bad. Maybe the horses were upset about the heat. And maybe the chicken was just hungry. As for the goat . . . I'm not sure what could have caused him to butt his way into the barn, but I guess I can worry about that some other time."

"So you're saying you're sorry?"

Heck, no, he wasn't sorry.

But then she swiped her hands through her hair, leaving the cutest streak of dirt right at the start of her hairline. And the idea that she'd gotten that dirt by cleaning his filthy windows kind of made him soften.

Kind of.

He sighed. "It's okay if you sing, but do you have anything in your repertoire less abrasive than disco?"

"I know a little Patsy Cline."

He nodded. "Good. Yeah, I like her. Now, can we do anything about cooking up some grub?"

She raised those arches of gold she called eyebrows. "*We?* You expect me to not only clean, but cook for you?"

Ah, there were those sparks he'd been looking for. "I said *we,* didn't I? Besides, if you'll remember correctly, you volunteered to clean. All I told you to do was sit."

"Touché." She at least had the decency to look chastised for having leaped to conclusions about his lack of character. "I don't mean to be cranky," she said, hands on her hips, "but I'm tired. Can we call a truce for a couple of hours? After that, we'll fight all you want. But first, I need some food and then a nap."

"Woman," he said, pushing himself up to swing his leg over the chair. "You just read my mind."

Belle's request had caught Boone off guard, as did his reaction to it. For the second time that day, she'd surprised him by showing a vulnerability that made him want to stop punishing her and start protecting her.

Once again, he got the impression that if she was a con artist, her talent was world-class, and that saddened him. For suddenly, more than anything, he wanted at least one part of her to be genuine.

Especially those parts to which he was most attracted.

Heading for the door, he looked over his shoulder to find her staring at him. "What?"

"I thought we were going to fix something to eat."

"We are. But first we have to haul in the food from the truck. Unless you've developed a craving for pork & beans."

Belle stuck out her tongue at Boone's feeble joke, then trailed behind him, hoping he had a few candy bars stashed among the necessities.

Unfortunately, after fifteen minutes of back-and-forthing to the truck, she got bad news.

No chocolate.

"Whew." After setting a case of canned fruits and vegetables on the kitchen table, Boone sighed. "It's really heating up out there."

Sweat trickled down his left temple, and his dark

T-shirt clung to the center of his back, but where his shoulder blades should've been were two odd humps— long and narrow.

Had he been in an accident? Had he—

"What're you looking at?" Boone asked, turning his back to the wall.

"Nothing." Belle dropped her gaze, shoving a mammoth box of Bisquick onto a shelf. Geesh, did he have to be so sensitive? All she'd been wondering was what had happened to him—not that his deformity detracted one bit from his looks.

Bummer.

Funny how he'd just been going on about how hot it was outside, 'cause she'd been thinking that if he didn't stop looking so darned cute, things were liable to heat up inside as well.

His cropped dark hair stuck out every which way. Inky stubble coated his angular jaw. And every muscular ridge on his body was genuine, earned by countless days' labor under blazing Texas sun.

"Now that you've seen what the kitchen has to offer," he said, "what looks good?"

"Truthfully?" She pulled out a chair at the table and sat. "After all that unloading, I'm too tired to eat." Between them, they'd carried about thirty boxes of food into the kitchen. Mostly staples like rice and beans, dried meats, pasta, and packets of freeze-dried camp food that only needed boiling water to become wholesome and complete, albeit tasteless, meals. Also there were boxes of powdered milk, and a few treats like popcorn and Twinkies.

"Can you cook?" Boone asked, straddling the chair beside her.

"Don't you ever sit normally in a chair?"

"Don't you ever answer a question before asking one?"

She leaned her head back and sighed, stretching her arms behind her head to lift sweat-dampened hair from her neck. "Yes, I cook. Mostly meat-and-potatoes stuff. My aunt taught me the basics."

"Good."

"Why?"

"'Cause I'm a meat-and-potatoes guy. Not that I'm implying I'm in any way attracted to you just because you can cook."

"Oh, no," she said, an impish grin lighting her eyes. "Never would I have thought anything like that. Because, hey, if I ever thought you were the least bit attracted to me, then I'd have to lure you into my marriage trap, right?"

As charmed as Boone had been by their light-hearted banter, as turned on as he'd been by the sight of Belle lifting her long, golden mane high off her neck, he was now that turned off.

Damn her.

When was he going to stop forgetting who he was dealing with?

This was no innocent girl from next door on his farm for an afternoon picnic. This was a conniving, cheating wench who'd set out not only to rob his mother, but undoubtedly him as well.

Internalizing that fact closed a steel door on his heart. It reminded him he was immune to her wily charms.

"Sorry I ate your Oreos," she said. "You should have told me you were saving them for a special occasion."

Damn, damn, and double damn the woman. How come every time he decided to be strong, she went and did something sweet?

"As much as you think you know me, Boone, you don't. I know what it's like to want something so bad that it becomes a physical hurt inside."

"You do, huh?" He narrowed his eyes. Why did he have the feeling they were no longer talking about cookies? Deciding to give her a taste of her own lying medicine, he said, "I know about wanting, too. You might not believe this, but I'm broke. What I want is to make a go of this farm, and the money I promised you was earmarked for seed and fertilizer. So, you see, whatever you *think* you want, I want, too. Only ten times worse."

She leaned forward. "Society columnists say you're worth millions."

"Gone."

"What do you mean, *gone*?" The shock marring her perfect features told him she'd bought his lie hook, line and sinker.

"Frittered away. When you have a mother like mine who likes to party, it doesn't take much to spend a million just like that." He snapped his fingers for effect. "Oh, sure, Mom still has an income, but she spent all of my inheritance."

"But I thought you ran the family business? You have not only an inheritance from your dad, but money from the companies you're in charge of, right?"

"Wrong," he said with a wry smile. "What can I say? You know that old saying about a fool and his money. As for my inheritance, none of that cash was legally mine until I turned thirty. Now that I have, I found out it was gone. Nice birthday gift, huh?"

It took everything Belle had in her to keep a straight face. Right. She no more believed he'd run out of money than she believed Santa was going to hand her a free and clear property deed for Christmas.

Still, if this was the way Boone wanted to play the game, she'd go along for the ride.

Making sure she was wearing the appropriately shocked expression by holding her mouth wide enough for a buzzard to fly in, Belle asked, "But weren't you furious? How could you take news like that so lightly? You don't even seem bitter."

He shrugged. "Easy come, easy go. Besides, there's not much I can do about it now."

"Wow." She shook her head. "But wait a minute." She scooted forward in her chair. "If you're so broke, then why all the fretting about me being a gold digger? And why haul me all the way out here?"

"You already know. To save my mother from embarrassment. But since we're being totally honest here," Boone said, cringing for his own growing passel of lies, "my mother is, um . . ." *Think, Boone, think. You're dealing with a scoundrel. Sky's the limit. Tell her the biggest whopper you possibly can to see just how low she's willing to go.* "Mom is"—he cracked his voice—"dying."

The instant that tears pooled in his hostage's eyes, Boone knew he had her right where he wanted her. And then he felt like a world-class ass.

"I'm so sorry," she said. "I didn't know."

"Would knowing have made a difference?"

"No." Blue eyes suddenly hard, she raised her chin a barely perceptible notch. "Like I already told you, Maude hired me. What it does make a difference in, is understanding why you went to such lengths to haul me all the way out here just to protect her reputation. You're wanting to make her last days on earth as stress-free as possible, right?"

Ashamed, Boone nodded.

"You know," she said, absentmindedly twirling a golden lock of hair, "this certainly explains a lot about her behavior last night at her house."

"What do you mean?" He leaned forward, bracing his elbows on the table.

"Well, not that you believed me the first time I told you, but she actually asked me to marry you."

Looks like he'd felt sorry for the princess a little too soon. Was she up to that again? She was even more conniving than he'd thought.

His jaw muscles working in fury, he said, "You have no shame, do you? It doesn't matter to you how many times you lie." But were they really so different? Here he was accusing her of lies, when that was exactly what he was doing to her.

Belle pushed her chair back.

No way could she just sit here playing nice knowing Boone took her for a low-life, everyday thug.

The man was off his rocker.

She didn't believe for one second that Boone was broke, but could Maude truly be ill? Surely even Boone wouldn't sink low enough to lie about something so serious. And no wonder Maude had been in such a hurry to marry off her son. She might not have much time left to hold a grandbaby in her arms.

On the other hand, if Maude truly was dying, why was Boone willing to spend the next six weeks away from her? So many things he said just didn't add up.

Ugh. Belle put her hand to her forehead, squeezing her temples between her thumb and forefinger.

This was all so much harder than she'd ever thought it would be.

"Have a headache?" her captor asked.

"Yes. Not that you'd care."

"I'm not the bad guy here, Princess. You don't have to get snippy with me."

"I'm not snippy. I just haven't had a good night's sleep in I can't remember when, and I haven't eaten since last night at your mother's party."

"What about all my Oreos?"

"Grrr!" Completely fed up with the man who wouldn't give her a second of peace, Belle charged at him, but in the instant that took, he leaped from his chair to face her head-on, readying himself for her in-effectual blows to his chest.

"Oh, no, we're not playing this game again." He grabbed her by the wrists, holding her firm but not overly tight, just enough to let her know he was in control.

The more she struggled, Belle realized, the more fu-tile was her task. No matter how badly she longed to lash out at the man, physically he'd always win.

A battle of wits, on the other hand . . .

"Just how long do you plan on holding me like this?" she asked from between gritted teeth.

"Long as it takes."

"For what?"

"You to calm down."

"Not going to happen."

"Yeah?"

"Yeah."

To prove her wrong, he released his hold on her wrists to place one hand at the back of her head and the other on the small of her back. He pulled her toward him, close enough for her to feel his heartbeat against hers.

"By God, woman," he said in a voice as rough as the grit she'd washed from the windows. "As long as I've known you, there's only been one way to keep you quiet."

"A-and how would that be?" Belle asked, barely able to breathe, let alone condemn herself for hoping he'd kiss her.

"I think you know." He did kiss her. Fast and hard. Hot and hungry. "I also think you wanna be kissed."

No, an alien voice inside her said, a voice that didn't match the yearning in her soul as this long, tall Texan once again lowered his firm lips to hers.

This time, he didn't seem in any particular hurry.

The kiss was a drawn-out, teasing affair.

Belle couldn't have pushed him away if she tried. No matter how much she claimed to hate this man, at the moment, forever would be too short a time in his arms.

But he's a pauper, the woman who had to pay the mortgage screamed. *He's keeping you here with the promise of paying you in six weeks, when odds are that if this kissing keeps up, you just might be leaving here with nothing more than a broken heart.*

But he tastes of just-picked mint, fresh from his great-grandmother's herb patch, the hopeless romantic in her was quick to point out.

Bottom line: As much as she knew it was the wrong thing to do, Belle craved more of Boone's kisses—badly.

Even if what they currently shared was only make-believe, she wanted just a sampling of what utter contentment would be like. A taste of an uncluttered life spent working the land, making a living side by side with the ones she loved. No more pretending she wasn't Ewan's mom. No more struggling to pay blackmail along with their mountain of bills. Just bliss.

Groaning, he deepened the kiss, slid his warm, work-roughened hand under her T-shirt to glide up her abdomen.

Hot sparks of excitement and anticipation licked her belly. Lord help her, she wanted him.

She hadn't wanted anyone or anything this badly since . . .

Since the night one reckless act had cost her so dearly.

"No . . ."she said, putting her hands against his chest. "Boone, stop. This has gone too far." His kisses were making her forget everything she'd worked so hard to save. Her family, farm and career.

"Princess . . ." Gaze heavy with passion, he moaned, "Please don't do this to me. I need you—*bad*. It's been a long time, and . . ." He released his hold on her to swipe his fingers through his dust-coated dark hair. "How about I triple the money I owe you? Come on, whaddya say? I promise we'll have an afternoon that'll blow your mind."

"What?" His request held all the romanticism of a cold splash of water. "Did you just offer me money to sleep with you?"

"Damn, Belle," he groaned. "I'm sorry. I just . . . I guess—"

"Save it." Aiming her index finger against the chest she'd only moments earlier wished to feel naked against her own, she said, "Never have I been so insulted. So utterly and completely degraded. Even worse, by your own admission, you don't even have any money to pay me with. I should've known someone like you would sink to this level."

"Someone like *me*? You're the con artist. Hell, at least I was honest enough to tell you I'm hot for you."

"Great. Want a prize?"

Turning away from him, she wiped annoying tears from her cheeks. Her cheeks still hummed from their brief contact with Boone's soft whiskers.

Honestly, if this whole fiasco ended in losing her job, she'd head straight to a shrink to learn how to control her emotions. All this crying was nuts!

"Take me home. I need to go right now," she demanded, hands on her hips, standing at the open back door, facing the weed-choked vegetable garden that both Henny Penny and the goat were having their way with. "*Please.*"

Her voice held such sincerity, such desperation, that at that moment Boone half wondered if his reasons for keeping Belle weren't altogether altruistic.

His mother was no fool. She could more than handle most of her own fights. More and more he suspected he didn't want to take Belle home for the very bullheaded, very selfish reason that not only did he want her body, but he was intrigued as hell by her mind.

What made her a thief one minute, then a handywoman the next? All in the same twenty-four-hour period, she'd dazzled the cream of society *and* his ill-mannered goat. She looked equally at home in a formal evening gown as she did in a pair of his boxers and a raggedy T-shirt—her only adornment being a sexy sweat sheen.

Maybe he didn't want Belle to leave because he wasn't done with her.

He didn't trust her further than he could throw a stick, but she'd become a puzzle to him. A puzzle he couldn't wait to piece together.

"Boone?" She interrupted his thoughts with the same lyrical voice that could sing off-key one minute, then say his name so sweetly the next. "I want to go home."

The ever-growing dark side of him said simply, "No."

To which she replied, "I hate you."

Without glancing back, she stomped off the back porch to storm across the yard in those ridiculous boots he'd loaned her.

In seconds, she left his line of sight, but he still couldn't tear his gaze away.

"You might not like me now," he said, lips turned into a determined smile. "But you know what they say about that thin line between love and hate."

Slapping his hat back on his head, he grabbed a can of pork & beans from the cabinet, then headed for the barn.

The challenge of opening the can with his pocketknife, then swallowing the beans down cold, should, at least for a little while, take his mind off the princess.

Chapter Seven

"Henny," Belle said, her lower back aching from having spent the past two hours slaving to make the chicken coop habitable. "Has Boone always been this obnoxious? Or do I just bring out a special streak of ornery?"

A slow gurgling *cluck* was the hen's only reply before flying the coop in favor of once again pecking at what little grew in the garden.

"Leaving so soon?" Belle looked down at herself and grinned. She guessed she didn't blame the bird for finding a new companion. She was a wreck.

To counteract the day's heat, she'd pulled the bottom of her T-shirt over and through the collar, forming a halter. The boxers she'd tied tight, then rolled down the drawstring waistband, allowing the shapeless garment to ride low on her hips. She'd plaited her thick hair into a single braid, then tied it at the bottom with a strand of kitchen twine. Not exactly a new fashion statement, but at least it kept her hair from wisping about her face.

After sweeping at least twenty years' debris from the

coop floor, hammering at least thirty planks back into their rightful place on the wall, fixing the wire mesh door, then dragging a hay bale from the barn to fill the nests, finally Belle stepped back to view her work with pride.

As much as Boone didn't deserve her help, the chicken and rooster deserved a safe home. Boone was just lucky a creature of the night hadn't already taken off with his flock, meager as it was.

"Baaaaah." The goat wandered up to inspect the latest in luxury poultry accommodations.

"Don't you worry," Belle told him. "I'll work on your house tomorrow. Your days of roaming free are soon over, too."

He snorted, then stole a clump of hay from one of the nests, chomping contentedly despite Belle's most condemning stare.

"Shoo!" she hollered, chasing after the bearded beast with the broom.

Who she really wanted to nail with that broom was her human companion.

She was one of the most noble-bred Fairies, for goodness sake. Never—not even in her childhood days—had she told a person she hated him, but at the moment she'd said the ugly words, she'd meant them.

Never had she been so offended, so utterly hurt.

How dare he offer her money for sex!

Even worse, how could she have even briefly considered not just making love with him, but for free?

Just like Ray, Boone had a raw energy about him.

Some mysterious magnetism sucking her in.

No matter how much she wanted to believe she hated him, she was terrified she might actually be falling for him.

It didn't matter that he not only didn't deserve her, but he didn't like her beyond the purely physical bond which he kept proving was alive and well between them. It didn't even matter that he professed to be broke. His claim of poverty only made him that much more attractive. After all, she was broke, too.

Why was it that when he'd been rich, she'd thought she wanted nothing to do with him, but now that he claimed to be struggling, she had the strangest yearning to struggle with him?

No, she told herself. *You're doing exactly what he wants you to by believing his cockamamie story. Boone Wentworth is rich. Rich beyond your wildest dreams.*

Now was not the time to let down her guard and go all soft on him.

As for his farm, that was another matter.

In the short time she'd been on the place, she'd formed an attachment. A sweat equity.

This mangy stretch of prairie reminded her of home. The struggles she'd fought her whole life to win.

But at home, all the mindless jobs had been done. The only tasks left to tackle were the really big ones, like figuring out how to pay the second and third mortgages. Which was why she couldn't let her guard down around Boone for even a second.

Despite what Boone had told her she could and could not sing, Belle hummed a Donna Summer disco hit while taking her shovel back to the tool shed.

It was a short walk, maybe ten yards, and along the way, she admired a stand of wildflowers. They'd look pretty in the antique pottery vase she'd spotted while cleaning the kitchen.

Nearly to the shed, she kicked aside an empty five-gallon bucket, only to get a nasty surprise.

101

Coiled up, not at all pleased at having his house overturned, sat a rattler poised to strike.

Oh, God.

While she'd seen plenty of snakes, never had she seen one quite this big—or crotchety. And never, no matter how many reptiles she saw, had she ever felt good about being in their company.

"Boone!" she wailed, hoping the high-pitched desperation in her voice carried to the field.

When he didn't answer, she called out again, trying to stay completely still, wishing the cagey snake would turn tail and run.

"What?" Boone finally hollered, sounding too far away to be of any immediate assistance.

"Help! I—"

The snake rattled again, this time real slowly.

Twin beads of sweat trickled down the sides of her face. Her heart pounded.

What should she do?

If she darted to make a run for it, the snake might lash at her as she ran. Sure, she had on her ruby slippers, but they only rose midway up her calves. If it struck any higher, with no protection on her legs, this far from a doctor, she'd be a goner.

"I need you, Boone! Please . . ." The realization that she could die in this place hit hard. Tears blocked her throat as she again tried calling for help. "Boone . . ."

Visions of Ewan and Aunt Lila and Uncle Philbert flashed through Belle's mind. Mental snapshots of her mom and friends and even cherished pets. And oddly enough, though his was the last face she'd have expected to see, she saw Boone. Giving his horses affectionate pats and extra pails of feed. She saw him laughing with her during one of their few moments of peace.

Coming in close for a kiss . . .

And then he was there, not just a figment of her imagination but a flesh-and-blood hero, poised to save her life. "Don't budge an inch, Princess."

The snake rattled.

"W-what are you going to do? D-do you have a rifle in the house?"

She chanced a glance his way, and what she saw spooked her more than the snake.

Boone's eyes were crazy.

Dark.

Heart racing, Belle licked her lips.

What was the matter with him? Was he on the verge of having another of his spells?

Boone knelt before the snake, seemed to lock eyes with it, then, in the same instant as the rattler struck, he snatched it just beneath its fangs.

An unearthly growl left Boone's throat, and his expression was not of this earth. Eyes squinted. Strong white teeth bared, he looked entirely capable of ripping the snake's head off with his bare hands.

Instead, Boone laughed, then flung the snake's writhing body fifty feet into the tall weeds at the yard's edge.

"Oh my God," Belle said, quivering head to toe.

Boone was still laughing, shaking his head as if handling that snake had been more fun than winning a blue ribbon at a county fair.

He eyed her, and Belle, trembling fingers to her throat, backed away.

"What's wrong?" he asked.

"N-nothing." She took another step back.

"What? You don't like heroes?"

"Well . . . sure. Of course. Thank you. It's just that . . ." What he'd done in saving her was of course heroic, but also downright creepy. No one she'd ever encountered, Fairy or mortal, had ever wrestled a snake.

It was—well, it was just plain weird.

He took another step toward her, crazy-dark eyes sparking with what she could only guess was adrenaline.

"As my reward," he said, closing the gap between them, clamping his hands round her upper arms, "I'm going to kiss you."

"I think . . ." What? What could she possibly think when he stood this close, clouding her mind and judgment with screaming thoughts of his power.

If he was that unafraid of a snake, what other demons might he tackle? He would never be so weak as to bow to blackmail like she'd done.

How wonderful it must be to possess such strength.

How wonderful it must be to be possessed by such strength.

"I think," he said, his mouth mere inches from hers, "you think too much." Backing her all the way to the side of the house until the rough adobe bit her shoulders, he kissed her with such urgency, such savage, stormy intensity, she lost sight of everything in her life but him.

He became the very air, transporting her to a danger zone where nothing was as she had known it. Here, with him, she was no longer pretty in pink as a Tooth Fairy should rightly be, but wicked in black leather and fleshly greed. And for the moment, that was enough.

It was all she could ever remember wanting.

He was kissing her, kissing her.

She was falling, falling.

And then he stopped, crushing her in a hug that seemed more for his benefit than hers.

"What's happening?" he said, the words but a warm cloud in her hair.

"I d-don't know." Her heart drummed in her ears. On so many levels, this—being with Boone—wasn't right. She knew that, so why couldn't she pull away? Why was she clinging to him as if he were saving her yet again?

"I-I'm sorry," he finally said.

She looked up at him, and his eyes were back to safe silvery gray.

Had she dreamt their darkness?

Their kiss?

She nodded.

"I don't know about you," he said matter-of-factly, "but I could use a swim."

Eyes narrowed, she looked at him. *Really* looked at him. Just like that, the dark power she'd so willingly drowned in was gone. All her senses were firmly back in place.

Dizzy, weak, she put her fingers to her throbbing temple.

How? What had just happened? Why did she feel as if she'd downed a full bottle of champagne?

"Belle?" Boone persisted. "You wanna go for a swim? I have a spring-fed pond that's—"

"What's wrong with you?" she said, the queasy tremble back in her limbs.

"Come again?"

"You're not right," she said, inching down the wall of the house, ignoring the adobe's bite on her hands. "In here." She tapped her head.

After shooting her a grin so handsome it stole what little remained of her breath, he glanced down, kicking a dried clump of dirt near the toe of his right boot. "Why don't you like me, Belle? Am I that hard to stomach? Have I been mean?"

"In comparison to what? It's not as if I have another kidnapping experience to compare this to." She turned away from him to head toward the porch, but Boone wouldn't let her off that easy. The woman had wormed her way under his skin, and he wanted—no, *had*—to know more about her.

Chasing after her, he shouted, "I thought that kiss was our way of declaring a truce."

"This latest one?" she shouted over her shoulder. "Or the one just before you offered me a ton of cash—cash you supposedly don't even have—if I'd sleep with you?"

"Hey!" He dashed in front of her, then had to run backwards to avoid being trampled. "I apologized for that. Can I help it if it's, ah, been a while in *that* department? I don't know what made me say such a thing. It was wrong, and again, I'm sorry."

Belle was surprised by how much Boone's apology mattered.

But then, why wouldn't it?

To Fairies, *I'm sorry* meant the world.

No, it *was* the world.

Acts of kindness and genuine repentance were the only things standing between good and evil.

Light and Dark.

Belle took a deep breath, reminding herself about

what happened the last time she'd wound up in the arms of a sweet-talkin' Texan.

She'd gone home alone and pregnant.

From the field came the sound of one of the work-horses anxiously snorting and jingling its harness.

Grateful for the interruption, she said, "Sounds like somebody needs you a whole lot worse than me."

"You're some piece of work, you know it?" He shook his head. "I just saved you, but here you are, acting like I've done something wrong. I try being your friend, but you act like you'd be more comfortable keeping me as your worst enemy. I give up, Princess." He threw his hands in the air, then let them smack against the thighs of his dusty jeans. "I don't know what you want."

That's two of us, she longed to say, but instead she muttered for the umpteenth time, "What I want is for you to take me home."

"Forget it," he said, " 'cause that's the one thing that's not gonna happen."

For the longest time they stared at each other, standing close enough for Belle to see the stony challenge written in his gray eyes. A fine layer of dust had settled across the upper portion of his dark T-shirt where sweat caused it to cling to his rock-hard pecs.

Staring her in the face were two distinct handprints. *Her* handprints.

Guilty heat crept up her cheeks.

Had she really touched him *there*?

If she dragged that T-shirt up, up, up . . . kissing a trail from his collarbone to his navel, would his skin taste of salt where her tongue might accidentally, or maybe wholly intentionally, touch?

As if he knew her every wicked thought, his nostrils flared.

His pupils darkened and widened.

Why, when she'd told herself repeatedly how much she despised him, could she not get over her silly longing for him? Honestly, she was acting like a schoolgirl with a crush.

For goodness sake, the man was a kidnapper!

Pursing his lips the faintest bit, he puckered up and blew her a mocking kiss. "While you're standing there deciding what to do, I'm going to finish my row." He winked. "Holler if you run into any more trouble."

Trouble.

The word fit him to a tee.

As he sauntered toward his neighing horse, Belle felt his blown kiss as distinctly as if he'd pressed it to her lips.

Why she'd ever called on him for help with that snake she didn't know.

She should've just saved herself.

In fact, how many times since starting the whole princess gig had she told herself she'd do just that?

And yet here she stood, pulse still curiously weak and unsteady after their latest encounter.

Stepping onto the back porch and into the small patch of slightly cooler shade, she surmised that back home she had too many responsibilities to indulge in even the slightest whimsy. Especially whimsy involving a man who, by the very act of offering to *buy* her affections, had proved to be no more of a gentleman than that bull-riding beast Ray.

At the back door, she kicked off her ruby slippers, which landed with twin thuds on the wood plank floor.

Inside, she paused in the kitchen while her eyes adjusted to the difference in light.

The house had held tight to the coolness it'd stored overnight, and she was grateful for the ten-degree temperature swing.

After stealing a Twinkie from the sainted box Boone warned her to stay out of, she padded into the living room, where she sat on the leather sofa, punching dust from a rose-colored tapestry throw pillow before sticking it behind her head, then lying down.

It felt good to stretch out.

Almost as good as it felt to have a moment's peace from Boone.

Unwrapping her Twinkie, then taking a big, yummy bite, she remembered the last time she'd felt such an instantaneous, all-consuming reaction to a man. But what had that gotten her? Nothing but heartache.

Well, except for Ewan—he never failed to bring her a good dose of joy. But every day that passed with her having to pretend she wasn't so much his mother but a friend brought on a brand of heartache all its own.

Belle closed her eyes, thinking back to the spring her son had been conceived.

She and her supposed best friend, Josie—a fellow Tooth Fairy candidate—had been sprung from the Dallas Training Academy for a long weekend. After borrowing Josie's brother's vintage white Mustang convertible, they took off on a road trip, breezing down arrow-straight Lone Star State roads with no cares other than where to pull over for grub.

In the one-horse town where they stopped for the night, a rodeo had been under way, and as dusk turned to darkness, they cheered calf ropers and barrel racers and daredevil bull riders.

After the night's winners were announced, they discovered the bulk of the riders were staying at their motel.

Josie, never having been a shy girl, invited herself to the barbecue going on down by the pool.

Back in those days, Belle had been more into her studies than finding a lifelong companion—after all, if she was chosen for the honor of becoming a Tooth Fairy, there was that whole celibacy vow—but that was before she met Ray. Before she gained firsthand knowledge of the multitude of ways a bull rider had of showing a girl just how much he liked her without saying a single word.

One of the rodeo queens set up a boom box, and the slow, sad twang of beer-cryin' country music filled the night air.

Ray danced like he rode, tight and hard, and by midnight, when most everyone else had gravitated to bed or off to mull over the day in intimate groups, Ray took Belle by the hand, leading her across the starlit parking lot to his truck.

"I want to show you something," he said, his voice smooth as the night air kissing her bare shoulders.

He held open the door to a small camper attached to his rusty Ford. Earlier, he'd explained that he couldn't afford a room at the motel, but since his friends were staying there, he figured the owner wouldn't mind him parking his rig there for the night.

Once Belle ducked her head to follow him inside, he turned on a faint light at the head of a built-in bed.

The single room with a closet-sized bathroom was stuffy, so Ray wound open the one cantilevered window.

The place smelled of a manly mix of saddle soap and leather. A hint of loose tobacco.

A jumble of plastic dishes polluted a tiny stainless sink, and the splattered remains of what she guessed to be chili were glued to the stove.

"Ray, darlin'," she teased. "You're a P-I-G, pig."

He tipped his hat and winked. "Why, thank you, darlin', that's the nicest thing anyone's said to me all day."

"So?" she asked, spinning a slow circle where she stood. "What did you want to show me?"

He flashed her a wicked smile of white teeth and complete confidence in his sex appeal. "What did you think I wanted to show you?"

In the time it took to catch her breath from her attraction to his smile, he clenched her tight, curving his meaty hands about her waist and settling his firm, hot lips on her mouth.

Ray was her first experience with a man.

Sure, she'd been on lots of hayrides with lots of different boys, but this was no boy, and the burning hunger in the pit of her stomach told her flat out that Ray would never be satisfied with a childlike kiss.

Though she was nineteen, she was, of course, still a virgin.

She'd held tight to her virginity, believing it was a gift to be given to her future husband, long after her Tooth Fairy duties had been fulfilled. After spending just one evening with this Texas charmer, though, she knew he was the man she'd always dreamt of meeting—even if he was a mortal. For whom but her soul mate could she have ever felt such pure need?

Even if she would soon be bound to a ten-year period of celibacy, if he truly loved her, they could secretly be married; then he'd wait until her promise to the Fairy Council was honored.

111

That was why when he slid his hand down the curve of her backside, then up and around to cover her breasts, she said, "Ray, honey, don't you think we're moving a bit fast?"

"Ain't no such thing as fast when two people are in love. Haven't you ever heard that?"

He one-by-one unbuttoned the closures on her sundress, then leaned low to suckle her right breast.

She gasped.

The sensation was hot and biting.

Instant, exquisite torture.

She tried pushing him away, but his logic seemed so right. How could what they shared be wrong?

That night, nestled amidst a tangle of sheets with a cowboy named Ray, she lost not only her virginity but her heart, and the next morning, when she woke to bright sunshine streaming through the trailer's tiny window, she'd never been more content.

Ray tenderly kissed her awake, made love to her again, then left to bum a shower from his friend's motel room.

She did the same, shyly confessing to Josie where she'd spent the night.

Once dressed, she headed to the convenience store across the street to purchase eggs, bacon and juice. Then she cooked her lover and soon-to-be-husband a wholesome breakfast, washed his dishes and made his bed.

Her future home tidy and breakfast cooked, she sat back to wait for her man's return.

An hour passed, and just about the time she'd grown worried, a knock sounded at the door.

She opened it to come face to face with a gorgeous, dark-haired, charmingly petite rodeo queen dressed in red from the tips of her silver-trimmed boots to the top of her custom-made red felt hat.

"Ray here?" the queen asked in a darling country twang.

Belle hated her on sight.

Heart pounding, Belle shook her head. "Last I heard, Ray was in Room Fourteen taking a shower."

The woman narrowed her eyes, then took in the proprietary way Belle stood in the door wearing one of Ray's white T-shirts and holding one of his dish towels. "Great," she said in a less-than-enthusiastic tone. "Thanks."

Across the drive, the door to Room Fourteen swung open. Ray poked his head outside. "Felicia! Over here! Damn, baby, I didn't expect you till tonight."

Swallowing past a hard lump of anger and embarrassment for having been so gullible, Belle tortured herself by watching Felicia sway her curvaceous hips all the way across that parking lot and into Ray's arms.

All hope she'd harbored of the woman being his sister was lost as soon as their hug developed into an epic kiss.

"Lordy, I missed you," Ray said, his words carrying along with the chatter of wrens on the early-morning breeze.

"Me too, sweetheart. You know I had that parade down in Austin, but . . ." As she stepped inside the room, shutting the door behind her, the door to Room Twenty-One opened and Josie stepped out.

When Belle raced out of the trailer and back to her room, flinging herself across the bed she hadn't slept in, she thought the worst of her shame was over. But a month later, when her period was late, she knew the worst was yet to come.

113

Tests confirmed she was pregnant.

She'd immediately dropped out of the Academy, claiming she needed time to think about taking on such a huge responsibility as becoming a Tooth Fairy.

She'd gone to stay with her mother, who lived in a Washington State commune full of free spirits who wouldn't see a young unmarried pregnant girl as a problem, but a blessing.

Belle's mother had become pregnant with her while she'd been on active Tooth Fairy duty. According to Aunt Lila, the scandal was all anyone talked about for years.

Belle's mom, Violet, had been run out of the Fairy Kingdom in shame, losing her wings, job and above all, her place in the world.

Because of that, Belle's mom left her to be raised by Aunt Lila and Uncle Philbert—technically, since they were the brother and sister of Violet's mom, the pair were Belle's great-aunt and great-uncle, but to her, titles hardly mattered as they were the only family she'd ever known.

Though Belle occasionally heard from her mother, and knew she loved her, it hadn't been the same as if she'd grown up beside her. Belle knew she was taking a risk in bringing Ewan back to the farm where she'd been raised, but a Fairy's word was sacred, and when she'd sworn to the Council that out of the goodness of her heart she'd taken Ewan into her home as an orphan, they'd believed her.

When she'd subsequently rejoined her class at the Academy, then gone on to ace each portion of her training as if she'd never even been gone, the whole matter was forgotten.

Forgotten by everyone, that is, except Josie—who'd

miserably botched both the tooth weight ratios and flying spell portions of her final exam. Even worse, her psychological testing showed her personality unsuitable for working with small children.

Josie's family was furious when, instead of earning a Tooth Fairy assignment, she was given the embarrassing duty of Traffic Fairy.

Day in and day out, Josie willed stoplights to turn.

Say a mortal was late for work and wishing for all lights to be green. Josie—and others of her kind—were charged with turning the lights red, so that the mortals might have time to calm themselves before continuing on with their days. Everyone knew Traffic Fairies performed important tasks, but the jobs weren't all that prestigious.

Anyway, not long after her first month on the job, Josie showed up on Belle's family farm just in time to catch her practically floating into her beautiful pink tulle Tooth Fairy uniform. Still wearing her drab gray Traffic Fairy uniform, the usually flashy Josie had been furious. Furious enough to blackmail Belle over the issue of Ewan's birth.

Knowing what'd happened to her own mother after she'd become pregnant while on the job, Belle couldn't take the chance of drawing an ounce more of Josie's wrath, so she'd agreed to pay her an outrageous monthly sum to keep quiet.

Wiping a few tears not only for the mother and son she so desperately missed, but for her lost innocence, too, Belle shifted on the sofa.

Old folks said we must learn from our mistakes, and if Belle learned one thing in her life, it was to never, *ever* fall for another mortal Texan.

To this day, Ray Parks didn't know he was a father.

How many other women had he taken advantage of in that dilapidated trailer?

A trailer that reminded her of Boone's time-worn house.

She sniffled.

A house where, for all she knew, he'd brought countless women.

You don't really believe that.

"Yes. I do," she mumbled in a reed-thin voice. "Just like Ray, he cares about nothing but himself and the—"

"Princess?" The sound of the back door swinging open caused her to jolt upright.

Speak of the ornery devil.

"I'm in here," she called out, wiping stupid tears.

"Well, come in *here*. I've got something to show you."

Where had she heard that line before?

Still, she did as he asked, only to get the surprise of her life.

Chapter Eight

Standing in front of the open door, golden rays of setting sun silhouetting his rangy frame, was Boone with an antique copper bathtub.

A bathtub!

The prospect of soaking in a steaming, sudsy tub made Belle tingle in anticipation. "Is that what I think it is?" she asked, putting aside her constant suspicion to cross the room and finger the tub's smooth, time-worn surface.

"Sure is. My great-grandmother was rumored to have been quite the beauty, and just to torment my great-grandfather, she made him fill this with steaming water every single Saturday night. 'Course I'm sure he was richly rewarded for his troubles," he said with an incorrigible wink that somersaulted her stomach. "But just to prove I'm not the ogre you think I am, I spent the last thirty minutes cleaning this old tub for you, and I'm willing to spend the next thirty minutes filling it, all for the low, low price of your forgiveness."

While he stood back, grinning at his ingenuity, Belle scowled.

What was he up to this time?

Could his sudden generosity really be nothing more than an attempt to mend their fences?

"Well?" he asked expectantly. "Don't I at least get a thank-you hug?" He looked so darned handsome she almost succumbed, but common sense won out when he added, "I'd take a friendly kiss, too, if you have one to spare."

"So this is a peace offering, huh? I'll bet what you were really hoping to do is get in there with me."

He shrugged. "Can't blame a guy for trying."

"In your case," she said, "I can."

An hour later, Belle's tummy was full with two more Twinkies and she'd sunk up to her neck in strawberry-scented bubbles that Boone's mother had given him for Christmas the same year he'd gotten his flashy red boots. He said she'd been on a red theme.

Not only had Belle forgiven him for his earlier strange behavior, but she was ready to give him the friendly kiss and hug he'd requested.

Darkness fell swiftly on the prairie, and flickering oil lamps lent the kitchen a soft glow it lacked in the harsh light of day. With little effort she imagined herself back in Boone's great-grandmother's time, relaxing in this tub when its copper surface must've gleamed like a new penny.

She'd have spent the day tending her garden and baking, anticipating the night ahead when, for a few all too brief hours, the everyday world of backbreaking work would fade to make room for pleasure.

Closing her eyes, Belle sighed in contentment, listening to Boone pluck out a tune on his six-string guitar.

Who'd have thought at the start of this long day that she'd end up so utterly at peace?

Yes, Ewan and Lila and Philbert still needed her.

Yes, the mortgage and Josie's blackmail payments still had to be paid.

But with Boone's ballad floating through the calico curtain serving as the door between the kitchen and living room, her problems seemed another lifetime away.

"Princess?" Boone called out. "You all right in there?"

She couldn't help but grin. "If you're asking if I need my back scrubbed, thanks but no thanks."

"Sure. No problem. Just being neighborly."

He plucked a few more notes before she asked, "Boone?"

"Yeah?"

"What was your great-grandmother's name?"

"Tallulah. Why?" He'd stopped playing, and she sensed his presence on the other side of the curtain.

"Just curious." She truly didn't know why she'd asked, just that she needed to know. For whatever reason, she felt close to the woman she'd only seen in a photograph but whose presence was reflected in countless loving touches scattered throughout the house. The needlepointed sofa pillow, Boone's bedroom quilt, the threadbare calico curtains—from all those womanly embellishments, Belle knew Tallulah had loved this place as fiercely as she'd loved her man and children.

Belle shivered.

Oh, how she one day wanted to experience that same kind of love. That same contentment.

119

"Your water still hot?" Boone called out.

"Yep."

"Good." He didn't budge an inch from his spot by the curtained door.

"Is there something I can do for you?"

"As a matter a fact," he said, "I'm needing a snack. We kind of skipped dinner."

Gazing at the water, she realized that however indecent she was under the bubbles, all Boone would be able to see of her was from the neck up. Should she be a good sport and let him grab a bite to eat?

"Okay," she said, making a split-second decision to go with her heart on this one. One good deed did deserve another, and after this bath, she surely did feel a good deal better. "Come on in."

"You sure?" He peeked around the side of the curtain. She nodded.

"Great." Bounding into the room, he looked pointedly away from her and toward the back door.

It was kind of hard for Belle not to get a good look at him—or at least his jeans-clad hindquarters and strong, T-shirt-clad back—as he scooted through the narrow space between tub and cabinet.

"Let me just grab a can of beans and I'll be on my way."

Belle sucked in a swift gulp of air.

He might as well have been grabbing a handful of diamonds for all she cared, as her sole focus was on his T-shirt, beneath which the twin ridges on his shoulder blades seemed to have grown a couple of inches longer and about a half inch wider.

What was wrong with him?

Were the elongated lumps a fast-growing cancer?

Was that why he had such mood swings?

Could it be that not only had his mother been stricken with a deadly disease, but he, too?

What were the odds?

"Ah," he said, "got one."

Normal, Belle thought, sick at the thought of how much this man must be keeping from her. *I have to seem normal while figuring out what else he may be hiding.*

"Don't—"She cleared her throat. Speaking normally through a throat thick with tears was no easy feat. "Don't you get sick of pork & beans?"

"Nah. It's all a matter of perspective, you see." He turned to look at her, momentarily forgetting her location in the tub, and hastily turned back to the cupboard. "Oops. Sorry about that."

"It's okay."

The back of his neck flamed an even deeper red than his farmer's tan. "Anyway," he said, "where was I?"

"Perception."

"Oh, yeah. Like I was saying, you just have to convince yourself that pork & beans are the food of the gods. Which, if you think about it, they really are."

"How so?"

"High in protein and low in cost. Could there be a better combination?"

"I see your point." She didn't, but in her current state of undress, she figured it might be prudent not to start a food debate that outlasted the coverage of her bubbles.

When he turned to make his exit, he bumped his kneecap on the tub's edge.

Reaching forward to rub his wound, he dropped the can into the water, where it not only splashed water onto Belle's freshly scrubbed floor, but smashed the big toe of her left foot.

121

"Boone!" She winced from the sharp pain.

"Sorry," he said, kneeling as if he meant to go bobbing for beans beneath the sudsy waters. Before she could tell him in no uncertain terms that his hands were *not* to reach below her iridescent covers, he did just that.

Biting his lower lip, face furrowed in concentration, he said, "Just give me one more second and I'll—" When his hand touched far more than his can of beans, he jerked back as if struck by that rattler.

"*Boone!*" she shouted.

"Sorry," he said again, flashing a naughty grin that didn't look the least bit apologetic.

"You are not! You did that on purpose!"

"Prove it." He'd gotten her with her own logic that time, and as he sat back on his haunches, hands dripping with warm water and white suds, he flicked a few bubbles her way.

She ducked, but not fast enough to avoid a speck of white that landed on the tip of her nose. "Why, you . . ." Forgetting that in light of his apparent affliction, she ought to be careful with him, she heartily fought back, but in earning her title as the bubble-fight champ, she'd forgotten that the only thing covering her birthday suit was her soapy ammunition.

Not thirty seconds later, after the laughter died down and they—and the floor—were soaked, Boone unashamedly watched as the princess's leftover giggles turned to out-of-breath awareness.

Their gazes locked, and she crossed her arms over her breasts, but not quick enough to keep Boone from catching an eyeful that made his jeans fit uncomfortably tight.

Damn, he'd known she'd be one hell of a tasty dish, but nothing could have prepared him for the truth of what those silky white bubbles had hidden. In the brief flash he'd seen of her at his mother's, he'd missed the fact that her breasts were big and high and crowned with dusky-rose nipples he'd much rather feast on than beans.

The voice in his head told him if he wanted them— her—he could have them. All of her. It was but a simple matter of taking that which he desired.

"You know I want you," he said, ignoring the voice.

She swallowed hard. Nodded.

Her pale blue eyes grew impossibly wide.

What was she thinking? Was it hunger for him that made her lick her lips? Or fears *of* him?

The old Boone said, "You also know I would never do anything you didn't want."

Liar, the voice said.

He put his hand to his temple, warning the voice to stop.

She nodded again.

"Then why aren't you saying something?" he asked. "Hell, you haven't been this quiet in all the time we've been together. Come on, Belle, tell me what's on your mind."

"You really want to know?"

"Well, yeah, why wouldn't I?"

"Because at this very moment a—"

"Damn! What was that?"

Belle couldn't keep from laughing when the Make-Out King got bit on his rear end by a Goat Queen.

He spun around to face the two-and-a-half foot tall menace. "Mabel. How the hell did you get in here, and where have you been?"

"Hmm, looks like while you've been ogling me, somebody else has been on the make for you."

"Not funny, Princess."

"I think so."

The goat bleated her agreement.

"Women," Boone said, using the tub edge to help stand. "How did she get in here?" He grabbed the goat by the scruff of her neck, then led her out of the kitchen and onto the back porch, as she grumbled all the way.

"Treat her gently, Boone. She looks like she might be pregnant."

"Great," he mumbled from outside. "Just what I need, a cocky princess and a knocked-up goat."

"Look on the bright side," she quipped. "At least now we'll have milk."

Boone strode back through the door and slammed it before glaring at her, then heading for the living room. "She had to have come in through one of the windows."

Now that she didn't have an audience, Belle rose from the tub. Boone had left her a thick navy blue towel, which she wrapped around her body sarong style.

Though her hair was dripping, she couldn't resist seeing what Boone was up to. "Well, Sherlock?" she asked, poised in front of the kitchen curtain. "How did she get in?"

"Right here." He pointed at a flapping screen.

When the goat popped her head back through and bleated, Boone scowled, pushed poor Mabel back, then pulled the window down just low enough so she couldn't get in.

Dissolving in a fit of laughter, Belle struggled to keep her towel on, while sidestepping Boone's wrath.

"Think this is funny, do you?"

"What I think is that you need to put bars on the windows to keep your livestock out."

"You're right," he said, "and then I'll put you at the top of my list of creatures that need to stay out." While he talked, he steadily moved closer until they stood toe to toe, chest to chest. The evaporating moisture on her skin caused her to shiver, as did the undisguised heat in Boone's gaze.

If only for a few minutes, that damned goat had interfered with Boone's intentions, but now, for the second time that evening, laughter turned to breathless anticipation.

Only this time, Boone knew no goat would be coming to the princess's rescue.

"You ready for this?" he asked, not sure he recognized his own voice. He backed her up, pinning her to the wooden cabinet with its pressed-tin counter.

Was the cool metal nipping at the hot, soft flesh of her back?

"I—" There she was, once again licking her lips. "I don't know what you mean."

"Don't play the innocent with me, Belle. I know this isn't your first time."

Her left hand made a slow rise to cover her mouth. "How could you . . ."

His nostrils flared. "I smell it. You want me—*bad*."

How he'd done it, Belle couldn't fathom, but much to her secret shame, Boone was right—on both counts.

In spite of cold/hot warning chills running through her, she felt powerless to the hold he had on her. She'd become a string puppet, awaiting his touch to tell her her next move.

Her right arm ached from the effort of holding the towel. His dark, dark eyes told her to drop it. To grant him access to not just her body, but her soul.

Drop it, a voice inside her said. *Don't be afraid. It—he—won't hurt you. He'll only bring you pleasure beyond your wildest dreams.*

"Yes," she said, softly parting her lips, breathing on shallow puffs of hot, moist air.

Nipples hard, straining to him, she gripped the towel tighter.

"What's wrong with me?" she murmured.

Nothing's wrong, the voice said. *Go with this. With him.*

Boone braced his hands on the counter, pinning her in between.

She felt trapped.

Sheltered.

Afraid.

Excited.

Guilty.

Most of all, unbearable anticipation.

Like a great winged beast, he swooped down upon her and her warring emotions, crushing her mouth in a kiss fueled by starvation.

He still had his hands on the counter, but she wanted them on her, skimming up her back, dragging down that wet, cold towel.

She craved his heat as if his hands were the sun.

Seeking the heat—only the heat—she abandoned the towel, letting it fall along with her every inhibition. She was no longer a noble-bred Fairy, but merely a woman.

Just as Boone was merely a man.

She slid her hands up the inside of his T-shirt, exploring the ridges of his abs. The hard planes of his chest. His skin was warm, sprinkled with hair she knew would be dark and rough and satisfying to the itch gnawing her breasts.

"You taste like candy," he murmured, straying his kisses to her neck before returning to her lips.

From outside, a breeze lofted through the partly open window, chilling her fever-damp skin.

No, she wanted heat.

Boone's heat.

Its heat—whatever *it* was.

The chill persisted, bringing along with its discomfort a jolt of conscience.

What was she doing? Standing here naked with her hands on Boone's chest.

She had no business kissing him like he was the moon and stars and everything wonderful in between.

"No . . ." she said. "We can't. This is wrong."

"Yes, Princess . . . we can. Damn, can't you feel it? How everything about us being together is right?"

She removed her hands from the glory of his chest to run them through her damp hair at her temples.

She had to think.

What was she doing here?

She'd taken vows—not only to the Fairy Council, but to her son. She'd promised both her innocence. Her allegiance.

Something sinister inside her laughed. *To Fairies*, it said, *isn't telling the truth paramount to all else? Yet look at you, Belle, lying to yourself about not wanting to be here, standing naked in Boone's arms, just as easily as you lied to the Council about the true origins of your son. To a creature such as yourself, supposedly incapable of lies, have you ever wondered why they come so easily to the tip of your forked tongue?*

"Boone?" she said, eyes tearing, voice wavy and unsure.

"Yes," he said into her hair.

"I'm scared."

"Me, too, Princess. Me, too."

She looked up, deep into his silvery gray eyes. "What should we do?"

Crushing her in a hug, he said, "After I tuck you into bed, I'm going out to the barn."

Though the thought of being apart from him all night somehow felt even more wrong than for the two of them to be standing here together, with her naked, she nodded. She was not at all afraid when he gently lifted her into his arms and carried her to bed.

"I didn't wake you, did I?" Philbert asked Maude over the phone long after he'd brewed the evening coffee, done the supper dishes, then settled Lila in front of her shows. Darnedest thing. She was crazy for those mobster series. Fancied herself some kind of Fairy crime boss. The whole obsession was unnatural, if you asked him. But seeing how nobody was askin' him, he—

"Not only am I awake," Maude said with one of her signature brassy snorts, "but you couldn't have called at a worse time. I'm right in the middle of a Panties for Parkinson's fund-raiser."

Philbert swallowed his latest gulp of coffee down the wrong hole, coughing up that old proverbial storm. "Panties for Parkinson's?" he managed at last.

"Oh, you don't have to go acting all shocked about it," Maude said. "Having Belle do her princess act kinda livened things up 'round here. Well . . . my friend Maryvale Clawson has a second cousin who's a real live Victoria's Secret model, and seeing how *Pastries* for

Parkinson's wasn't drumming up much excitement on advance ticket sales, we thought—"

"Yeah, yeah," he said, "I get the point. But I'm telling you, we got bigger problems than some disease."

"Parkinson's is a serious affliction, Philbert. Each year it strikes tens of thousands of—"

"Yeah, well, my problem could very well destroy the whole world if we don't figure something out."

Maude rolled her eyes. Honestly, sometimes Philbert could be so melodramatic. "Would you kindly move it along there, stud? I got a major Hollywood hunk out in my grand entry hall shakin' his tight buns in one of those man-thongs."

"Focus, Maude. Did you hear about it?"

She giggled. "Oh, my—the fabric is gray silk with a silver sequined elephant trunk covering the important stuff—if you know what I mean."

Ignoring her, Philbert said, "Heard on the evening news there were two more earthquakes today. Turkey and Spain. They caused terrible tidal waves and flooding. People are dead, Maude. Thousands are dead."

"Oh, dear, this next stud is all dressed up for a safari. *Rrrrrr*," she said with a sexy roll of her tongue.

"The Darkness . . ." Philbert said, his right hand trembling to such a degree that coffee sloshed out of his cup, scalding him, warning him, he'd sent their precious Belle off on a gamble she had one chance in a million to win. "It's coming."

"*Woo-hooooo*! I'll tell you who's *coming*, old friend, and it's not—"

Click.

Maude frowned at the phone, then tossed it onto the nearest Moroccan-style pillow couch she'd had brought in for the night.

Honestly, that old coot needed to lighten up.

Too bad he wasn't here to see this latest sex-kitten starlet slink her way down the staircase in her emerald-green snakeskin pasties and panties.

Maude giggled.

Pasties & Panties.

Talk about the perfect name for next year's event!

The darkness was complete, yet Boone's vision unnervingly clear.

I'm waiting, the voice said.

"No," Boone said back, writhing from side to side on the bed he'd made for himself out of hay bales in the barn's loft. "No, I'm not ready. There's so much left to do."

You don't have to be afraid of me, my son. I am you. Embrace me. Embrace the power that is yours for the taking.

"No. No, I don't want it. What you're doing to me—to her—it's sick. Wrong."

The voice laughed. *Did it feel wrong this afternoon? Was it wrong when the life-or-death power of me raged through your limbs when you stared that snake in the eyes? You could have easily ripped its head off, you know. In fact, doing just that probably would have been good for you. A good first lesson in exactly the kind of creature you'll soon enough become.*

"No."

Was it wrong when you could've taken that pathetic woman right there in the dirt? You know you wanted to. You know how hard your need made you. You could've easily taken her again tonight in the kitchen. What kind of man are you? The voice laughed. *If you're even a man at all.*

"Get the hell out of my head," Boone said, clawing at his hair, no longer sure if he was asleep or awake.

Alive or dead.

How can I leave your head, the voice politely inquired, *when I'm already in your soul?*

"No, that's a lie."

Is it? Care to try denying the wings sprouting from your back?

"No," Boone said, thrashing his head from side to side. "No, they're not there. They're not real. None of this is real. Not you, not—"

Imagine the power of soaring above this pathetic earth. Imagine the power of swooping down upon your defenseless prey. Imagine—

"Stop it! Stop it! Stop—"

"Boone?" The voice was different.

Soft.

"No!" Boone cried, convinced the softening must be another of *his* tricks. "I *will* fight you. I will, I will, I—"

"Boone, please," Belle said, hand on his arm, giving him a light shake. "Wake up. It's just a dream."

"No," he said, returning slowly to what was real. To Belle, gazing at him through the eyes of an angel, her pale hair taking on the light of the moon. "No, it wasn't a dream, but a nightmare."

She sat beside him on the bales he'd arranged into a bed. With a couple of saddle blankets as the first layer, and quilts and sheets after that, the pallet was comfortable enough, but not very large. Not nearly large enough to keep her at a safe distance.

This time, the voice had been closer. *Deeper*. More intent on finding whatever it was it sought.

"You know," Belle said, smoothing his hair from his

forehead, "when my little boy has nightmares, he always tells me that talking about them helps."

Boone raised his eyebrows. "You have a son?"

The slight rise in his tone told her he found the very idea inconceivable.

Swallowing hard, she nodded. "His name's Ewan. He's not really mine, though," she said, covering the familiar ache in her heart that came each time she told the lie. "I, um, took him in when he was just a baby. A friend of mine found him lying on one of the front pews in her church. She couldn't keep him, so she asked me to—and I did."

"You took in a child like he was just a stray puppy?" He shook his head.

"What do you mean? What else could I have done?"

"I'm not saying it like it was a bad thing," he said. "I—hell, it's been a long night. I'm in awe. What you did—it's noble."

"Thank you."

"You're welcome."

After a long time of just sitting there, trying to look anywhere but at him, Belle said, "About that nightmare, Boone. You'll get back to sleep faster if you tell me about it. You know, kind of get it out of your system."

He violently shook his head. "I can't—could *never*—talk about it."

"Okay," she said, shying away. "But if you ever change your—"

"I won't."

Chapter Nine

Boone woke the next morning to both a headache and straw spearing him in a not-so-pleasant assortment of places.

Sun streamed through the open hayloft door, illuminating thousands of dust motes. The air smelled gentle. Of fresh-cut straw and Dandy and Daffodil's oats. Leather and horseflesh.

On the surface, it should have been a great day.

Trouble was, those things on his back burned.

And then there was the voice.

The darkness that clung to him like a bad smell.

Hand to his throbbing forehead, Boone shook his head. It was all too much.

Too much to think about, and definitely too much to be forced to live with. Oh, sure, he supposed there were worse ways to die, but these nightly visits were starting to feel like some sort of curse.

And then there was the princess.

If Boone truly was the honorable man he kept proclaiming to the voice that he was, he would have already taken her to the nearest town and put her on a bus headed home.

Lord, he hated to admit it, but the princess was growing on him. Which made the battle raging in his head that much harder to bear.

On the one hand, there was the voice—urging him to take her.

In the dirt.

On the kitchen floor.

Anywhere he damn well pleased.

But what small portion of his former self he still recognized wanted to protect the princess from whatever monster he was becoming.

Not only that, but if they did sleep together, he was going to have to get naked. What was he going to tell her about those damned things on his back?

Does it really matter? the voice said. *You have to know she's only out to con you. Any good she's done here has only been for one cause—lining her own empty pockets with* your *money. Sound familiar?*

A sickening vision of Olivia kissing her golf pro flashed through Boone's weary brain.

But even as he remembered Olivia, he recognized a vital difference between her and Belle. The night he'd seen Belle gliding down his mother's staircase, he'd identified the warrior's spirit in her eyes.

Even more confusing was her gentle way with animals, and even with him. Last night, when she'd come to him in the night, she'd had an intrinsic calmness that warred with the idea of her being out to trick him.

Or was she just that good at the game?

No way. She had a little boy.

Did she?

With a frustrated groan, Boone scrambled to his feet, then descended the loft ladder.

How was he going to make it through the next few weeks with her there? How was he going to make it all the way to the end all on his own?

No matter how much he might doubt her sincerity, he didn't want to—couldn't—let her go. He was so damned scared of dying alone. And knowing that ticked him off all the more.

Dandy and Daffodil softy whinnied their morning welcome.

"Hey, you two," he said, still around the corner from their stall. "What do you say we—"

"Aren't you pretty," a lilting feminine voice said after making a few obnoxious kissy noises. "Yes, you are." *Kissy, kissy.* "You are the prettiest horse in the whole wide world."

In no mood for niceties, Boone whipped around the corner as if coyotes were attacking his beloved plow team, but what he saw was worse than any ordinary coyote—it was the princess, smooching his horses!

And from the sound of it, they were smooching her back—the traitors!

He was just about to tell her to get away from his horses—and him—when he caught a whiff of whatever she was hiding under the dishtowel-covered plate she held out to him.

"Good morning," she said with an impossibly pretty, shy smile. "We didn't have much supper last night. I thought you might be hungry." She removed the towel, revealing an omelet and fried potatoes.

"Good God, woman." Holding the steaming grub un-

135

der his nose, Boone groaned his pleasure. "What're you trying to do to me?"

She beamed. "Oh, here," she said, handing him a fork. "You might need this."

He took a bite and happily sighed.

Belle beamed. "You like it?"

"Oh yes." He took another bite, this time taking time to admire the view. Her blond halo was all mussed from sleep, and her v-neck T-shirt showed a tantalizing bit of throat he'd like to—whoa! Hadn't that line of thought gotten him in enough trouble just last night? "I, um, didn't figure you for a cook."

She raised her chin. "I can do lots of things that might surprise you."

"Oh, yeah?" He shot her a bad-boy grin. "Like what?"

"Like castrating bulls."

"Ouch."

"Take that as a cue to keep your mind out of the gutter."

"Yes, ma'am," he said, taking another bite. "You eat yet?"

She shrugged.

"What's that mean?"

"There weren't enough eggs or veggies for two omelets."

"Here," he said, forking off a bite and holding it up.

She shook her head. "I made that for you."

"Then I should be allowed to share."

"Yeah, but—"

He held the fork in front of her mouth. "Open."

She stubbornly refused.

He touched the tines to her lips, wanting to ignore the jolt passing through his hand and arm, up his chest and throat, into his own lips as her sweet mouth opened, taking in not just the fork and the bite of omelet, but him.

While she chewed, she looked away.

"Good, isn't it?"

She nodded.

"So you'll take half?"

"Boone, I—"

He loaded his fork with her second bite, then held it to her lips. Like a good little girl, she opened her mouth, and he slid the fork in.

A second later, he was taking another bite for himself, thinking about where that fork had just been. And about how stupid he was for being jealous of a freakin' piece of metal.

"Henny," Belle said as the noon sun baked the grass she'd just whacked. "I do believe my making breakfast for Boone won him over, don't you think?"

The hen ignored her to scratch for a bug.

"Well, it doesn't matter what you think, because I know how much he enjoyed my cooking."

Not to mention how much you enjoyed that sexy-assin mind game of him feeding you!

Belle raked faster.

Having found a sickle in the tool shed earlier that morning, she'd decided the tall grass around the areas where she'd be working had to go.

Unfortunately, all that chopping had made a big mess, and raking wasn't at the top of her favorite-activities list. What she really wanted to do was spend more time in the kitchen, whipping up a meal that would make Boone's taste buds water.

But why?

Well . . .

She raked harder.

Knowing that she was waffling on her opinion of Boone didn't make the knowledge any easier to bear.

Who knew why she was softening toward him?

Maybe because of the surprise bubble bath he'd provided, or the way he'd looked so vulnerable in the middle of the night. How he'd wolfed down his part of the omelet like one of Ewan's starving strays.

Whether he admitted it or not, he needed her.

And she had this compulsive thing about needing to be needed.

Not good. No, wherever this was heading, it couldn't be anywhere good.

She already had a family, home and career needing her attention. She had no business finding satisfaction in tending to not only a miscreant like Boone, but his little house on the prairie, too! And as for how she got butterflies in her tummy every time she thought about his kisses . . .

She stooped to pick up a tumbleweed carcass, then flung it into the pile of grass.

Was it the power behind those kisses that made her so determined to leave her healing mark on this place? On him?

Oh—way to go on not thinking about it, Belle!

Okay, but since she obviously was thinking about it, was it the kissing that made her feel connected to him? And made her feel that on some basic, instinctive level, he was a fellow struggler in life? For whatever reason, he, too, was fighting to save his farm and a family member he held dear.

Just the thought of Maude being terminally ill brought tears to Belle's eyes.

And say Boone was telling the truth about being

broke. What a generous man he was, to give his mom free rein with his nearly empty wallet.

Considering the style to which Maude must be accustomed, Belle couldn't even fathom the financial load Boone must be bearing.

Surely he could have found a better way to raise money than with this farm, but who knew? Once Belle helped whip it into shape, he just might make a profit off his land after all.

And if they failed to make a profit, well, then they'd just bring their loved ones out here to live with them. She could home-school Ewan, and maybe Boone could convert one of the sheds into an extra bedroom where Aunt Lila and Maude could sleep.

Philbert might get a kick out of setting up residence in the barn.

Pausing in her work to gauge the size of the tool shed, Belle grinned at the mental image springing to life. Maude Wentworth, the Grande Dame of Clairemonte Falls, sleeping in a converted tool shed—now, *that* would make society tongues wag!

But the important thing was, everyone Belle loved would be together.

Whoa! Did she just say that everyone she *loved* could be together? Was she lumping the man who only yesterday she'd considered a low-down, dirty, despicable bum into the same category as the people she held most dear?

She put renewed energy into her raking.

Even if loving every living thing on the planet was part of her official job description, she couldn't possibly love Boone Wentworth.

It just wasn't possible, and to prove it, she performed three hours of yard work in thirty minutes flat.

* * *

"Mmm," Boone called out that afternoon, stepping onto the porch with hat in hand. "What's that delicious smell?"

The princess opened the door. "Hey, there, cowboy."

"Hey, yourself." He didn't want his heart racing at the sight of her, but Lord, how it did.

Her long hair hung loose and sexy, and the way she wore his plain white T-shirt halter-style, showing off her curves—*damn*.

Good thing he had her out here all to himself or she'd start a bachelor stampede. As for how his red plaid boxers had settled low on the bottom rung of her hourglass . . .

"What's cookin'?" he finally managed to ask.

"Come on in and taste for yourself. I doctored one of those cans of chili, then made salads from what little lettuce I managed to rescue from the goats."

"I've never been much of a leaf eater," he said, "but hungry as I am, it all sounds good." Quashing the urge to plant a kiss on her cheek, Boone yanked his boots off and tossed them in the corner by the door. Didn't want to go lousing up the cook's good mood by mussing up her clean kitchen floor!

Inside, he found the table decked out in a pretty yellow calico tablecloth. A pottery vase overflowing with wildflowers graced the table's center. Two mix-and-match place settings and salad plates loaded with baby greens completed the most elaborate spread the house had seen in the last seventy-five years.

"Damn," he said on his way to the sink to wash up. "You really went all out."

She shrugged. "Wasn't anything else to do."

"I see that you worked on the yard, too."

"Like it?"

"Sure. What's not to like?" He dried his hands on the dishtowel that had never before been hanging by the sink, then sat at the table.

"Oh, I don't know," she said, wincing as she pulled a steaming pan of what smelled like sweet cornbread from the oven.

Dear Lord, what had he done before she'd arrived?

And what was he going to do when she was gone?

Maybe it was just his imagination, but since eating her omelet that morning, he'd put a little more muscle into his plow work.

"I guess I didn't know how you'd take my fixing the place up," she said. "I mean, for all I know, you might have liked everything just fine the way it was."

"Yeah."

She scowled.

"I mean, no," he quickly said. "I kind of like the changes you've made." And he did like the changes to the yard and outbuildings. He liked how the house's door latch was fixed and the chickens no longer roosted in the kitchen. He especially liked hearing the faint sound of the princess's off-key disco songs as he plowed the field.

About the only thing he didn't like about her changes were those in himself.

He was starting to become attached to the woman, and for a man on the verge of dying, forming any sort of attachment wasn't a good thing.

Belle gestured for him to have a seat at the table, but instead he pulled out a chair for her. "The least I can do after you cooked is play butler."

Beaming up at him, she said, "Why, thank you, kind sir."

"You're most welcome, milady." He scrunched his nose. "Or would that be madame?"

"I thought madame was for married women."

"Beats me," he said, grabbing both bowls, then heading for the stove to fill them with spicy-sweet-smelling chili. "Man, this looks good," he said, setting Belle's full bowl in front of her. He filled his own bowl and set it on the table before returning to the stove to break off chunks of cornbread.

Belle winced. "How can you touch that cast-iron pan without a hot pad?"

"What do you mean? It's not at all hot."

"Boone, it's . . ." She narrowed her eyes. "Never mind. I guess it's none of my business."

"What?"

"Nothing. I don't want to spoil our meal."

"Nothing's spoiled. Just tell me what you were going to say."

She toyed with the cloth napkin she'd placed on her lap before looking his way. "It's just that the bread is still steaming. I took that pan out no more than two or three minutes ago, and then it was so hot it burned me through my oven mitt."

"Yeah, so? It's cooled down. See?" He held it out for her to touch.

She did, then flinched. "Ouch! I told you it was hot." She put her wounded index finger in her mouth.

"You've got to be kidding me," he said, drawing her finger out to look for himself. The tip glowed angry red, and already there were signs of an approaching blister. "Geez," he said, still holding her injured hand as he set the steaming pan on the table, then lowered himself onto the seat beside her. "I'm sorry. It didn't feel hot to me."

"That's okay," she said.

"No. No, it's not even a little okay. I hurt you." He raised her finger to his mouth, gently kissing it, then drawing it into his mouth, touching just the tip with his tongue, then plunging it deeper to lightly suck.

Her blue eyes grew huge. "Boone, stop. I—"

"What? You don't like being nursed?"

"No. I mean, yes." She shook her head, trying to free her hand, but she must not have been trying all that hard, seeing how he still had hold of it.

"Well?" he asked, eyebrows raised. "Which is it to be, Princess? Yes, you like me tending your wound? Or no, you'd rather I set you free?"

Though a moment earlier he wouldn't have believed it possible, her eyes widened further still. She parted her lips, and out came her cute pink tongue.

"Tell you what," he said, freeing her hand to let it fall safely back on her lap. "Seeing how you don't seem to have an answer for me, I'll do the gentlemanly thing by just letting you go."

Her breathing shallow, she nodded.

"Now," he said, rubbing his hands together, "I know I bought some hot sauce while I was in town. You seen it?"

"It's, um, in the cabinet to the right of the sink. But I already added quite a bit."

Standing, he shot her a wink. "Then just a tad more won't hurt." He found the bottle, rejoined her at the table, then frowned when some annoying plastic thingee at the bottle's top kept him from getting out more than a few drops at a time.

"That should be plenty," Belle said. "I've tried that brand. It's pretty hot stuff."

Boone rolled his eyes, then took off the plastic

shield and dumped at least half the bottle into his bowl.

After taking a bite of chili and smiling, he dumped the rest of the bottle onto his salad.

"Boone! Are you crazy? You're going to make yourself sick."

Fork poised at his mouth, he winked. "That mean you care?"

"Did I say that?"

He took a bite of salad, taking his own sweet time to chew. "Seems to me the question implied the sentiment."

"Seems to me any sane person would realize that if something happened to you, I'd be kinda hard pressed to find my way home." Picking up her fork, she impaled a wad of lettuce. "Therefore, it's in my best interests to keep you healthy."

"So you genuinely don't care?"

"Well . . . no."

Boone fisted his napkin.

Hardened his jaw.

"You don't have to get all cranky," she said. "It's not as if you brought me out here intending to make me your prairie bride."

True.

So why was he all of a sudden mired in a thick, black cloud of hopelessness?

For those few seconds when her eyes had brimmed with concern, his spirit had soared. He'd even briefly envisioned life with her.

He still might have been dying. He still might have had to deal with that damned voice in his head, but at least he'd have her. At least he wouldn't have to endure a moment more of the sheer terror gripping him every single night he spent alone.

"I'm sorry," Belle said, toying with the yellow cloth napkin she'd set beside her plate. "That came out a little harsh. I don't know what I'm saying. I guess while I was working this morning, I realized that maybe we aren't so different after all. I mean, I know you think I'm some kind of criminal with nothing better to do than scam people out of their money, but that's just not the case."

"So tell me why that's not the case. If you have a reason for what you did, let's hear it. I want to know."

"The reason isn't important. What's important is that you trust me on faith alone. On the fact that you know in your heart I would never do anything to purposely hurt someone, which is why when you told me your mother is dying, I . . ." Her words stumbled off, as once again her eyes welled with tears.

Great.

He'd known that that story about his mother dying was bound to come back and bite him. Was now the time to tell the princess that Maude had lower blood pressure than he? Or that his mother would surely outlive him?

"Listen to me going on," she said, using the back of her hand to wipe tears from her cheeks. "I swear, I get so tired of crying at the drop of a hat—not that your mother's ill health isn't something to cry about, but you know what I mean."

No, he didn't.

Because this time he was the one pulling a con. This very minute, Maude was probably with her personal trainer, Marquis, before lunching with the girls—girls whose exclusive club she was now a member of because of Belle, or should he say, the *princess*.

Truth was, Belle hadn't in any way hurt his mother.

She'd helped her.

And the whopper he'd told his mom about the princess and him hooking up couldn't hurt matters, either—at least it wouldn't hurt until he spoiled the whole thing by finally telling the truth.

Unless . . . maybe Maude would never have to know the truth if he and the princess hooked up for real.

Lord. Boone sliced his fingers through his sweat-dampened hair. Damn this sickness in his head. It was making him think crazy.

Be crazy.

The whole reason he'd hauled the princess out here was to protect his mom's fortune, yet here he was getting all sappy sentimental just because he was dying.

Steeling his jaw along with his heart, Boone reminded himself that people died every day.

The dying was easy.

It was making sure that those you left behind would be well cared for for the rest of their lives that was tough. No matter how much he feared kicking it alone, Boone owed it to his mother to protect her—no matter the cost.

The princess's speech about trusting was nothing more than a fishing expedition designed to learn more about his bank account. Had to be.

But still, he could not overlook her wonderful qualities. No woman but Belle could be not only as gorgeous as she was, but as incredibly capable around a farm.

For the first time in his life, he felt scared where his feelings for a member of the fairer sex were concerned.

Scared, and a little bit in awe.

Oh, sure, his mental pep rally on only viewing Belle

as the enemy sounded great on the surface, but at the moment, he couldn't imagine letting her go.

"Boone?" she asked. "You okay? That hot sauce getting to you?"

"I'm fine," he said, ducking his head just in case she looked into his eyes and saw that nothing could be further from the truth.

Scalding his forearm with a simple caring touch, she said, "Good. Tummyaches are the worst."

Forking another bite, wondering why she didn't stop touching him, never wanting her to stop touching him, he cleared his throat before asking, "Know that from experience?" That touch of hers, innocent though it was, brought to mind all sorts of intimacies.

It was the touch of a wife to her husband.

A mother to her child.

It wasn't the typical gold digger's paw.

He ought to know. With Olivia, he'd gotten more than enough of those touches.

"My son used to get them all the time. Poor little guy." She spooned a bite of chili and thoughtfully chewed. "Our doctor suspected a food allergy, but one day the aches just went away."

"Good." *Maybe those things on my back will go away.*

The voice in his head laughed. *Just like me, my child, let me assure you, they will* never *go away.*

"Mind if I ask you a question?" Belle said later that afternoon, hot and bored with raking. Much to her surprise, Boone had come to help by wielding the sickle. He said it was because she'd be safer in the yard if the grass was short—fewer snakes. But she'd seen the way he kept eyeing her clingy makeshift halter, leading her to conclude that the only snake left around these parts was him!

" 'Kay," he said. "Shoot."

"How long were your great-grandparents married?"

"Sixty-eight years—not counting the one when my great-grandmother left my great-grandfather to go live with her sister."

"How come?"

"Way I heard it, Great-grandpa liked showing hogs at the county fair. Well, one year he had a boar he thought was a shoo-in to win not only the local fair but state, so, not wanting to take any chances with something happening to the thing, he brought him in the house. My grandpa said his mother pitched a fit that could've been heard clear to Denver about that pig livin' inside, but his daddy didn't care. So, Great-grandma Tallulah packed up the kids and moved to her sister's in San Antonio until after the summer fairs."

"Well?" Belle asked, fighting the distraction of Boone's wicked handsome grin. "Did the pig win?"

"Nah. Livin' in the house like it did, it ate too many table scraps. The damned thing got so big my great-grandpa could hardly get it out of the house, let alone into the wagon."

Once her laughter died down, Belle gazed across the shorn grass at the man who in such a short time had become such a fixture in her life.

He had a wonderful laugh.

Loud and billowy, like he wasn't afraid of anyone knowing he was having a good time.

Hearing that story made her more convinced than ever that Boone came from honest, hardworking stock. Simple people who treated a small thing like a county-fair victory with the reverence it deserved.

Heck, she remembered her own 4-H wins like they'd happened just yesterday. "Did you ever enter anything in the fair?"

"One of those public-service diorama things, but we had a big storm the day of the judging and, unfortunately, my table sat right beside the door. Rain demolished my lesson on recycling before the judges reached my table."

"How sad," Belle said, her heart going out to the disappointed boy Boone must've been.

That mental image of him as a dark-haired little scrap who didn't look all that different from Ewan brought out her fierce protective streak toward all things defenseless. "I'm sorry."

He shrugged. "It's no big deal. Hell, that happened over twenty years ago."

"But still . . ." She couldn't keep herself from reaching out to touch his forearm.

She'd meant her touch to be comforting and sympathetic, but when her fingers curved around his tanned forearm, when she felt the sprinkling of dark hairs dotting her palm and the sinewy strength of latent energy in his muscle, it was all she could do to breathe, let alone remember what she was trying to comfort him about.

His dark blue T-shirt hung heavy with sweat, clinging to his chest and back and biceps. Though she'd noticed he was careful to keep his back facing away from her, she'd seen enough to know those bumps had grown bigger.

Was that why he kept his shirt on despite the heat?

Was he embarrassed?

Had a doctor told him to keep out of the sun?

She selfishly didn't care.

Her itching fingertips remembered the rock-hard ripples on his abdomen. Only it wasn't enough to have merely touched them.

She wanted to see them.

Now.

Take it off! Take it off!

The chant echoing through her head sounded like she was seated front row center at a male strip show.

What was wrong with her? Was she coming down with flu, or just a bad case of Boone-itis?

This man was hardly a sad little boy. He was a scoundrel who'd offered her money to sleep with him—a *lot* of money, which he'd earlier claimed to not even have. Even worse, he was handsome enough that she still pondered the notion of sleeping with him for free.

Chapter Ten

"Woman," Boone said, in the mood to wax poetic about the amazing veggie lasagna-like stuff Belle invented, "that dinner was so damned tasty, it may have just forever ruined me for beans."

Shooting him a dubious grin, she said, "Am I hearing you right? The man who said, and I quote, 'beans are the perfect food' is now claiming not to care for them?"

"Damn, you're a mean-tempered gal," he said, firing a grin right back. "Never give me a moment's peace."

"Me? Mean to you? Have you been planting wacky weed in that field of yours?"

He turned serious. "You think I'm mean?"

When he'd given her such an incredible segue for launching into yet another spiel on how much she'd like to go home, she couldn't understand why the words that tumbled out of her mouth were, "Well, I wouldn't say you're *mean* mean. You know, just kind of gruff. Only sometimes."

"Oh."

She couldn't tell if that meant he liked her response or was just pondering it, so she added, " 'Cause if we're talkin' about *mean* mean here, I've met some real doozies."

Raising his eyebrows, he said, "Really? You've had a guy do worse than kidnap you?"

"Technically, Boone, you didn't kidnap me, you *bought* me." His truly apologetic silvery eyes told her he was sorry for what he'd done, even if their terminology didn't match up. "Believe me," she said, tucking her hair behind her ears, carefully not looking his way, "I've had much worse than this happen."

Like losing my virginity to a rodeo cowboy, then single-handedly raising a sweet child who deserves a much better daddy than the deadbeat I chose.

Clearing her throat, she pushed her chair back and stood. This conversation was getting way too personal. The lasagna had been delicious. Why ruin it with an unappealing topic like Ray?

"Hand me your plate," she said, reaching in Boone's direction. "I'll do the dishes."

Not only did he not hand her his plate, but he stood, too. "Let me wash up."

"That's okay," she said, her plate already in hand. "I like washing dishes."

"Me, too."

"Don't lie."

"Why not? You are." He snatched up the lasagna pan and the watercress-salad bowl, then sauntered to the sink.

"Boone? Why are you doing this? I'd like to be alone."

"So be alone. While I wash up, you can have the whole living room to yourself."

Slamming the plate on the counter, she said, "Fine. Then I guess we'll both do the dishes."

"Great. That'll give us plenty of time to talk about what has made you cranky all of a sudden."

"I'm not cranky."

"Are too."

"Am not."

"Are too."

"Am—"

"Look, Princess," he said, putting a marshmallow-soft intonation on the "P." "I know you think I'm not half as intelligent as you, but I'm not a big enough oaf to have missed the catch in your voice back there." He set his plate gently on the counter to settle his hand beneath her chin, raising it until her gaze met his. "Want to tell me about him?"

She wanted so badly to take advantage of this suddenly soft side to Boone.

She wanted to use his broad shoulders to cry messy tears upon, to share how much she missed Ewan and her aunt and uncle.

She wanted to, so why couldn't she?

"I take it you're not ready?"

"No."

"That's cool." He removed his hand from her face, then turned to the sink. "Just know that when you are ready, Dandy and Daffodil think I'm a great listener."

His touch of humor couldn't have lifted her heart higher than if he'd told her a chopper was on its way to fly her home. Just like that, he'd dropped the subject, giving her permission to hold on to her personal woes, while at the same time letting her know that whenever she was ready for him to lighten her emotional load, he'd be there, ready to listen, ready to care.

He pumped water into the huge copper kettle they used for boiling and set it on the stove. "Feels like the fire's getting low."

"Yeah."

He reached for a log, then slipped it into the belly of the stove. Within minutes, the room grew ten degrees warmer while the two of them bustled about, trying to clear the table without making eye contact.

For all Belle's attempts to steer clear of her kitchen partner, the room was small, so while it was easy enough not to look at him, she couldn't avoid touching him.

Every time their forearms or hips brushed, stinging pulses of awareness shot through her, telling her to steer clear of this man who had no intention of settling down, let alone setting up housekeeping with a "con artist" like her. But it was no use. The more she tried to stay away from him, the more she succeeded in brushing against him.

The room had grown stiflingly hot.

That old yearning stirred in her belly at the thought of peeling off her damp T-shirt, then his, and sidling up behind this incredible hunk of man to press her breasts against his bare—

"Hey, Belle?" He stood in front of her, waving a dishtowel. "Water's ready. You wanna scrub or dry?"

"Dry."

Boone handed her the towel, wondering about her tight little grin. Hmm, could it be that Operation Heat Stroke—heavy emphasis on the stroking, especially him stroking her back into a good mood—was having a positive effect on the gloomy princess?

It was nice and hot in the kitchen, especially with the extra logs he'd added to the fire, but all was fair in love and war—especially in a war about taking Belle's mind off one lousy ex and putting it back on a great guy like himself.

She set the dishtowel on the counter and started winding her long hair around a just-washed wooden spoon.

Spiraling gold escaped her spur-of-the-moment up-do, framing her face in femininity while her clinging T-shirt showcased her heavy breasts.

"What's the matter?" she asked, arms up, still messing with her hair.

"Nothin'." Did she have no idea how badly he wanted her?

"In that case," she said, "you might want to hand me that plate you've lifted in and out of the dishwater three times in a row." Once he did as she'd asked, she said, "Good grief, it's hot in here."

Feels great, doesn't it?

He shot her a big smile.

Drying the plate in question, she said, "Whew, what I wouldn't give for an air-conditioner about now."

"You warm?" he asked, feigning surprise.

"Duh. You're not?"

Grabbing the lasagna pan, he shook his head, then dunked it under the suds.

"For real?" she asked, eyeing him hard.

"What?"

"You're not even a little bit hot?"

Dropping the pan back into the sudsy water, he dried his hands on the seat of his jeans, then offered one of them to the princess. "Come on."

"Where are we going?"

"You'll find out soon enough."

"But I don't have my ruby slippers. What if my friend the rattler comes back?"

Sick and tired of hearing babble when he wanted to hear happy sex-kitten mews, Boone literally swept her off her feet.

"There," he said, happy to see surprise rendering her speechless for once. "Now any snake wanting to get to your tender skin will have to tear through tough ole me first."

"Put me down," she protested. "I can walk, you know."

"Woman, for once would you let me take care of you?"

"But—"

He kissed the words right back into her mouth by sealing her full lips shut. Damn, she tasted good. Like tomatoes and sugary mint tea. Like hope and goodness and all the things he'd searched his whole life to find in a woman.

Could he be wrong about the princess being a con artist? Could he be wrong about wanting to give her the benefit of the doubt? After all, she thought he was dirt-poor, didn't she? If she were truly out to con him, wouldn't she have stopped his advances long ago?

The wooden spoon holding her hair clattered to the floor.

"Mmm," she groaned, her voice delivering that soft mew he'd moments earlier longed to hear.

"There," he said, finally pulling away to continue with his mission. "Wasn't that fun letting someone else be in charge?"

"I never knew you felt so out of control in my presence."

"Yeah, well, me neither. Not until I realized that everything I try to do for you, you have to go and either upstage me by doing it better, or bitch a blue streak about me never having done it in the first place."

"Give me an example," she said, driving him wild by nesting her cheek against the crook of his neck. Her recently freed hair was soft and tickling.

"How can you demand an example at a time like this?"

"A time like what?" she teased. "I wasn't aware we were in a crisis situation."

"Hell, yes, this is a crisis!"

A crisis in my pants!

He walked faster, praying that the cool of the well house would bring him blessed relief, especially since the relief he truly wanted was thus far just out of reach.

Finally they were there, and he set his damsel to her feet before working the combination lock on the door.

"Why do you keep this place locked?"

"Simple. This is where I keep my beer."

"Ahh. Should've guessed."

"What's that mean?" Her throaty tone caused his fingers to slip. "Now look what you did. I have to start over."

"I didn't do a thing. Besides, you're the one who's in such a hurry to cool off." When he turned to glare at her by the light of the moon, she stretched her arms high and yawned, stretching that clinging T-shirt to near bursting.

"You didn't do a thing, huh?" He squeezed his eyes shut tight, hoping that when he opened them the formerly innocent princess turned temptress would've disappeared. No such luck, but at least she'd crossed her arms. Peaked nipples out of sight, they should have been out of mind, but then her covering them only made him crave a good game of hide-and-seek. "Woman, you've done everything in your power to annoy me tonight."

"How so?"

"Look at you. Standing there all . . ."

"Yes? All what?"

"All . . ." She licked her lips, and he'd have sworn he felt the touch of her tongue on his mouth. Had he ever wanted a woman this badly? No. Which only made her teasing that much worse.

"Boone Wentworth," she said, "if I didn't know better, I'd say you don't have the best of intentions toward me."

Forgetting the lock, he slipped his hands around her waist, burying his face in her hair. "Believe me, I only have the *best* of intentions toward you."

"Mmm." She arched her neck, granting his lips access to her collarbone and throat. "As delicious as that sounds, cowboy, do you really think those intentions of yours are appropriate . . . Oh. Oh, my . . ." He'd foraged lower to draw on her peaked nipple right through her shirt.

"You were saying?" he asked, looking up with a naughty grin.

"Just that . . ." While Belle searched for words that wouldn't come, he carried on, taking the additional liberty of slipping one of his hands beneath her shirt.

She swallowed hard.

It was going to take all her willpower and then some to deny this temptation, but deny him she would.

Yes, she wanted with all her heart to plunge into the bliss of Boone's arms, but not only was it against her chastity contract, but Boone wasn't offering anything more than Ray had. Only in Boone's case, she'd already been given a glimpse into how much fun they might have as a full-fledged couple.

With Ray, she'd offered herself up for just one night, but now she was older. Hopefully, wiser. She wouldn't—couldn't—make the same mistake again.

Eyes closed, she gave herself the gift of his touch for a few more wondrous seconds, but then, eyes wide open, she gently pushed him away. "Sorry, Boone, I—"

"What's the matter?" he said softly. "You uncomfortable? I'm such an oaf. I could have at least carried you to the bed instead of the yard."

"That's not it."

"Then what, Princess? I can't hold out much longer."

"I'm sorry, but you're going to have to hold out for an eternity where I'm concerned." Or at the very least, the ten-plus years it would take to work out her current contract and her new!

"Huh?"

"Don't play dumb." Trying to calm down, she tucked flyaway strands of her hair behind her ears. "We both know what you want. I'd be lying if I said I didn't want it, too, but I can't."

His eyes narrowed. "You're kidding, right?"

"No joke, Boone. I don't ever intend to go all the way with you." At least not here. On this farm. But how many times would she fantasize in the private corners of her heart about what might've been?

He threw his hands in the air, then let them fall to his thighs. The smack pierced the innocence of nature all around them. Crickets and spring peepers, the gentle shush of the breeze whispering through tall grasses— all of that was now spoiled, just like her affection for Boone.

159

"Sorry you feel that way," he said, a knife's edge in his tone. "But at least now we both know where things stand."

"Just because we can't sleep together doesn't mean we can't be friends, does it?"

"Oh, so now you wanna be my *friend*? And I suppose you would have slept with me if I weren't broke?"

"Why are you bringing money into this?"

"Because that's what everything's about with you, Princess. Since I can't give you the expensive house and baubles you want, then you want nothing to do with me, am I right? I'm fun to play around with, but you don't want my dirt-stained paws getting on your high-maintenance bod, do you?" He put his hand to his forehead and winced.

Yes, the voice said. *Good. Let the little bitch have it for toying with you this way. She's nothing but a common tease, and you're a future king.*

"That's not what I said!" she cried. "You're twisting my words, making me sound like some kind of—"

"Con artist out to marry money? Is that what you were about to say?" He snorted. "Somehow I doubt it. You never have been big on telling the truth, but the way I see it, if it walks like a duck and quacks like a—"

"Hush, Boone. *Please*, just hush. I've told you a dozen times the truth of why I was with Maude, but you never once listened. You know nothing about me. You don't even know why I so desperately needed her money."

"Wanna know what else I don't know?"

She raised her chin. "What?"

He laughed. "Why I should even care. Once you answer that, Princess, then we'll talk about being friends. Until then, I wish I never had to see you again."

* * *

Long after Boone took off for the barn, Belle stood outside the well house waiting. For what, she wasn't sure. An apology? For Boone to finally wise up and realize she wasn't the bad girl he'd made her out to be?

But then, why did she even care what he thought of her?

Like she'd just told him, they were never going to sleep together. Just as they would never have a relationship that went further than what they currently shared: exactly squat.

Marching across the yard, she muttered under her breath, "If the creep prefers horses to me, more power to him."

Inside the house, she dead-bolted the front door, locked the back door, too, blew out all but one of the lamps, then, taking the lit lamp with her to the bedroom, vented more about the fact that Boone took her every word and action as additional proof of her being a con artist.

In the first place, she thought, nervous energy making her snatch the case off a down pillow, if she were a con artist, she'd have been the best in the business.

She never did anything halfway.

Secondly . . . well, she couldn't think of a second.

She took a deep breath.

This was no good.

She couldn't keep going from lust to hate.

There had to be a happy medium.

Before tackling the bottom sheet, it dawned on her that she might want to see if Boone had spare sheets to replace the ones she was stripping, so she headed for the dresser.

The bottom drawer contained a haphazard pile of blue jeans, socks and boxers, but no sheets.

One down, four to go.

Unfortunately, the next two drawers provided much the same results except for the addition of T-shirts in colors ranging from forest green to dingy grayish pink that spoke volumes about Boone's laundry skills.

Pulling open the top drawer, she expected to find more of the same, but instead found a thick pile of tissue paper.

Curious, she wisped the paper back, then sucked in a swift breath.

Nestled amid the tissue was a wedding gown, yellowed with age.

She carefully lifted it out and arranged it across the bed. It was still in remarkably good shape. None of the lace was torn, and an array of hand-sewn pearls glowed in the dancing lamplight.

"Amazing . . ." she said, her voice filled with somber respect for the garment's beauty.

Not thinking, just doing, she slipped off Boone's clothes to put on what she assumed had been his great-grandmother's dress.

She took her time unfastening dozens of tiny pearl buttons, then pooling the gown about her feet to step into it. Ever so slowly, she pulled it up, being careful not to damage it in her quest to see what kind of shape Tallulah had had. Had she been petite? Or tall and rangy like her heir?

Belle giggled when she realized she was holding her breath until she found out if the gown fit.

Skimming the luminous satin past her hips, her breasts, then finally high enough so she could slip her arms through the sleeves—only then did she look in the cheval mirror.

Only then did she exhale upon the realization that the gown and her body were a perfect match.

What were the odds?

She turned back and forth, fluffing her hair to mimic the shape of a veil.

Though she knew it would sound silly to anyone else, she couldn't help but wonder if this was one of those cases of things happening for a reason.

Was there a reason Boone's great-grandmother's gown fit so perfectly and had been so well preserved? Was the gown destined to be not only worn again, but worn again on *her*?

Belle gave herself a mental shake.

Good grief.

Was that the eternal Fairy optimist coming out in her, or what? Maybe the lack of protein and the late hour were making her delirious.

After all, woman could not live on beans and Twinkies alone.

As lovingly as she'd put the dress on, she took it off, folding it with care before settling it back in the tissue-lined drawer.

So much for her search for sheets.

Picking up the pillowcase she'd tossed to the floor, she put it back on the pillow, blew out the lamp, then crawled into bed, praying that sleep would come quickly.

But how could she sleep when the warm breeze fluttering the curtains brought with it restless stirrings of what might have been? As much as it hurt to admit it, she didn't want to be lying in Boone's bed, surrounded by his masculine smell, his very essence, without him beside her.

He was everywhere, yet nowhere.

She plumped the feather pillow, hoping a few good punches would make her feel better, but all they did was leave her more awake, more frustrated, more alone.

"Sorry to interrupt our regularly scheduled programming, folks," that boneheaded newsman from Channel 35 out of Oklahoma City said. He wore his brown hair all whuffed up like he thought he was some kind of rock star.

Philbert turned his attention back to his jigsaw puzzle of the Eiffel Tower in spring, only half listening until he heard the kid mention earthquakes.

"Lila," Philbert said, instantly more than a little sick at his stomach. The meat loaf his sister had prepared for dinner came up in a foul-tasting belch. "Turn up the volume!"

She grunted before setting down her knitting needles to grab for the remote.

"Put this one in the record books, folks," the newscaster said—this time louder. "Our friends over on the eastern seaboard just reported a major earthquake. Folks all the way from Wilmington, North Carolina, to Norfolk, Virginia, were shakin' and bakin' with this one. Fortunately, no one was seriously hurt—unless you wanna count the billions experts are saying this little burp from Mother Nature is going to cost in flood damage all along the coast. Our affiliate over that way on WKJB caught this amazing footage of the arrow-straight fault line leading all the way from the coast into Raleigh. Thanks for tunin' in, folks—and remember: Catch it live on Thirty-five."

Clutching his chest, trying unsuccessfully to soothe his raging indigestion, Philbert pushed himself up from his recliner and headed for the kitchen to make a call.

Like it or not, Maude had to be notified.

She had to know the likelihood that their plan had gone horribly wrong.

Two days later, on a morning so sweet and still it was just begging to be shared, Belle found herself quite alone, and stalking across the rough-cut lawn.

Desperate to fill her mind and heart with anything other than her latest tiff with Boone, she aimed straight for the tool shed, where she rummaged for paint to bring life to the shabby outhouse.

Spotting a few cans on top of a bowed rack of shelves, she shoved aside a pile of rusty tools to reach for them.

Though why she wanted to paint the outhouse was a mystery. She didn't want to be on this farm in the first place, yet she was becoming hopelessly attached to it.

Boone avoided her like the plague—especially around mealtimes.

Why she'd ever fancied herself falling for him she didn't know. Could she have become afflicted with that attachment-sickness that female kidnapping victims sometimes got toward their captors?

But, no, that didn't fit, because she hadn't been taken against her will.

She'd been bought.

The first paint can was stuck to the shelf, so she took

her frustrations with Boone out on it by giving it a fierce yank, not stopping to think that the shelf was fastened to the wall with only three rusty nails.

Crash!

The whole shelf came down on her feet.

Coffee cans filled with more rusty nails toppled, scraping her bare legs on their way.

"Oh, now that felt good," she said with a hop and a wince as she made her way out of the murky shed to inspect her wounds in bright sunshine.

"What's wrong?" Boone asked, coming around the corner of the barn, causing her more pain from the sight of his handsome, whisker-stubbled face than from any of her scratches. It was the first time she'd seen him since that night at the well house, and she hadn't realized how much she'd missed the creep.

His shoulders seemed broader.

His slow smile brimmed with danger of the strictly forbidden, wholly tempting type.

"Nothing's wrong," she said, hiding the fact that her heart raced like an excited kitten's. A ridiculous notion, considering that she was still so mad at him she could spit nails. "I just came across a shelf that decided to use my shins as its new support brackets."

He knelt to inspect her wounds. "Some of these look pretty bad. Why don't we go inside and I'll doctor you."

She could think of a lot better things to do inside, especially since he'd wrapped his hands around her calves. Heat from his fingertips seeped straight through her, reminding her how long it'd been since the last time they'd touched.

"Really, Boone," she said, "I don't think these little cuts are that big a deal." *Not enough to warrant another chance encounter whereupon the two of us almost hook up.*

Wielding his most wickedly handsome grin, he put her heart in peril. "Why don't you let me be the judge of that?"

He stood, then swooped her off the ground and into his arms—not the safest place for a girl trying to convince herself she wasn't developing a serious crush!

Chapter Eleven

Inside, Boone sat his patient on the tabletop, all the while wishing she had knobby legs more like Dandy's. Or maybe short and stumpy instead of long and lean and graceful and . . .

He gulped, skimming his fingers along her petal-soft left calf.

"Boone, really, if you'd just—"

He put his fingertips over her lips. "Would you for once let me do something for you? If you want, think of this as a selfish act on my part."

"How so?"

Because your thighs are softer than the down on a baby chick. "Because, I, ah . . . used to want to be a doctor and I, um, like to fix up wounded things."

"Really? Somehow I can't picture you as Doctor Boone."

"Yeah, well, try harder." At the sink, he worked the pump, figuring that the cool water streaming over his hands would make them feel better. Unfortunately, the water was so cold that, far from being refreshing, it had a chilly bite.

After jerking his hands free, then drying them on the thighs of his jeans, he turned back to his patient and all nine yards of her legs.

Damn.

Just like that, he was once again in trouble.

"Paging Dr. Wentworth," she teased. "Dr. Boone to ER—stat. Code blue, code blue."

He rolled his eyes.

Just his luck he had the only patient on the prairie with stripper legs and a hospital-based-sitcom mouth. "You laugh," he said, opening a tube of antibiotic cream he'd found in the first-aid kit in the drawer beside the sink. "But honestly, I think I'd make an awesome doctor."

"You think so, Neurosurgeon Boone?" She smiled, not just any old smile, but a brilliant one that held the power of the sun. "So how come you didn't go the premed route in college?"

"Maybe because I didn't give a flying flip about college," he said, spreading a thin layer of ointment over her wounds.

She frowned. "But you just said you wanted—"

"I know what I said. I lied." *Just like I've lied about everything else since you came into my life—especially about my attraction to you.*

"Why?"

He sighed. "Because running my hands up and down your legs is making me dizzy, okay? There, you made me spill my guts. Satisfied?"

"Are you serious?"

Princess, if you saw the mountain behind my fly, you'd learn a whole new meaning of the word.

Serious need.

Serious want.

Serious doubts over why he'd ever brought her here—to the farm, the kitchen—in the first place.

"Can we change the subject?" he asked. "I think we've talked enough about me."

"Yes, sir," she teased, giving him a mock salute. "So, let's see, what's a new subject we can safely discuss while you . . ."

As Boone continued administering physical therapy higher on her thigh, she sucked in a breath, grabbed hold of the top of his head to steady herself.

Cool.

He hadn't realized that his mere touch had that kind of effect on Her Royal Pain in His Privates.

". . . while you caress my inner thigh. Boone?" she asked, her voice barely there.

"Yeah?"

Their gazes locked. "I don't have any scratches on my inner thigh."

"Does that matter?"

Belle closed her eyes, savoring his touch, at least until he trailed the rough pad of his thumb in a maddeningly straight course down to her knee.

No, no. You're going the wrong way!

Move higher, firmer, deeper.

She squirmed on the tabletop. Was he feeling this same kind of all-consuming rush?

"Knock, knock," he said. "Anyone home?"

As she realized she still had her hands in his hair, her cheeks blazed. After tugging down her T-shirt hem, she safely tucked her hands on her lap. "You about finished?" she asked, not sure how much more doctoring she could take.

"Oooh, is Her Highness all hot and bothered?"

"No, I'm . . ." *Furious* and hot and bothered.

"Face it, Princess, you want me."

"No, I don't."

He leaned in so close that if she'd parted her lips, they'd be kissing. "Liar, liar, pants on fire."

"Hanging on a telephone wire." She tried scootching away, but he'd penned her in on both sides. It was no use. She was trapped. Trapped by a crazed Texan who had an army of red-hot ants in his pants!

"Admit it, you've wanted me ever since we first met."

"Nope."

"Say it, or we'll be here all day."

"Never."

"Not even if I do this?" He moved the millimeter it took to kiss her, instantly changing everything with the mesmerizing pressure of his lips. She wanted to stay mad at him, but, truth be told, she *was* a liar.

If she had her way, he'd take her right there on the kitchen table.

He'd take her fast—maybe even a little rough—all the way and then some.

"Mmm," he groaned. "I was a fool to sleep in the barn last night when I could have been in here with you."

His words reminded her of a question she'd been meaning to ask. "Speaking of which, where were you last night? You didn't sleep in the barn."

"How do you know?"

"I checked. After spending two hours cooking dinner for you, setting the table for you, even baking a cake for you—*you* never showed up!"

"Busted." She'd wanted him to be appropriately sorry for lousing up her evening, but all he did was grin. "I couldn't sleep, so I grabbed a few beers out of the well house. Finally drifted off to sleep on the front porch."

"The porch? You were right here all the time? Why didn't you answer when I called?"

"Princess, I really don't think—"

"Tell me!"

With the hem of his T-shirt he wiped sweat from his forehead, teasing her with a glimpse of his tight stomach—not that she looked. Well . . . maybe she'd taken just a peek, but only to assure herself it wasn't as tempting as she'd remembered. Unfortunately, she'd remembered right.

"I didn't want to tell you this, but—"

She put her hands over her ears. "If you have another woman out here, I don't want to know."

"Another woman? Are you nuts?"

"Then why does just the thought of telling me the truth have you sweating buckets?"

He sighed. "I might as well come out with it. Basically, I'm afraid of you."

Hands on her hips, Belle scrunched her nose and forehead. "That's got to be the single most ridiculous thing I've ever heard. Grrr. I'm not an advocate of violence, but if I were, you'd need a spanking."

"Mmm." He winked. "Spank me, Princess. Spank me."

She shot him a dirty look.

After putting on the last of her Band-Aids, he left her to rummage through a drawer beside the sink. "What can I say? You're a dangerous distraction. Shoot, you cook good, clean good . . ." *Look good.* "For all I know, it's part of your con."

Suspecting that his true mission in the drawer was to avoid her, Belle hopped down from the table to tug him by his shirtsleeve to face her. "Would you get over it, Boone? Not everything I do or say is a con. For the last time, your mother *hired* me. I'm broke, okay? Flat-out busted, only I'm too stubborn proud to have told you sooner. Back home, I've got my own farm to save, along with a son, elderly aunt and uncle, and more or-phaned pets than a stupid zoo. My uncle and your mom go way back, and I guess he showed her a pic-ture of me, and she told him I looked like a princess. That's when she got the idea to hire me to play the part."

Those old familiar pools in Belle's blue eyes dug a sick pit in his stomach. Sure, he supposed her confes-sion could be just another carefully rehearsed speech, but somehow he doubted it.

Plain and simple, he was starting to think that his con-stant distrust of Belle had way more to do with his wounded pride over being duped by Olivia than his true belief that Belle was ever out to scam his mom.

That said, why had he brought Belle here?

Why couldn't he bear to let her go right this minute?

After eating a lunch of beans, then dinner of beans, Belle was itching to try her hand in the kitchen again, but she'd starve before cooking another feast for the thickheaded Texan plucking an out-of-tune ballad on his guitar.

Wiping her hands on a dishtowel she'd unearthed from the back of the hutch, she hollered above his playing and a sweet-smelling downpour, "Can't you get that thing to sound any better than a stuck hog?"

"Sure. Why don't you come in here and sing with me? Then we can sound like two stuck hogs."

"Ha, ha." She set down the oil lamp she'd been pretending to clean. Boone had insisted on doing the dishes, so to avoid him, she'd been inventing chores all evening long. "Shouldn't you be heading out to the barn?"

"Nah. It's raining." He looked up from his melancholy rendition of "Home on the Range." "Anyway, I figured since we got that whole issue of me being afraid of you out of the way, it'd be safe to sleep inside. You know, sort of a test for me to face my fears."

Hands on her hips, she said, "If you plan on living to see dawn, drop it about me being scary." She was a Tooth Fairy, for goodness sake! No one was afraid of her—ever! The very thought ticked her off—and she was never angry. Which just showed what an emotional mess Boone was making of her normally kind heart!

"Oh, really?" he asked with one of his sexy-slow grins. "Just for kicks, let's say if I had a choice between being seduced by another of your delicious bowls of chili or being eaten alive by a rabid pack of prairie dogs—"

"Oh my gosh." Belle's hands were back on her hips. "I can't believe you're complaining because I'm too good a cook."

He shrugged.

Because there was nothing better to do—not to mention the fact that she was tired of pretend cleaning—she plopped down on the rocker across from him. "What's on TV?"

"Knowing my luck, *Misery*."

"You're just full of laughs tonight, aren't you?"

He rested his guitar against the sofa. "You don't find me amusing?"

"Oh, amusing, yes. Entertaining, no."

"Princess, I'm hurt. The girls I went to college with lined up round the block for a chance just to see me, let alone *kiss* me." He winked.

"Yeah, well, all the girls at my school always did think Texas girls had poor taste in men."

"Ouch." He clutched his heart before faking death by rolling onto the rag-rug-covered floor. He landed on his back, and for just an instant, pain registered before he'd slipped his cocky self-assuredness back in place. "That hurt sooooo bad," he teased. "And here I thought I was irresistible to all womankind."

"Sorry to burst your bubble there, cowboy, but probably all those women liked you back when you had money. Now that you're just another down-and-out dirt farmer, a woman would have to be crazy to pair up with you." *Crazier still to worry about those things growing on your back. Do they hurt? Is there anything I can do to make them feel better?*

"Gee, Princess." He scrambled to his knees, crossing the short distance to where she sat, pinning her in the chair with his hands on the arm rests. "Is it just me? Or every time we kiss, do you get hotter?"

Belle rolled her eyes. "Do you have to be so crass? Last time we kissed, I was just delirious from lack of sustenance, okay?" Not to mention overexposure to him.

Held at a safe distance, Boone was resistible, but up close and personal like this, she was having problems remembering even the basics like breathing, let alone big-ticket items like her name.

And he smelled so good, like an honest day's work. Like sweat and dirt and horseflesh, and good old-fashioned manliness that she hadn't smelled on a man since . . .

Well, since Ray, but that was just coincidence, because Ray had never put in an honest day's worth of anything—let alone *work*.

" 'Fess up, Princess, what you were delirious from was *need*." He leaned closer, flustering her all the more with bean breath that should have been offensive, but on him smelled sweeter than a whole row of convenience-store mints.

"I have no needs," she said, determined not to ever again fall under his spell, a challenge made even worse tonight by the romantic patter of rain.

"Everyone has needs . . . all sorts of 'em." Rocking her and the chair toward him, he planted a kiss on the base of her throat. "Take me, for example. Right now I have a need for—"

"Nope. Nope, not going to happen." Belle squirmed out from beneath him to stand in front of the cold stone hearth.

Boone didn't seem in the least dissuaded by her flight. Sitting back on his heels, wearing that disgustingly handsome Texas-sized grin, he innocently asked, "What'd I do? All I was going to say was that I have a need for a Twinkie—assuming you haven't eaten them all." He cast a dashing wink her way before heading into the kitchen.

Whew. With him gone, she let out the breath she hadn't realized she'd been holding.

Gracious, what that man did to her with just a glance, let alone a touch. She wanted so badly to give in to the enchantment of this place, to weave a spell between Boone and herself that could never be broken, but first she had to remember why she was here.

She had to remember that the children across her region depended on her to transform the pain of losing baby teeth into a magical, joy-filled rite of passage.

She had to remember that back home, her son and aunt and uncle were depending on her to save their farm. And that, as good as Boone's farm was starting to look, hers must be steadily looking worse.

Uncle Philbert had taught Belle everything he knew about running the place, but he was getting on in years and wasn't as good at handling the livestock as he used to be. At least Belle had managed to get the garden planted before leaving, much to Lila's dismay. Belle didn't much like wearing gloves when working with earth, but that spring, in light of her upcoming princess gig, her beauty consultant had insisted.

Looking at her hands, she saw that they were in desperate need of lotion. She couldn't play the part of a princess now even if she'd wanted to, and an even sadder fact of the matter was that the role she really wanted to play was the part of Boone's girl.

Belle's hand flew to her mouth.

Thank goodness she hadn't given voice to such a ludicrous thought. Helping out a friend in need was one thing, but forming a true bond with him? And since when had Boone become a friend? Last time she knew, he'd been nothing more than a kidnapper convinced she was out to con him. Even worse, she'd taken a vow of celibacy! Granted, she only had two years left on her current contract, but she'd already told the Fairy Council of her intention to re-up for another ten.

Eek! That added up to twelve long years without Boone's kisses!

"I found two Twinkies," he said, sauntering back into the room. "Want one?"

But then, see what ever-increasing obstacles she was up against? The man was a study in contradictions.

From anyone else, a gesture like that would be common courtesy, but for a man who loved his Twinkies like Boone did, this offer had the dewy beginnings of a relationship written all over it. "No, thank you," she said. "You go ahead."

"Thanks." He popped one into his mouth while unwrapping the other.

Just the rustle of the plastic wrapper made her stomach growl, but that was okay. Watching him scarf the cakes would at least clear her guilty conscience about the five others she'd eaten but blamed their disappearance on the goats.

Bite swallowed, Boone asked, "What were you so deep in thought about just now? You're not still mad at me for hiding out, are you?"

Yes. But what good would telling him do? She shook her head.

"Well, then? What's up?"

Shrugged. "Guess I'm a little homesick."

"Tell me about him—Ewan."

The part of her that was still mad at Boone thawed. He'd remembered Ewan's name. "He's eight, with the most amazing blond hair."

"Just like his momma, huh?"

"No. It's just a coincidence that we . . ." Belle started to tell the lie of how a friend of hers found Ewan on a church pew, but instead, looking into Boone's silvery-gray gaze, she found herself in the unthinkable position of telling the truth. "Yes. Ewan has my hair and eyes."

"How come you told me earlier he was an orphan you took in?"

"Why do you care?"

Shaking his head, he shot her a slow grin. "The

whole time we've been together, you've been making this huge hairy deal about not being a con artist, yet from the very start, you lied to me about your son. I just want to know why."

Belle's pulse pounded in her ears.

Oh, sure, she'd be happy to tell him the rest of the truth, but somehow she didn't figure him for the type to believe in fairies of any kind—let alone the Tooth Fairy!

Tightly lacing her fingers on her lap, she said, "It's not just you I lied to about Ewan, but everyone."

"You mean some guy knocked you up, then refused to do good by you and his son?" Boone's eyes turned dark.

"H-he doesn't know."

"The father? Or son?"

Belle pressed her lips tight.

"You've got to be kidding me. Neither knows?"

Unable to speak through the tears gathered at the back of her throat, she nodded.

"So who does know? Your aunt and uncle?"

Belle shook her head. "I shouldn't have told you."

He leaned forward, eyes darker than ever. "Why did you?"

Those eyes. It was as if Boone held the power to see straight through to her soul.

She shivered.

"It's getting late," she said. "Where do you keep your spare sheets? I'll make up the couch for myself. I'm ready to call it a night."

"No."

"What do you mean, no? You might have a wallet fat enough to keep me out here, but that doesn't give you the right to tell me what to do."

He touched his forehead and winced. "You're making me angry," he said, voice throaty and low. "You don't want to make me angry."

She raised her chin. "Oh, so now just because I won't tell you about my sordid past, you're going to throw a tantrum?"

"That's the problem," he said, gripping the arms of his chair so tightly that his knuckles shone white. "I'm not sure what I'll do."

Chapter Twelve

Belle kicked the sheet off her bare legs. Already she'd lain in Boone's bed for an hour, listening for the smallest creak announcing his return. So far, all she'd heard were overly chirpy crickets and an annoying mosquito whine. What she wanted to hear was an apology for his running out on her. Which was stupid, considering that as spooky as his eyes had grown, she'd pretty much wanted him to go.

Why was she having such a hard time remembering why she was here?

It wasn't to play house, or because she was caught up in the dewy first stages of a relationship, but plain and simple because she'd been paid.

On the flip side, now that Boone knew the whole truth about why she'd so badly needed Maude's paycheck, he should wholeheartedly support her decision to take on that princess role.

But then, why did she care if he supported her? What did it matter if he liked her, or thought she was the worst pond scum to ever pollute the earth?

It mattered because of how much she'd grown to respect him in the past few days. He knew what he wanted out of life and wasn't afraid of working hard to get it. In fact, he'd sacrificed everything for his love of his mother.

Belle had thought her own goals had been similar to his, but now she wasn't so sure. If she'd really been working toward saving her farm, would she be so content whiling away her days weeding Boone's garden? Fixing Boone's chicken coop? Watching the play of sunlight on Boone's muscular forearms as he worked his plow?

She sighed.

This was getting her nowhere.

Tossing off the sheet completely, she got out of bed to stand at the window, hoping the warm breeze that smelled of approaching rain would cool the curiosity blazing in her gut. Curiosity centered on one question: How long would it be till she was once again in the arms of the infuriating man who could so capably work a plow team yet so gently treat her wounds?

Boone was such a mystery.

His moods shifted from comical to enraged to seductive in under thirty seconds, yet even when he'd hauled her kicking and screaming—not to mention biting—out of his mother's house, he hadn't hurt her.

Despite his harsh words that night, she knew he would never hurt her.

He didn't have the capacity to hurt.

For goodness sake, the man claimed he'd slept on the front porch to avoid being seduced by her cooking. And even tonight, he'd insisted on sleeping in the barn again even though she'd offered to sleep on the sofa, giving him the bed.

A floorboard creaked behind her, and she looked over her shoulder to see the object of her thoughts.

He stood in a sliver of pale moonlight dressed in boxers and nothing else. If her cold feet hadn't told her she was fully awake, she'd have thought his striking profile only a dream.

"Can't sleep?" he asked, stepping into the shadows to stand beside her at the open window.

"Heartburn, warden . . . from all the beans this joint serves." She hoped her half fib hid the real reason she couldn't sleep.

Him.

He nodded. "Sorry. I've had a few of those rough nights myself here lately. Think we ought to eat one of the chickens for Sunday supper?"

"Tempting as that sounds," she said with a sad laugh, "when we only have a flock of two, that might ruin our chances of increasing the local poultry population."

"Yeah, guess you're right."

They stood silent in the oppressive heat.

Somewhere far away, a coyote yipped.

Closer, cicadas hummed while a few stubborn crickets kept up their chirps. Apparently, no other creatures of the night were having such a tough time making small talk, so why did Belle all of a sudden feel charged with a vague sense of unease?

"Why are you here?" she found the courage to ask.

"I needed to see you."

"To apologize?"

"For what?"

She laughed. "You don't remember that not-so-subtle threat?"

He shook his head, and in the moonlight his eyes shone silvery-gray in a face so handsome it took her breath away. Just as she'd requested in her heart that afternoon, he stood before her bare-chested, muscles honed to an unimaginable degree.

She wanted to touch him—all of him—so badly the tips of her fingers burned, yet she stood there frozen, unsure what to do.

Finally she asked, "W-what do you remember about our argument?"

"We argued?"

Oh, this was too much. "Boone? You sat right out there in the living room telling me that if I didn't tell you every private detail about my past, you'd be angry, and that there was no telling what you might do."

Hand to his forehead, he groaned.

"What's going on with you?" she asked, reaching up to touch his shoulder. Just his shoulder.

He violently flinched.

"Nothing's wrong," he said, backing deeper into the shadows. "I should go. I never should have come."

"Tell me," she said, following him into his world. "You know something's wrong with you, don't you? I mean health wise."

He shook his head.

"Does your illness have something to do with those things on your back?"

"How do you . . . I mean . . ." He washed his face with his hands.

"Tell me," she said, drawing his hands down. "Trust me. Maybe I can even help."

"I'm beyond that," he said, voice raspy with what she could only guess was pain. "I shouldn't have come."

"Boone, please don't shut me out. Whatever's wrong, let me help."

As if someone had flipped a switch inside him, he stood taller, grinned, then asked, "Do you like fish?"

"What's happening to you? You're scaring me."

"What are you talking about?" he said, voice perfectly normal, perfectly charming as if none of their previous conversation had taken place. "I mean, yeah, fishing can be scary when you don't catch anything, but, woman, we're going to catch a bushel."

Ha! At the moment, the only thing she wanted to catch was a ride to the nearest psychiatrist!

"Well?" he asked. "Are we going, or what?"

Before she could fathom a reply, he pulled her close, dizzying her with a simple, eloquent kiss.

"Get to sleep," he said, tenderly mussing her hair to the accompaniment of a sudden drumming rain. "I'll wake you at first light."

Lips pursed, forehead furrowed, Belle didn't figure she'd need a wake-up call, seeing how she was too creeped out by Boone's split personality to sleep.

"Princess, wake up. You've got a bite." Boone scowled at her before taking her pole, then reeling in her catch.

She stirred, but only to reposition herself, resting her head on his lap.

Lord, how he wished she'd get on her own side of the dock. The temptation of having her spread like a buffet on his lap was torture.

Any sane person would've long since taken her back across the Oklahoma state line, but then, judging by the steady worsening of his symptoms, he was about as far from sane as a man could travel and still be rational enough to think about it.

With a minimum of motion, Boone wedged the

fishing-pole handle beneath his thigh, then gently nudged Belle off his lap and onto the leather jacket he'd brought for her. With last night's rain, the air was damp. He didn't want her to get cold.

As soon as he had her settled, he reeled in a two-pound catfish, took it off the hook and added it to the stringer before baiting the hook and plopping it back in the water.

Probably, he mused, it was a good thing the princess had slept through that. Seeing how soft she was toward animals, she'd have demanded he set the fish free, and knowing how it seemed like lately he did exactly what she wanted him to, he'd probably have done just that—which would only have resulted in them eating beans again for supper.

Ugh. Just the thought made him shudder.

"Huh? What? Did I miss something?"

"Only catching your first fish." From his perch at the end of the dock, he shot her a grin. "He was a pretty one, too."

"How big?" She yawned.

"Definitely a keeper."

Just as he'd known it would, her forehead creased. "You know, if it means saving this fish's life, I could probably eat another can of—"

"Yeah, well, I can't, so nix that idea right there."

"You don't have to be so grumpy."

"I'm not grumpy, just hungry. Which reminds me, want some beans?" He held out the half-eaten can he'd opened for breakfast.

"Give me my pole," Belle said, making a face to show him just how much she didn't want another meal of beans. "Let me show you how fishing is done."

A few minutes and no bites later, a gnat did a slow buzz of Belle's nose and she swatted it away.

The temperature had been climbing, and tipping her head back, she closed her eyes, letting the morning sun sink deep into her skin.

A bullfrog croaked.

Tall grasses swaying at the pond's edge hummed with insects.

What a perfect place to while away a late-spring morning with the perfect man.

Too bad that after his latest bizarre episode, Boone no longer fit that bill.

Stealing a glance at his strong profile, at his shock of dark hair and silvery-gray eyes, Belle tried not to think of just how attracted to him she was. But even if she didn't have her celibacy vows to deal with, there was no way she'd let herself become any further emotionally involved with such an obviously unstable guy.

Sure, she'd been worried about those things on his back, and his headaches, and eyes that changed color with his every change in mood. And then there'd been that weirdness with the snake, and the corn-bread pan and the hot sauce and—

Belle rubbed her temples.

Good grief.

After each of those incidents, she'd told herself it had been just an isolated oddity in an otherwise normal day. But added up, when each quirk was added to the whole, the picture she was getting of Boone wasn't exactly flattering.

More like downright spooky.

That duly noted, why was she still so physically aware of him?

189

No—if she were honest, she wasn't merely *aware* of the guy, but turned on to a degree no Tooth Fairy should even think about, let alone contemplate acting upon!

But if she were fair, the guy did have his sweet moments. Finding her ruby slippers. Bringing her the tub. Always insisting on cleaning up after dinner. Helping her cut the grass. Bandaging her legs. Even this morning, how he'd brought her his jacket.

These two radically different sides of him made no sense.

Near a fence at the far side of the pond, butterflies fluttered over a wildflower patch of burgundy winecups, bluebonnets and yardstick-tall thistles. The warm breeze swayed pussy willows and cane. Watercress and lilies graced one end, and a gently sloped mossy bank the other.

A bank made for lovers. . . .

Her gaze strayed to Boone's powerful profile. His strong chin and nose. And those lips.

Would he try kissing her again? If he did, would she be strong enough to turn him away? Or would she—

Focus on the scenery, Belle.

Her gaze fell to his broad shoulders, then lower to the bulging biceps below.

She licked her lips.

The natural *scenery*, she chided herself.

When they'd sat for twenty minutes without getting so much as a nibble, Belle asked, "What are we using for bait?"

"Worms."

"Euw," she said, scrunching her nose. "That's the problem. You can't offer up one living thing in the hopes of catching another."

"Huh?"

Already she was reeling in her line. "Haven't you heard of karma? We must give the fish a fighting chance. If we give him a good fight, then he will give us a guilt-free meal."

He looked at her as if sunflowers were sprouting from her ears. "Have you lost your mind?"

"No," she bristled, her hand on the still-dripping sinker and hook. From the tip of the hook clung a shriveled worm, its gray guts bared to the world. Belle shuddered. "Now, see? This just isn't right."

After tenderly removing the tiny creature, she set her pole on the dock, then stood, bare feet soaking in the radiant warmth on the sun-bleached planks.

"What are you doing now?" Boone asked, disturbingly close on her heels.

"Putting him back in the ground."

"*Him?* How do you know it's not a her?"

"Actually, dear," she sweetly said, cupping his whisker-stubbled cheek, "he's an *it*. Worms are asexual—just like you're gonna be if you don't lose that frown. Here you go, little worm," she said, digging out a spot for him in the shade of a big rock. "Live long and prosper."

"Give me a freakin' break," Boone said on his way back to the dock. "What is this, a worm funeral?"

"Of sorts. Only he isn't dead yet. Maybe he'll even make it. Worms have amazing regenerative powers, you know."

"Can't say that fact has ever been high on my list of must-knows."

Crossing her arms, she flounced away. "Figures."

Boone had no intention of letting *her* off the hook that easy. Who did she think she was, dissing him like that? "Not so fast," he said, gripping her elbow. "You've got some explaining to do."

"I thought we were out here to fish."

"We are, but first tell me what you meant by that asexual bit. Were you implying that I, in some way, fall short of being a man?"

She giggled, and the sound infuriated him.

"Quit it," he said.

"I can't."

Well, he darn well knew how to not only fix that, but how to prove he was a one-hundred-percent, grade-A manly man. Grasping her by the shoulders, he reeled her in for the kiss of all kisses.

Finished, he took a step back to survey his results.

"There," he said. "Now say I'm not all man."

The princess looked dazed.

She yawned. "That's all you've got in your arsenal of love?"

"Who said anything about love, Princess? I'm talking about the fine art of seduction."

"Oh, you are some piece of work. My goodness, you need a spanking."

"Bring it on, Princess. You know how I like it rough."

When he winked, she playfully pummeled his shoulder.

"Ready to get back to fishing?" she asked, working overtime not to be charmed by his wicked handsome grin.

"Only if you're ready to be humiliated when I catch twice as many as you."

"Sure about that, stud?" Her all-woman, all-knowing smile told him he was in big trouble. Then she leaned forward.

Her hair blocked his view, but she was doing something against his chest, something that left clean-scented softness rubbing the underside of his chin, something that—snip. "What the . . ."

Beaming, she held her prize clamped between her teeth.

It was a button.

A button from his lucky plaid fishing shirt!

"What'd you do that for?" he all but growled.

"You said we were down here to fish. I needed tackle."

By the time the hot sun hung directly over their heads, Belle was up five fish to one. Not that she was bragging, but she did get a thrill every time Boone glowered when she squealed about getting another bite.

She could easily have kept up this game all day as punishment for that cocky kiss, but what would that have proved? She wasn't out to completely humiliate him, just tame him a smidgen.

"Ready to call it quits?" she asked her sullen companion while reeling in her line.

"Never."

"Come on. Let's go. I'm hungry."

"I'm not leaving until I've caught more fish than you."

"You can't be serious."

"Damn serious."

She sighed. "Look, I wasn't going to tell you this, because it's an old family secret, but my uncle discovered that button trick years ago. It's all in the way you skip it along the bottom. It reflects sunlight. Works even better with a shiny silver one."

He didn't look convinced. "So you're saying you tricked me to catch more fish?"

"Yeah. I tricked you. So there. Now can we eat?"

"Are you going to tell me what that asexual crack meant?"

"We're back to that again?"

Holding his hand to his chest, he said, "You hurt me, Princess. I'm talking real, honest-to-goodness, physical pain."

For a second he almost had her, but then she spotted the giveaway twinkle in his silvery-gray eyes. "The only thing hurt on you is your male pride."

"Male pride, huh? I'll show you male pride."

It was a good thing she hadn't had her pole in hand or he could have impaled her with the force of his tackle.

"There," he said, tickling her ribs. "Here's how I'll get back at you for that crack."

"Stop!" she wailed, squirming beneath his wriggling fingers. "I hate being tickled!"

"Good. Then I'll do it some more." He sat astride her, tickling her hips and stomach and underarms and . . .

He came perilously close to her breasts. Close enough for her nipples to harden. Close enough for her giggles to turn to raspy breaths.

"Oops," he said, his eager expression looking more like he'd meant *Oh, boy!*

Leaning back on her elbows, she shook her hair back over her shoulders. "Are you getting off of me anytime soon?"

"Wasn't planning on it," he said, cupping his hand to her cheek, tumbling her heart with one of his dreamy Texas-sized grins. "Do I have to?"

Chapter Thirteen

Somewhere in the middle of Catfish Cooking 101, Boone figured it ought to be illegal for a woman to look so good coated in cornmeal.

"Okay," he said, shaking off his attraction to the princess long enough to finish the lesson, "now that we've added the secret stuff, take each of these nuggets and dunk it in the beaten egg, then dredge 'em through the meal."

"Huh?"With the back of her hand, she rubbed the tip of her cute nose.

Lord help him, but if that had been anything but raw egg and cornmeal on the end of that nose, he'd've thrown her onto the table and licked it off. As it was, he could hardly think back to what he'd been trying to teach her.

"Boone?" she asked. "I don't know what you mean about dredging. I thought that's what backhoe guys do to silt-filled ponds."

He shook his head.

It was going to be a long afternoon, but that was

okay with him. One thing they had plenty of was time. Time for kissing and licking and caressing and—

His stomach twisted.

Who was he trying to kid?

The one thing they didn't have was time.

He was dying. And if he needed proof, those things growing bigger by the hour on his shoulder blades would be happy to oblige, not to mention the voice that'd left him mercifully alone for a good long stretch of the day—which explained his almost jubilant mood.

"Boone?" She put her sticky hand on his forearm, and never had he more enjoyed being dirty.

"Right," he said. "Dredging. What you've got to do is drag each of these nuggets through the meal. That's called dredging." Stepping behind her, he took one of her small hands in his. "Here, let me show you."

Together they picked up a piece of fish and slipped it into the slick beaten egg.

The egg was cool. Belle hot.

Dropping the catfish, he spread her fingers, fitting his own in between, easing them in and out in a way it'd take no lessons to understand.

Instantly rock hard, he groaned, closed his eyes on the surging swirl of sensations.

Streaks of red and orange met his closed eyelids, shimmering, strobing, stroking levels of light.

He didn't just *want* her.

He *had* to have her.

Know her intimately.

Irrationally.

In ways he had no right to ask.

Squeezing his eyes shut harder, he willed the more perverse parts of his needs back to sleep. Later, under the shameful blanket of darkness, he'd admit his secret cravings, but until then, no.

What remained of the old Boone was selfishly having too much fun in just sharing their day.

Fighting the dark, screaming for light, for the innocent glory it implied, he slowly backed away from her, from the table, then turned to the sink to pump fresh, cool water from the well.

Only the reality of it was that the cold water stung like acid.

Jerking his hands free, drying them on a dishtowel, he closed his eyes and imagined how water used to feel. Cool, crystalline blue easing over him, healing him, making him feel human and righteous and good.

Finally he dared to exhale.

There.

He'd beaten it.

Willed the darkness away with sheer, heartfelt might.

"You okay?" the princess asked, too close behind him. Too close for him to even try to hide those things on his back.

But then, what was the point, when she'd already asked about them? Who was he trying to kid?

"Yeah," he said, his voice cracking. "I'm good. You, uh, do the rest, then plop 'em in the fry pan when you're done. I'll be right back."

"Where are you going?"

He ignored the even bigger questions in her tone: *What's wrong with you? Did you just have another of your spells?*

When he finally turned to face her, her gorgeous blue eyes loomed as big as the damned skillet. Her weepy expression was a regular Hallmark card chock full of sentimentality.

He didn't want her worry—especially not her pity.

All he wanted was a good hard ride.

Plain and simple—hot sex.

He put his fingers to his forehead. Why now? Yeah, he was dying. Duh. But, dammit, couldn't he have at least ten minutes of peace? Would it be too freakin' much to ask?

Yes, the voice said. *Anything you do without me is too much.*

"You're already a great cook," he said to the princess on his way to the back door. "Just fry those up and you'll be good to go."

Hands slick, sweat-sticky T-shirt clinging to her full breasts, her wistful smile held sincerity and hope. It plainly said, *Take my hand. Let me help. Whatever your problems, we'll tackle them together.*

"Where are you going?" she asked again, her voice small and maybe scared.

Straight to hell.

"This here's gettin' a little odd," Elmer Gentry said at the Oakville coffee shop Tuesday morning while Philbert tried to unstick the lid to the sugar shaker.

Darned thing—always getting stuck in the humidity. If he had a lick of sense, he'd move. Somewhere nice and dry. Phoenix maybe. He'd visited there. . . .

"Says here," Elmer said to the rest of the old farmers assembled—George, Victor and Orville—before tapping the front page of that morning's *Tulsa World*, "they just had more of those earthquakes. This time three in an arrow-straight row. Twenty-foot-deep crack leads all the way from the coast of North Carolina through Cookeville, Lebanon and McKenzie, Tennessee. Bunch

of them wackos out in California say the world's fixin'
to split plum in half."

"All I got to say," Orville said, liberally spooning
sausage gravy onto his biscuit, "is that if the end is
comin', I ain't followin' this low-cholesterol diet Pearl's
got me on for one more minute."

"Whoa, there, fella." Orville put his hand on the
sugar shaker Philbert still held upside down. "I'm all
for *you* goin' off your diet, too, but don't you think
you're goin' a bit overboard?"

Philbert swallowed past the lump of fear in his
throat, the one making it hard to breathe, to see what
his friends were all gaping at.

The sugar had finally come out—*all* of it.

A caramel-colored mountain now resided where his
coffee cup had once lived, while a stream of hot coffee
dripped off the table and onto his lap.

Philbert knew he needed to clean up the mess, but
he physically couldn't. The shock of this latest news
rendered him powerless to do anything but stare.

"Carla!" Elmer shouted. "We're gonna need some
rags over here!"

"Good morning, Henny. How are you?"

Boone frowned.

From his perch at the barn-loft window, through ears
working so keenly it hurt, he heard her gabbing a mile
a minute to the poultry.

What did she have to be so damned chipper about?

He hurt.

Everywhere.

In his muscles.

His spirit.

His soul.

Three weeks had passed since he'd walked out on their catfish-cooking lesson. Three weeks since he'd battled the demons inside him and resisted the impulse to rip off Belle's clothes and have his way with her right there on the kitchen floor.

Until then, he hadn't realized the strength of those dark urges growing within him, but at that precise moment—that moment pierced with not just sex, but hope for a future not tainted with fear—animalistic urges had rushed so hard and fast between his legs, he'd actually felt dizzy.

It was then he'd realized how urgently he had to have her—urgently enough that he'd felt capable of following through on those urges—even if it meant taking her against her will.

Every day became more of a love/hate struggle.

Did he love Belle or despise her?

The one aspect he couldn't question was her knack for keeping the place presentable. She was doing an amazing job.

The few times he'd ventured into the house for more beans, he'd found that she'd scrubbed the place spotless, even scouring the curtains until their colors glowed. The place smelled incredible, too, like the orange oil his mom's housekeeper gave him to use on the antique woodwork.

The yard was immaculate, as was the front flower garden. He'd watched her mix up a manure medley that she sprinkled on the plants, and as much as he hated to admit it, they were all thriving. Even the vegetable garden was coming along better than it had since his great-grandparents had been alive.

She'd thoroughly charmed the livestock, and now, thanks entirely to her, he was the proud daddy of five cute-as-a-button chicks he secretly visited after she went inside for the night. Mabel had had her kid, and Belle milked the proud mama daily. He'd even seen her standing on the front porch spreading what he could have sworn was butter on a biscuit.

Squinting into the sun, ignoring the stabbing pain the action brought on, Boone licked his lips, glancing Belle's way. Her long pale braids made her look as angelic as a grown-up Heidi.

The fact that she looked like an angel should've rammed the point home that she was off limits.

Should've.

All it really did was up the stakes by haunting him with those same old dark cravings to drag her down off her innocence and into his perpetual night.

"Booooone!"

Damn. What was she doing in his barn?

"I know you're in here. Like I tell you ten times a day, you're not solving anything by hiding."

"Who said I'm hiding?" he stubbornly pointed out. "I'm *avoiding.*"

"Whatever you're doing, could you please come down?"

"No. I'm busy."

"Doing what?"

"None of your business."

"Boone, please don't be ugly." Through openings in the widely spaced floorboards, he watched her cross her arms. His keen ears picked up her weary sigh. "Look," she finally said. "I'm worried about you. I'm just guessing, but you probably need to see a doctor."

"I don't need anything."

She glanced up to his voice, and if only for an instant, their gazes locked.

Tears shimmered in her big blue eyes.

Knowing he'd brought on those tears hit him like a pitchfork jammed into his gut. He didn't want to hurt her. Never wanted to hurt her. But he didn't know what else to do.

He couldn't stand being in the light.

It hurt too damned much.

Just as being around her hurt by making him crave the kind of normal, everyday life he knew he'd never have.

He dragged in fresh air, sinking to his knees. "P-please go," he said. "I'm fine."

"No," she said, crossing to the loft ladder. "You're not."

"What're you doing?" he asked, rising to his feet, eyeing her eye the ladder.

"What's it look like I'm doing? Coming up to talk some sense into you."

Taking advantage of his growing strength, before she had a chance to mount the first step, he ripped the sturdy oak ladder free of its nailed supports, effortlessly lifting all twelve feet over his head to settle it among the rafters.

The princess drew her trembling hands over her mouth, then took off running for the house.

Boone slunk deeper into the shadows, deeper into his despair, waiting out the day so he could live during the night.

"I truly hate that man," Belle said under her breath the next morning.

Nights had become torture, filled with so many

frightening noises that she'd resorted to hiding beneath stifling covers, waiting for the dawn.

Now that dawn had finally come, all she craved was more sleep. Never had she been so tired. And seeing how badly she needed to pee, never had she wished more for indoor plumbing.

Oh, well.

She rose from the bed, giving her ruby slippers a shake for critters before slipping them on, then shuffling out to the facilities.

The rooster crowed, and she shot him a dirty look.

Turning back to the outhouse, she gasped, drew her hands to her mouth.

It was . . . beautiful.

Had Boone done this?

Well, of course. He must've. But how? Why?

The once raw-wood outhouse was now a luminous pale pink that he must've mixed from the old cans of red and white paint in the shed. She walked closer, admiring the intricate white-and-blue flower chain winding around the top and down each front corner.

She creaked open the door to find the inside new and improved as well—not only pink, but lined with hundreds of sweet-smelling bluebonnets tucked in mason jar vases.

Was all of this Boone's way of apologizing for his strange behavior? Was he saying she was right? That he did need to see a doctor, but needed her help to get there?

Wiping tears from the corners of her eyes, she said, "Yes, Boone, I'll help," before stepping inside and pulling shut the door.

From his perch high in the shadows behind the loft window, Boone eased his eyes closed and smiled.

* * *

Straight from the outhouse, Belle had gone to the barn to thank Boone for his surprise, but, just as it had been the day before, the loft ladder was pulled up, and if Boone was up there, he wasn't saying a word.

Okay, fine.

If he didn't want to talk, she'd communicate with him in a whole other way.

Which explained why for his breakfast she was placing a plate filled with a steaming veggie omelet and fried potatoes on top of an old trunk she'd dragged over to where the loft ladder used to live.

"Boone!" she called up. "If the reason you don't want to see me has something to do with those things on your back, I don't care about them," she said. "They don't change the way I feel."

Which was?

Some of the time—okay, lately *most* of the time— she was afraid of him. But then he had these moments—pockets of the way he might be were it not for whatever sickness must be eating away at his brain. Like his painting the outhouse, teaching her how to fry catfish or bringing her a coat in case she got chilled. And then there was the way he kissed her. Hungry and deep that made her breasts swell and stomach tighten.

She took a deep breath. "Okay, well, I suppose you're probably sleeping or something, but if you're not, thanks for the outhouse. It was a really great surprise." From somewhere deep inside, she found a little laugh. "If you find you can't sleep again tonight, feel free to plow that unused corner of the garden. I, um, found some mystery seeds in the hutch I thought it might be fun to plant. Shoot, wake me up, and we can work on it together."

The way we used to work around here together.
Laughing.
Sweating.
Kissing.

"Anyway," she tagged on, her voice suddenly thick with emotion—worrying about Boone, halfway loving Boone, "I guess that's it. I, um, brought you breakfast. I'd like to sit with you while you eat, but if you don't feel up to company, I understand."

What she didn't understand was how he could be so sick as to hole himself up in the barn all day, then spend all night painting. But, keeping that question to herself, as she'd done with so many others, she cast one more look up at the shadow-filled loft, then headed back to the house.

Belle returned with creamed-corn casserole for lunch and spaghetti for dinner. Both times, she tried talking some sense into the man she only felt was hiding in the rafters. Both times, she never caught a glimpse of him or heard him exhale.

If it weren't for the empty plates she found, she'd doubt he was even there.

That night, she contemplated staying up to watch him, but in the end decided no. If he had become some creature living only for the dark, she didn't want to know. Couldn't handle knowing. So she hid under the covers, terrified yet again she wouldn't find sleep. So physically exhausted, she couldn't do anything but sleep.

Closing his eyes and taking a deep breath, under cover of a moonless night, Boone worked the long-forgotten section of the garden the princess had requested he plow. As he labored, his mind wandered over times he and Belle had shared.

He saw her strutting around his yard in that halter-top contraption, treating his livestock with a tenderness most women reserved for cooing babies. He saw her with a smear of egg and cornmeal across her nose as she worked her heart out cooking him a wholesome meal. He saw her on her hands and knees scrubbing his floors, washing his sheets, his curtains, and before he'd moved out to the barn, she'd even washed his clothes.

The entire month she'd been on the farm, she'd done nothing but give while all he'd done was take.

Which brought him around to the issue of when he'd take her home. It had to be soon—before those things on his back grew too large for him to sit behind the wheel of his truck.

Ending one row, easing the horses around for another, he used his forearm to wipe sweat from his brow.

It was a chilly night.

Damp, with eerie swirls of ground-hugging fog.

He shouldn't be sweating when he craved a nice long soak in Belle's tub. Preferably with her arms wrapped around him. But then lately, he couldn't keep track of the things that shouldn't be happening to him but undeniably were.

His sensitivity to light.

His keen hearing—even now his ears ached from chirping crickets and spring peepers that sounded more like the blaring horns of midday Dallas traffic than mere bugs.

The mood swings. The things on his back. That relentless voice that wouldn't let him say a word when every bone in his body screamed with wanting to tell the princess how much he appreciated her gifts of meals. That damn voice paralyzed him for long, agonizing stretches at a time, locking him deep within his own terrifying mind.

Shaking his head like a horse shaking off gnats, Boone worked the land.

And when he was done with that, he stalked the land, finding Belle more flowers to strew across the tops of his latest gift.

Finished, he slunk back to the barn where animals like he'd become deserved to be.

He *had* been listening.

Gazing upon the freshly plowed garden, breathing in the rich scent of turned soil, taking in the sweet charm of the wildflower blanket hugging the dirt, that was the one thought occupying Belle's mind.

Boone *had* been listening to her yesterday morning.

And if he'd heard her joke about him plowing, had he heard everything else? About how much he needed to see a doctor? And how if only he'd do it soon, some doctor out there might be able to do something to help.

Satisfied that at least she'd made a bit of progress in getting into his thick head, Belle once again went through the routine of preparing his meals, only to leave them at the foot of the loft.

Once again, she implored him to seek help.

Once again, he didn't answer.

But that was okay.

Now that she knew his rules, she understood the game better. A game she fully intended to win.

That night, just after setting down his macaroni and

cheese and canned spinach, she upped the stakes of the game by making one more request.

"If you find yourself not sleeping," she called out, "the tool shed needs shoring up."

Getting no answer didn't dampen her spirits. If anything, it only made her look forward to the night—even with all its scary noises.

Tonight, once and for all, she would get Boone to see her way of thinking or die trying.

On her way out of the barn, though, despite all her bravado, despite the day's lingering heat, she shivered, wishing she'd kept that *die* part out of her internal speech.

Hours and hours later, Belle's butt hurt from sitting behind the shed, waiting for Boone to show.

She yawned.

Swatted at a whining mosquito intent upon making a meal of her left knee.

Where was he?

It had to be pushing two a.m.

A rustling in the tall weeds at the yard's edge drew her eye. What was out there?

A coyote? That wretched snake?

Just thinking about the snake made her skin crawl, so she got to her feet, shuddering about a whole lot more than the night's chill.

"This is silly," she said softly, glancing toward the barn.

She was sick of playing this stupid game, sick of worrying about a man who didn't have the common sense to look after himself.

Enough.

Tonight. Right now, they were going to hammer this out.

Marching to the barn, glad for at least the sliver of moonlight guiding her way, she started to plan her speech.

Should she go with the anger that pumped through her with each step closer to Boone's hideout? Or should she play the compassionate friend? Which she was, when she wasn't so all-fire ticked.

Yes, the painted outhouse was pretty.

Yes, the flowers and plowed field had been nice.

But all she really wanted was for them to talk.

Barring that, she wanted to go home.

Pretend she'd never even met him, let alone had the misfortune to care.

In the barn, she stumbled through the darkness, re-assured by a soft, breathy snort from one of the horses. Her internal memory of countless trips made to Boone's new home guided her.

She felt for the ladder, but as usual, it wasn't there.

Fine.

She didn't need a ladder.

Fueled by a sudden rage that that infuriating man would put her through this, Belle built a tower of trunks and boxes and saddle blankets upon a sturdy base of baled hay.

Up and up her tower climbed, stoked by frustration.

Why was he doing this to her? To them?

She climbed higher still, heedless of her tower's sway.

Why couldn't he see that what they shared was spe-cial? Their friendship unique? For it to flourish despite the way they'd met, that had to mean something. Why couldn't he see how fantastically fragile their bond truly was?

Up and up she climbed, legs quivering from the height, yet she used her unease to feed her determination to find him. Find out what he'd been hiding. Find out if anything of the old Boone—the one she'd halfway convinced herself she loved—remained.

She was almost there, stretching her arms high, arching her fingers to meet the loft floor.

Teeth gritted, she made a final stretch, but found nothing but air.

Nothing but a falling, terrifying scream.

"*Booooone!*"

Umph.

Where she'd expected to meet with hard ground, she met warm, yielding flesh. Boone's flesh. She knew from the strength, the achingly familiar smell.

He cradled her, kissing the top of her head.

She clung to him, arms around his neck, crying against his chest.

"My God," she eventually calmed enough to whisper. "If you hadn't been there, I might've . . ."

There was no need to finish the sentence. They both knew what had almost happened.

Strong hand cupping the back of her head, he drew her mouth to his for an urgent kiss. Tongues sweeping, exploring, she melted against him.

For all their differences, this was what truly mattered. His kiss was what made her adoration—her need—for him swell.

Clinging to him, his strength, the goodness she knew was still inside him, she said, "Why, Boone? Why won't you talk to me? Why do you insist on hiding?"

She felt him shake his head. "It's complicated."

"Talking to me? Sharing a meal? A laugh? What's so hard about that?"

He set her to her feet. "You'd better leave."

"Why? So you can be in here all by yourself, stewing in your pain? Speaking of which, what exactly are your symptoms, Boone? Are they so bad you think no one else in all the world would have ever felt them before? Do you think no doctor can help?"

Gripping her hard by her shoulders, Boone gave her a shake. "I *know* no doctor can help. Now, just get back in the house and leave me the hell alone."

Quivering, crying, Belle looked at him, wanting, aching to see the man, but only finding shadows. Once again, he'd managed to vanish. Once again, she was left with nothing to keep her company but her own tears. Once again, she was left hating the man she'd only moments earlier been convinced she loved.

Chapter Fourteen

After spending what little was left of the night tossing and turning before finally falling into a fitful sleep, Belle woke with a savage headache she hoped caffeine would cure.

She slipped on her ruby slippers for a quick trip to the outhouse, then came back inside to build a fire in the stove's always hungry belly.

While waiting for the coffee to perk, she tried fooling herself into believing the night had never happened.

Her fall, her conversation with Boone—both had to have been bad dreams.

Right, she thought with a bitter laugh.

She could try fooling herself all she wanted, but the bitter truth was that the cruel, fingerprint-shaped bruises on her upper arms couldn't have been imagined any more than the dull ache in her heart.

The man she knew would never have handled her so roughly.

He saved you.

He hurt me—more than he could ever know.

The scent of coffee made her stomach growl. Never had she wished more for a simple fix. A granola bar or bowl of Cheerios. Everything out here was so much work. Nothing came easy. Not sleep or going to the bathroom or her next meal.

Sagging into a chair at the table, she rested her face in her hands.

The most work of all was trying to figure out her feelings for Boone. Sometimes hot. Sometimes cold. Always exhausting.

A knock sounded at the back door.

She looked up, stomach lurching, to see Boone, grim-faced and haggard, eyes hidden behind dark glasses. Were the growths on his back causing his navy blue T-shirt to stretch so tightly across his powerful chest?

Swallowing hard, she willed her pulse to slow.

For the first time since meeting him, she didn't know what to say. A thin wood door and window were the only physical things standing between them, but emotionally, they might as well have been oceans apart.

He took a deep breath, then said, "I'm sorry, Princess. So very, very sorry."

As if he'd said "open sesame," Belle creaked the door open, as well as a tiny bit more of her heart. "This is the last time, Boone."

"For what?"

A hard laugh spilled from between her still kiss-swollen lips. "I don't even know why I bother trying to get to know you. The goat's more civilized." With the back of her hand, she wiped a glistening tear from her cheek.

Boone held out a ragged bundle of flowers.

Every part of him longed to be the one wiping those tears from the corners of her eyes, but he couldn't. Just as he couldn't stand to see her in pain, he couldn't ever again let himself get too close. "Please," he said. *I need you. At least your friendship, since I can't have more.* "Don't give up on me just yet. And, hey, I brought you these."

A faint smile lighting her red-rimmed eyes, she shook her head. "And you think *I'm* the one who's a piece of work?"

She accepted his flowers, then headed for the sink.

Taking the open door as his invitation to follow her, Boone walked inside.

He couldn't remember the last time he'd been in his own house. The first thing he noticed were the homey smells. Gone were the scents of livestock and decades' dust. In their place, scents of home. Orange oil and fresh-baked bread. Sun-dried linens and a lingering trace of strawberry bubble bath. "I, ah, like what you've done with the place," he said.

"You sound surprised by the changes."

"I am."

"Why?"

Truthfully? Because he hadn't expected a trussed-up con artist to also be an incredible homemaker. Or for that matter, a damned hard worker. The princess ran circles around him in farm productivity, the knowledge of which only made him doubt his first impressions of her that much more.

"Never mind. I see the answer written in your disapproving look. You think I did all of this just to get into your good graces. You think my cleaning this all-but-abandoned house was only to con you out of all those piles of money you *don't* have, right, Boone?"

He said nothing. How could he when her assumptions were true?

215

"I'm right, aren't I?"

He nodded.

"Have you ever thought about what my motivation would be for all those supposed crimes? Have you ever thought that, deep down, like I already told you, I might have a darned good reason for needing money? And that beyond that surface need, I'm an honest, hardworking person who's never once asked for a handout?"

She still held the flowers in her hand. Shaking petals called him an ass. Three painful weeks of separation called him a fool.

While he'd set out to protect her from the creature of darkness he'd become, all he'd done was punish them both.

Finally, like a switch flicking on in his head, he realized just how pigheadedly slow he'd been in accepting the fact that she was no more a con artist than he was.

"Oh, God, Princess," he moaned. "I'm so, so sorry." For burying her in his problems. For ever doubting her. For ever even bringing her to his farm.

He ached to go to her. To wrap his arms around her and tell her with his body just how sorry he was, but his feet felt frozen to the floor. "How could I have been so wrong about you?"

She shrugged. "Under the circumstances, I have to admit that first impressions went a long way toward tainting your opinion of me. That woman you met, the princess, she's not the real me."

With a sigh, she reached into the cabinet beside her for her favorite pottery vase. She filled it with water, then plopped the flowers inside.

It was such a simple thing, but the sight of the

woman he'd come to think of as his, doing such a quintessentially feminine task, tightened his throat.

How could he have wasted so much time on petty bickering? On being afraid?

"Want to introduce me to the *real* you?"

"What's the point? It's not as if we can go back. You obviously need medical attention. Besides that, every day you've kept me on this farm, I've shown you the real me in a thousand different ways, and yet every time you saw me, you grew to dislike me a little more."

"I don't dislike you."

She busied herself by rinsing the few dishes cluttering the sink. "Right. And we should be expecting a pizza delivery boy to ring the doorbell any second."

"We don't have a doorbell."

"My point exactly."

We.

He'd said *we* don't have a doorbell, and the princess hadn't even noticed his fumble. Could his unintentional slip have been more? Was his mind trying to tell him something that he was too stubborn to have otherwise admitted?

He didn't know how or when it'd happened, but somewhere along the way, maybe the first time she'd fallen asleep using his shoulder for a pillow in his truck, maybe the first time he'd made her laugh, or saved her from that snake, or even last night when she'd fallen right into his waiting arms, the princess had become an intrinsic part of him.

A part he never wanted to let go.

The mere thought made his lungs short on air.

How many times had he told himself that, after what he'd gone through with Olivia, he'd never love again?

217

But had he ever really loved her? Had he loved the way she smelled and smiled? The way her hair shone in the early-morning sun?

No, but he had grown to love all of that and more in the princess. The problem was, the day was coming, and coming soon, when he'd have to take that long drive into town to set her free.

How many more warning signs did he need to show him he was being a greedy, inconsiderate fool for keeping her here on this farm?

That was why he was here in the kitchen with her now—to take her home.

But if you asked her, maybe she'd want to stay.

There was a world of difference between being told you *had* to be somewhere and *wanting* to be somewhere. But then again, what had he ever done for her to make her want to stay?

"What's got you so deep in thought?" she asked, drying her hands on a dishtowel as she headed into the living room.

He trailed after her. "You."

"Oh?" She picked up a well-thumbed cookbook that looked older than his truck.

"Surprise, Princess. I do think of someone other than myself on occasion."

Though she didn't look up from the book, he did spy her golden eyebrows lifting. "How interesting. Please, do go on."

Oh, how those smartypants lips of hers needing kissing, but he sensed that any further attempts to assert his manhood just might be the straw that broke the princess's back.

Nope, from now on, he'd play it cool. He wouldn't take her home just yet—what precious little remained of the old him couldn't let her go. Soon, but not quite yet. And if sometime during their last hours together she begged him to let her stay, to ride it out with him to his life's bitter end, well . . . that'd be swell.

"That was the best meal I've had in a long time," Belle said with forced cheer, putting her napkin beside her empty plate. "Funny how I thought I was a pretty accomplished cook, but had never fixed something as simple as fried catfish."

He shrugged, toying with the latest bottle of hot sauce he'd emptied.

This was the second time she'd made catfish since he'd taught her. This morning, after she'd made him two eggs and fried canned ham for breakfast, he'd gone out to the well house and brought her the fish he'd stored there overnight as a surprise.

She'd tried pretending that things were better between them. Maybe well on the way to returning to how they used to be. But the time had come to abandon the Fairy side of her, perpetually looking on the bright side, in favor of facing facts.

After spending the rainy day together, reading, talking, bumming around the house, it wasn't too hard to see that this Boone was not the same man she'd met all those weeks ago.

This man's mood was consistently dark, as were his eyes—the few times, like now, she'd seen them when he'd removed his glasses.

Truth be told, there had been a couple of times during the day when he'd scared her. Never because of cruelty, but unpredictability. Worst of all were times like this morning when he'd taken her hand and led her to the well house to see the fish.

Just inside the cool, dark shelter, he'd drawn her into his arms for an exhilarating ride. Kissing her until she knew that making love with him would be like clinging to him while they rode a motorcycle down a dark, desolate highway at a hundred miles per hour—no lights, no helmets, no protective leather.

Two of them against the wind.

Naked, fast and hard.

"You did good," he said, drawing her back to the present. The warm, dark kitchen was lit only by wavering lantern light and the white glow of his feral smile. "You're a quick study." He fingered his last fish nugget. "Sorry—about the night I taught you to make this. I didn't mean to run out on you."

"So why did you?"

The question hung between them like a line neither dared to cross.

Then he laughed, and the sound washed over her like cool rain. Why did he keep doing this? Showing her irresistible glimpses of the man he used to be?

Oh, how she'd learned to love the sound of his pleasure. She liked how it bubbled from deep inside him. How it made her feel lucky to be the one with whom he chose to play.

How would it feel to hear that laugh while he played *inside* her?

Her cheeks burned.

He tossed his napkin beside hers and pushed back his chair.

The sight of those two scraps of yellow that'd had been on their laps and touching their mouths hit her with no less intensity than a kiss, which was why she was looking away when Boone said, "Guess I'd better head back to the barn."

"You're kidding, right? You're just going to take off yet again?"

"Would you feel better about it if I washed the dishes first?" He shot her a slow grin.

"What would make me feel better is knowing why you keep running away. What are you trying to hide?"

"Nothing," he said, teeth gritted as he plucked the empty tray of fish from the table.

"Oh, Boone, stop." She rose from the table to put her hand on his forearm. It was hard with muscle. Pulsing with heat. "I know about whatever's wrong with your back. I'm not blind, you know. I can see it's getting worse."

"Mind your own business," he said, turning to the sink, turning those *things* on his back toward her.

She slowly raised her hand to the bump on the right, grazing it with a curious fingertip.

As if she'd burned him, he flinched, whipped round to face her with eyes as impassable as black ice. "Don't touch me," he ground. "Don't *ever* touch me again."

She took a step backward, only to pause and raise her chin.

He growled, shattering the century-old glass tray into the porcelain sink as he turned for the door. He thought escape was to be his, but he was wrong.

She was there, trailing after him, touching him again.

"Why, Princess?" Like an injured wild dog, he railed around, expression fierce and unyielding. Terrifying. "Why do you persist when I've warned you to stay away?"

"Because, Boone, I'm more worried for you than I am afraid. Tell me." Hands pressed flat to his powerful chest, she begged, "Tell me what sickness has hold of you."

"I . . . will . . . not," he ground out, words elemental and raw. He looked down. "I *cannot*."

221

Timid, yet ever more determined by the faint soften-ing of the darkness in his eyes, she raised her hand to his cheek, to lend him a fraction of her eternal hope. "Why, Boone? Why?"

Grasping her hard by her shoulders, he gave her a savage shake. "Because I'll hurt you, okay? You're right. I'm not in my right mind. I want to . . ." He looked away, swallowed hard. "I want to do things to you—*with* you. Unholy things that should never even be spoken, let alone shared."

"No," she said, cupping his cheek, wanting to help him instead of more logically walking away. "That's not you talking, Boone. I'm not sure who it is, but—"

"Why won't you listen?" he said. "Why do you insist on testing me?"

"Because you'll pass any test," she said, clinging to him. "At least tell me what you think is wrong."

He abruptly released her to put the heels of his hands over his eyes.

He groaned—an unearthly, agonized howl.

"No," he said, viciously shaking his head. "I won't do that to her. You can't make me."

Cold/hot goose bumps sprung along Belle's fore-arms and her stomach roiled, queasy with dread.

What was happening?

Why did Boone sound as if he were waging a war within himself?

He groaned, fell to his knees.

Heart pounding, she looked to him, to the door.

Was now the time to run, or to kneel beside him, helping him in any way she could?

Hugging him from behind, she unintentionally grazed her breasts against the growths on his back. Feverish heat gripped her mind and soul, seizing her

222

like a hungry bolt. Suddenly it wasn't enough just to touch him; she wanted more.

To not just be with him, but to *be* him.

Feeling caught on the spokes of a sinfully wicked web, she raised her T-shirt up, past her waist, over her breasts and head.

She was hot, so very hot.

No longer thinking rationally but instinctually.

While Boone held his head in his hands, she slowly drew his shirt up as well, wanting her bare breasts against his back. To feel the heat of him—the strength.

"W-what are you doing, Belle?"

"Shut up," she said.

She raked his shirt over his head, baring his back in unimaginable glory.

Those things on his back . . .

They were wings.

Glorious wings, growing larger by the second, glossy black feathers rich and sumptuous to her touch.

"They're beautiful," she said, rubbing the sensitive tips of her nipples against them. "*You're* beautiful."

Groaning, he turned to her, slipping his fingers under the fall of her hair, dragging her mouth to his.

He seized her lips in a moment of startling clarity, drowning her in unspoken emotion, kissing her like she'd never been kissed before—like she'd never truly *lived* before.

"Oh, Boone . . ." she whispered when they stopped tasting, exploring for air.

She rained her fingertips along the sharply defined planes of his face.

His eyes were dark, dangerously dark, yet she ignored their warning in favor of clinging to him again.

"Take me," she said, clearly out of her mind yet never more in focus.

He buried his lips in the hollow of her neck, grazing, moaning his need.

Her conscience screamed for her to run away from this terrifying man/creature as fast as she could. Yet the desire throbbing hot sweet wet between her trembling thighs still yearned.

He ducked his head lower, drawing hard at her breasts.

He suckled and she cried out in pleasure pain, burying her face in his hair.

His wings grew larger still, rising well above her in gleaming black glory.

They were terrifying in their beauty.

Mesmerizing in their power.

Never in all her life had she seen anyone—anything—like him.

Fairies whose positions called for flight were outfitted with removable wings that worked through spells, but these—these were a part of Boone. A part she ought never to have seen.

Only one race in all the world grew its own wings.

A Dark race that lived out their lives in Earth's fiery underbelly, thriving on gleaning their own pleasure from mortal pain.

Demons, Devils, Dark Souls—take your pick of names, they all meant essentially the same thing: Boone was her sworn enemy. He was stronger than she was, outfitted with mind-melding powers she couldn't even imagine. Ultimately, he'd be charged with the duty of destroying not only her, but all Fairy-kind.

He was a Bogeyman—or at least well on his way.

That fact alone should have sent her scurrying on

her way—into the fields, anywhere out of his enormous psychic range—but strangely enough, she could not—*would not*—leave him.

He stopped kissing her to fix her with his powerful stare. He rose slowly to his feet, bare-chested and primal, his beautiful black wings only accentuating the breadth of his shoulders and chest, the rock-hard ripples of his abs.

Rising above her, he was a god—and she his all-too-willing servant.

Taking her hands in his, he drew her to her feet. He smoothed his powerful fingers along her chest, following the gentle sweep of her shoulder blades. She arched her head back and groaned, and he leaned forward, grazing her throat with his hot, beseeching mouth.

"Belle . . ." he said, skimming her hair back from her forehead, gifting her with a look so earnest, so sincere, that tears welled at the back of her throat. "I never meant for this to happen." He stared a moment more, then said, "I never meant to pull someone so innocent into this mess I've become."

Hugging him close, she nodded against his chest.

"A while ago," he began, warm breath fanning her forehead. He slid his fingers through the hair at her temples, easing her head back, guiding her stare onto him. "You offered to help. I—"

"Yes," she said, swallowing hard. The words were all sincere, all Boone, yet his eyes still shone that terrifying inky black. What did it mean? Was he too far gone to be saved? Was it even possible for a Dark One of his obviously growing strength to be stopped? "Only I . . ."

"What?" he demanded. "What aren't you telling me?"

Stepping back, her trembling hand over her mouth, she shook her head.

"Tell me."

Battles raged within her.

Part of her wanted to wrap her arms around him as she would a hurt child, cuddling him and cooing that everything would be all right. But if what she suspected about him were true, nothing would ever again be right.

Advanced Darkness was akin to rabies. Once it took hold, there was no guaranteed cure.

Shaking her head, shaking her ever-rising fear, she asked, "Don't you know what's happening inside you? Can't you feel it ripping you apart?"

"All I feel is it ripping *us* apart."

"That's just it, Boone. What I now know is that if it weren't for your *darkness* pulling me in, there would be no *us*."

"My darkness?" He laughed. "That's good. What is this? Some whole new level of con?"

She rolled her eyes.

"Or wait," he said, eyes black as a moonless night. "This is the part where when I don't believe I'm growing a freakin' set of wings all because I'm turning into the devil, you tell me I've got some rare form of cancer that's only had three other documented cases in the history of the world. But for the low, low price of a cool million, you, and you alone, hold the power to save me."

Tears streamed down Belle's cheeks as she knelt for her T-shirt, intent on hiding her secret shame. Trembling, she tugged the T-shirt over her head.

Only just then did she feel the full impact of what she'd done in ever agreeing to come with this man.

Her family, her farm, her beloved position as Tooth Fairy—all of it was at terrible risk.

Though Boone might not even realize it, just as he'd held the power to have torn off that rattlesnake's head, he could do the same with hers.

She'd once sensed that he'd never hurt her, but now she wasn't so sure. Now, instead of throwing herself into his arms, she wanted to run—*needed* to run—lest everything she'd ever loved or held dear vanished with one furious sweep of his wings.

Raising her chin in a forced show of bravery, Belle said, "Please, Boone, take me home."

"Yes," he said all too easily.

Sick lead filled her belly and heart.

What had she done?

She couldn't allow him anywhere near her farm!

Ewan, Lila, Philbert—they were all vulnerable to his powers. When he reached his full strength, all three could be wiped out from the force of just one of his mighty blows.

Her entire Fairy line extinguished.

"Foolish girl," he said, throaty voice bearing no resemblance to the man she'd once loved. "Your fear is leading me right to them." Before she'd processed his words, he wrapped his powerful right arm about her waist. Smiling lean menace in the room's waning light, flexing his great wings, he said, "Fasten your seat belt, Princess. We're going for a ride."

Chapter Fifteen

Soaring through the night, clutched to this great man's—great beast's—side, drenched in the clouds' cool mist, and an intoxicating feral scent making her crave all things wild, Belle knew she should be afraid, but how could she when what she truly felt was electrifyingly *alive*?

Her Tooth Fairy wings worked more like the transporters on *Star Trek*. Sure, as a Tooth Fairy she had to know her general direction, but as long as she knew the child's address and recited it in a proper spell, pretty much all that comprised her brand of flying was willing herself there.

That was how she managed so many stops per night.

But this—this was *real* flight.

Wow.

Every beat of her heart pulsed awareness into limbs tingling with life.

Once, she'd sleepwalked through time, but now—now she had to experience everything.

Everything.

Exotic foods—caviar, champagne and curry.

And flowers. Orchids. Sexy, sultry, sinful flowers blatantly opening, spreading, luring beasts of all manner to lap them with their tongues.

Belle shivered, and Boone—or the man who had once been him—tucked her closer against his solid frame.

At the farm, he'd been cold—utterly mindless of her feelings. But this small gesture must mean that part of the warm and funny man she'd come to know must still live inside.

On and on, much as he'd once driven her across moonlit fields, they now flew—at one with the moon and stars. And once again he was silent.

Trapped in his own thoughts?

His own fears, as she was in hers?

What was he planning on doing with her? With her son, aunt and uncle? If he truly was becoming a Dark One, would he just kill them all on the spot and do something heinous like drink their blood?

She'd led a sheltered life, and Dark Ones were not a subject widely spoken of.

So why did she now want to speak of nothing but the terrifying race? Even worse, why was she no longer scared, but curious?

Boone dove them into another cloud.

Her nostrils flared, granting entrance to the cool mist. She raised her face, flying straight into what man—or woman—had no business being part of.

She laughed, becoming one with the wind.

Yes, this was good.

All of it.

The man.

The sky.

The dark swirl of questions transforming her into Eve after taking her first decadent bite of the apple.

But then, just as quickly as they'd ascended, they started their glide down. Fiery heat radiated from Boone's skin, and his sweat mixed with the clouds, forming a hot/cold contrast reminding her all too much of the battle she should be waging in her head.

Yes, she should be glad they were going down, hopefully to land safely on her farm. Where she could run and warn those she held dear.

But then there was the other side of her, loving this experience, this man, not caring who he was, just that he was.

That he existed.

That she existed.

That together their existences might merge into one.

"Boone—that's it!" she cried. "My farm. How did you know?"

He didn't answer, but then, if there was even a chance of the scary Boone answering, maybe she didn't want to know.

Closer and closer they came. She knew the dear lines of the seventy-year-old house as well as her own face. She knew the yard light, swarmed with moths, and the porch light, golden, warm and inviting.

Spring peepers sang out a welcome.

The air, moist and thick, smelled of dew-damp grasses and fecund pasture.

This was where she belonged.

Who she truly was.

All of the other—she could hardly remember what she'd been thinking before now. Now, here, home. It was all that had ever mattered.

The ground swelled to meet them in a terrifying rush—ten, nine, eight, seven—*boom*.

Boone, being the taller, hit the ground first with a shock that shook through them both.

Her own landing was gentler, because he'd cushioned her fall.

She turned to thank him, but his hand slithered from her waist and he crumpled to the ground.

"Boone?" Her voice barely a whisper, she knelt beside him, brushing back dark hair from his fevered forehead.

She was a mom. Her palms and fingers knew the degree of her son's fevers by touch. Just as she knew when Ewan was genuinely sick, or just carrying on because he didn't feel like going to school, she now knew something was very wrong with Boone.

"Can you hear me?" she asked, giving him a light shake.

Nothing.

Not a groan or sigh.

It was as if, aside from the raging fever, he was vacant inside—in his soul.

"Talk to me, Boone. Tell me what I can do to help."

"You there!" came a shout from the house.

Philbert?

Belle looked that way only to be blinded by a flashlight shooting off the porch.

"Stop right there, or I'm calling the law!"

Cool relief shuddered through her. Her uncle would know what to do. "Uncle Philbert!" she cried. "It's me—Belle."

Still holding the flashlight in her eyes, he inched off the porch.

The screen door creaked open, and out popped Lila, long hair up in her nightly pink rollers.

Behind her, tail wagging, loped Ewan's old hound, Digger.

Tears welled in Belle's throat as she rose, running to throw her arms around her dear uncle. "Oh, I've missed you," she said, full-out crying now, unable to fathom how she'd stayed away so long.

"Belle," he said, smoothing her hair. "You're safe. You got away in time."

"Oh, hush, you old pain in my patootie." Lila stepped up behind them, and Belle released her uncle to go to her aunt. "You keep up like this, and before long she'll be believing in aliens."

"It's true, Lila, only you're just too darned stubborn to—"

"I'm no more stubborn than you—"

"Me? Why I'll have you know that—"

"Would somebody please tell me what you two are arguing about?" Belle said, hands fisted on her hips.

"Belle," her aunt said, anger replaced by a warm smile. "I'm so glad your home. Tell me all about the big parties you've been having at Maude's. Did she serve more of those cactus cream puffs?"

Some things never changed, and her aunt, thank goodness, was one of them. Here they were, apparently facing a genuine crisis of some sort if her uncle was to be believed, and all Lila cared to talk about were the sweets Maude served at her parties.

Digger nudged his cold nose under Belle's palm. She gave his head a rub.

"That him?" her uncle asked, shining the beam on Boone's wracked form.

Back at Boone's farm, for those few seconds when he'd so roughly taken hold of her and swept them both into the sky, she'd been scared. But now, seeing him this way, his bare-chested, blue-jeaned body hugged into a fetal pose, his great black wings limp with sweat, her heart ached for him.

She went to him.

Digger followed, licking Boone's nose.

"No!" Philbert barked, dragging Belle by her arm back. "Don't touch him. It might be a trick."

"What?" She slowly turned to her uncle. "What are you saying? He's obviously hurt. And anyway, what do you know about him?"

The old man snorted. "I'll guaran-damn-tee I know a helluva lot more about him than you do."

Lila gasped. "Philbert Moody, I've never heard you cuss like that in all my live-long days."

"Yeah, well, there's a lot you don't know about me, Lila. I also have a penchant for Cuban cigars and take the occasional poke of fine whiskey. At least I used to before you took it upon yourself to suck all our purses dry."

Lila gasped.

Belle cringed.

What now? Laugh? Cry? Run screaming?

Lord knew Lila needed a good talking-to after the stunt she'd pulled, but not like this. Not out in the damp, dark yard where she could catch a chill. And not in this heartless, crass way, popping her bubbly spirit. There were plenty enough serious souls in this family, Belle thought. Poor Lila didn't need to become another one.

Stepping beside Boone, Philbert kicked the backs of his thighs.

Digger growled at the older man.

"What are you . . ." Belle tried to tug her uncle back, but he coldly shoved her away.

"Lila," he said, "go on in the house and take Ewan and his big ole prying eyes away from the window."

Belle glanced that way, and sure enough, there was her son. Her heart went out to him. He looked for a second like he might wave, then darted back behind the red-and-blue Spider-Man curtains.

She desperately wanted to take him into her arms, but her legs wouldn't move. Ewan was safe. With that in mind, she couldn't leave Boone. Not like this.

Her uncle kicked Boone again, and this time, Belle sank beside him, protecting his body with her own.

Digger cowered beside her.

"No!" she cried. "I won't let you do this."

"Get away from him, Belle. There's more going on here than you can even imagine. It's bigger than you."

"I'm not stupid," Belle said, swallowing hard. "I know he's a Dark One, if that's what you're worried about."

"My God, Belle, you say that as if it's no big deal." Expression thunderous, as if he'd like to give her a kick, Philbert said, "Wake up, girl. I warned Maude there was a chance of this happening, but she didn't believe me." Shaking his head, he turned his back on both her and the potential monster who lay at their feet. "Don't you get it?" he asked, turning back to her, allowing her to see the tears glistening in his eyes.

Up to that moment, Philbert had been everything to Belle. Not just an uncle, but father, teacher . . . friend. But this man standing before her. This man, she'd *never* known.

"Upon maturity," he said, his voice defeated, "Boone's sole mission in life will be to destroy ours. Maude and

I knew there was a chance of this, but she said, *no*. Her son was past his thirtieth birthday. There was no chance of this side of him making an appearance so late. And you—sweet as you are, you've always been able to lie. Fairies don't lie, Belle. Don't you see? I—we—had to step in to help. Getting you together, it was just a precaution."

"You knew?" Sick, hot dread roiled in Belle's stomach. "You both knew this was happening to him, yet you still set me up? What does that say about your capacity for lies, Uncle? What gives? Are you a Dark One, too?"

Shoulders hunched, her uncle abandoned Boone to stumble across the lawn and sag onto a porch step. Cradling his head in his hands, he said, "My lies were only to save you. I never thought it would come to this. That he was this far gone. Maude probably had her suspicions, but I suspect she thought that, if anyone, you'd be the one to save him—especially since . . ."

"What?" Belle left Boone to lower herself onto the step beside Philbert, taking his hand in hers. Digger stayed with Boone. "What is it you're not telling me?"

He shook his head.

"Tell me. I deserve to know."

Behind them, the porch door creaked open. "Belle?"

Turning, rising, arms outstretched to her greatest source of joy, Belle buried her face and worries in her son's hair. She breathed him in. His kid sweat and soap and shampoo.

Philbert said, "Boone has to die, Belle. Maybe . . . you, too."

"Stop this, Philbert." Lila cast him a ferocious frown. "Not now. I won't discuss this in front of Ewan."

"Did you bring me anything?" the boy—her dear,

dear son—asked, cheerfully oblivious to the treacherous undercurrents.

"I'm sorry, sweetie," Belle said, drawing him into another hug. "I wanted to, but it wasn't that kind of trip."

Digger loped, ears flopping, tail wagging, to her son.

"What kind was it, Belle? Did he . . ." As if stuck on his own question, Philbert looked away.

"Where've you been?" Ewan asked. "Lila said you were in some big fancy mansion doing work for an old lady, but—"

"You know what?" Belle said, forcing cheer. "I promise to tell you everything in the morning, but right now it's late. You've got school in the morning, and your uncle and I need to talk."

"I don't care if you talk," Ewan said. "Me and Digger'll just sleep on the porch swing."

"Sure you will," she said, ruffling his hair. "Over my dead—" At just saying the word *dead*, her throat tightened and her eyes welled.

She made the mistake of glancing across the yard at Boone's still form.

Ewan's gaze followed. "Who's that?" he asked, bounding off the porch, Digger hot on his heels. "Is he hurt? How come nobody's helping—aw, cool! Does he have wings? *Awesome!* How come—"

"Bed, Ewan. Now."

"Aw, man."

"*Now*," Philbert barked.

Ewan gave Belle another fierce hug, then, taking his dog by the collar, slumped into the house, letting the screen door slam behind him.

"Did you have to be so cruel?" Belle asked her uncle, a hint of desperation shading her voice. "What's wrong with you?"

Who are you?

"Stay here," he said, setting off across the yard. "If he so much as breathes on you in the wrong way, holler."

"But where are you going?"

"To get an ax."

"Whoa, whoa, whoa," she said, chasing after him. "Correct me if I'm wrong here, but this isn't about getting a jump on the winter log pile, is it?"

"Nope." In the yard light's glow, he unlatched the hook joining big double barn doors, yawning them wide.

"Then what are you doing? Because if you're planning what I think you are, you can just forget it. Boone might have a few dark moods, but basically he's a good guy."

"You would say that," he said, locking his fingers around the ax throat.

The barn smelled richly of worn leather and fresh straw. Not the sort of place where one would contemplate hacking a man to death with an ax!

"He's dangerous, Belle. He has to be stopped before . . ." Her uncle looked like he'd been on the verge of elaborating but had thought better of it.

"Before what?" she asked, once again on the chase.

"Before he wakes up and kills us all. Right now he's in a state of hibernation. It's the only time we can be sure to kill not only him, but the evil within him."

"Uncle Phil, are you listening to your own words? He's the son of a dear friend of yours. His wings, the mood swings—there has to be some other explanation than him becoming a Dark One. I *know* him. He would never hurt me, you—anyone."

His expression grim, he asked, "Are you prepared to

stake your life on that knowing? The lives of myself and your aunt? Ewan?"

Was she? Could it really come to that?

In the time it took her to think the questions, Philbert was already back to Boone, raising the ax.

"Noooo!" she cried. "You can't do this. He's a good man, he's just—"

"Get in the house, Belle."

"No! If you kill him, you'll have to kill me, too."

"Let's hope it doesn't come to that. Surely you're not too far along that things can't be stopped."

"*Things?*" She shook her head. "This is crazy talk. It's me you're talking to. Tell me what's got you so spooked that you're willing to take this man's life right here on your front lawn—even if it means harming the girl you've raised from birth."

"Stand back, I'm telling you. The only way to do a proper job of this is while he's in this state. Flying took a lot out of him. Right now he lacks strength to get into our heads, but once he wakes, it'll be all over except for mopping up our blood."

"No," Belle said, rushing around her uncle to crouch by Boone's side. "Killing isn't our way."

The older man snorted. "Just like lying isn't either, dear niece? Yet how many whoppers have you told since taking your sacred oath? The fact that you stood before the Fairy Council able to lie through your teeth about Ewan's true birth mother ought to be proof enough that each and every one of us are capable of doing things we never thought possible, given the right motivation. My God . . ." He bowed his head. "Look what's become of me."

"I lied to protect my son." Belle said, chin raised. "To

make sure he was raised with me—the person who loves him most in the world. Don't you think that was an honorable lie?"

"Is there such a thing, Belle?" Mouth set in a grim line, he shook his head. "I'm already too late to save you, aren't I? He got to you. *They* got to you."

Philbert took a step closer with the ax.

Belle clung all the harder to Boone's strong shoulders and back, hugging herself to him, willing him to wake, to help her out of what by the minute was growing into a more impossible situation.

Crying now, trembling, she buried her face in his hair, dragging in his familiar smells and strength. "Boone," she implored in his ear. "Wake up. Please, you have to come back to me. The *real* you—you have to come back. The kindhearted man who jury-rigged your old boots to fit me. The man who fetched me that old copper tub. The outhouse—remember how you took a whole night to surprise me by painting it pink?"

"Step back, Belle. This man, he isn't who you think. Like a cancer, he has to be cut out of your life." Philbert once again raised the ax.

"Our kisses, Boone . . ." Salty-tasting tears mixed with her words, Boone's heat. He was hot, so very hot. He needed a doctor. He needed understanding and love. "Please, Boone. Remember those kisses. Us. Remember the day at the pond. The times we made love."

Only they hadn't made love, had they?

That part was only a dream, wasn't it? She couldn't be sure. The details. All of it. Her mind was clouded with pearlescent beads from her past. All strung together in a lovely chain starting and ending with him.

Boone.

She would no more let her uncle destroy him than she would let him hurt Ewan.

"Step away, Belle." His footfalls crunching on the sparse grass and dirt, her uncle crept closer, closer. "I promise this is what's right."

"What do you know about right?" she asked, her eyes shut against the porch light that only moments earlier had seemed hopelessly weak and now burned her eyes.

"Oh, God," he said, shaking his head. "Please don't make me do this. Why are you making me do this?"

"Philbert!" Lila called across the yard. "What in heaven's name are you doing with that ax?"

"I'm sorry," he said, making the sign of the cross on his chest. "I wish it didn't have to be like this, but—"

"No!" Lila screamed. "Philbert, for heaven's sake, no!"

"Boone, wake up!" Belle cried, shaking him, realizing for the first time that she loved him wholeheartedly. "I need you. I can't fight my uncle alone."

"Belle," Philbert said, eyes crazy, ax held high. "For the last time, get out of my way. I have to ram this ax straight through his heart or else we'll never be free."

Sobbing, Belle clung to Boone, incapable of understanding how her life had gotten so out of control.

If losing Boone meant being free, she didn't want to be free!

"Philbert," Lila urged in one of her rare somber tones, her hands cupping his shoulders. "Get hold of yourself. Think about what you're doing."

"I *am* thinking, Lila, and it breaks my heart to say it, but we were wrong—about everything. We thought the Light in these two would overrule the Dark, but we were so very wrong."

241

"Hush," Lila said. "There's no need for her to know. Not now. Not after all these years."

"What?" Belle said, tears streaming her cheeks. "What have you been trying to hide?"

Her uncle tightened his grip on the ax.

Lila looked to the ground.

"Tell me!" Belle cried, clinging to Boone all the harder. Grateful at least for this momentary reprieve.

"You hush," her uncle said to her aunt. "If it weren't for you trying to keep up with that no-good Julep, none of this would even be happening. I never would've met back up with Maude. She never would've asked for my help. Our baby girl never would have been exposed to this kind of risk."

Lila bristled. "So now you're saying it's my fault that that no-good niece of ours got herself mixed up with the likes of Darious?"

"Fie on you," Philbert said, spitting on the ground. "How dare you even mention his name in my presence?"

"Because it needed mentioning—'round about twenty-eight years ago on the day of this dear girl's birth."

"D-Darious?" Belle dared ask. "Is that the name of my father?"

"*Was*," her aunt said. "He had his way with your mum, then we never saw him again. Philbert warned her never to get mixed up with a mortal, but not only didn't she listen to that bit of advice, she'd had to go and sleep with a Dark One. She had to . . ." Lila broke off in a fit of tears. "Look at me," she sobbed. "To this day, I still can't bear to speak of it."

"Then don't," Philbert warned.

"Oh, but you think it's perfectly acceptable to hack

these two young people to death for the crime of being born to the wrong set of parents?"

"It's not for us to say, Lila. We didn't write Fairy Law, but it is our duty to follow it."

Lila stopped crying long enough to laugh sharply. "Oh, like we did a real humdinger of a job with that when we took in Ewan—adding our lies to Belle's."

"We didn't know for sure the child was hers," Philbert said.

"We knew."

Belle looked up to catch the only two parent figures she'd ever known fix each other with such ominous stares, her breath caught in her throat. This was all too much. Was Lila really and truly implying everything Belle thought she was? That not only did Lila and Philbert know Ewan was her son, but that she hadn't just been born out of wedlock, but that her father had been a Dark One?

That she herself was half Dark One?

The very thought was inconceivable.

More than she could possibly process.

Was that why she'd felt drawn to Boone? Was that why now, even knowing that when he woke he might destroy them all, she still couldn't bear to see him destroyed?

"Stop!" Trembling hands covering her ears, she shook her head. "Please, both of you. This has to stop."

"It's too late for that," Philbert said. "From the day of your conception it was too late. From the day of Boone's. Two wrongs don't make a right, Belle, and what Maude didn't tell you was that she'd been seduced by a Dark One as well. The man Boone thought was his daddy wasn't. She'd hoped the changes in Boone weren't signs of him embracing that part of himself, but obviously they were."

"And so now you're just going to kill him and me, then go on living with our blood on your hands?"

"I knew from the start it might come to this." Unspeakable sadness shadowing his face, he shrugged. "Half my life, I've prepared. Out there on that farm, you've been isolated, Belle. You haven't seen the destruction the two of you matching up has caused. Earthquakes. Tidal waves, terrible floods. People are dying, Belle, and he is to blame. Indirectly, you are to blame. Boone. And Darious. King of the Underworld. Your own father has waited a long time for two dark entities as strong as you to pair up. Already the power has started to flow. And now that it has, there will be no stopping you. The child will grow inside you and—"

"Child?" Belle shook her head. "No, Uncle. There can be no child. We've . . . I've . . ." She bowed her head. "However sorely I might've been tested, I've been faithful to my celibacy vows."

Lila perked up. "Is that true? Because of the Darkness flowing through your veins, though you might not have known it, you've always held the power to lie."

"It's true, Auntie. I swear."

Philbert said, "You swore to the Council and us that Ewan was not truly your child. You lied then. Who's to say you're not lying again?"

"Would you listen to yourselves?" Belle said. "You've known me all my life. Why are you acting like this?"

"Because of me." Boone was awake, and judging by the black in his eyes, he wasn't happy.

Chapter Sixteen

"Boone," Belle said, cupping her hand to his still-feverish cheek, "you're okay. I've been so scared."

"You've been scared . . ." He pulled her into an emotionally charged hug. "What the hell happened? Where are we?" Before she could answer, he caught sight of her ax-wielding uncle. Flinching, he asked, "Who's he, and why is he aiming an ax at my chest?"

Lila clapped her hands together and laughed. "Oh, good, company for dessert. I made cherry pie. Belle, does your fella like cherry pie? It's made from that filling we put up last summer."

"Woman," Philbert said, glancing his sister's way, "have you lost what little remains of your mind?"

Hands on her hips, Lila asked, "What's that supposed to mean? Clearly the boy's no Dark One waiting to gobble us up in our sleep. You were wrong, Philbert. I was right. Now, let's all end this foolishness over a nice piece of pie."

* * *

"My poor baby . . ." The next morning, Boone could hardly breathe from the strength of his mother's hug. She'd arrived by chartered helicopter far earlier than most sane people would even wake up. "Now, don't you worry. I canceled my European tour to be with you through this entire ordeal."

"Thanks, Ma."

Belle's clearly deranged, ax-wielding uncle had held him prisoner in an upstairs guest room overnight, and while Boone was thankful that he hadn't had another blackout, he hadn't the heart to tell the old man what he probably already knew: It would take a hell of a lot more than either an oak bedroom door or an ax to stop him were he to once again be taken by whatever force was toying with him.

Anyway, it was good to have his mother there—even better to still have Belle and her flighty aunt and Ewan. Philbert, Boone could easily do without.

"This is all my fault," Maude said with a dramatic sob. "What have I done?"

"Knock it off, Ma," Boone said, freeing himself to stand at the kitchen window, bracing his hands on the counter. "You didn't do anything. It just . . . well, whatever's happening inside me, it just is. There's nothing either of us can do."

They were grateful to be alone for this scene. He assumed that Belle was showering after getting her son off to school, Lila was still in bed, and Philbert was out checking his livestock. Boone had offered to help, but the old man wanted nothing to do with him.

Unbeknownst to the whole crew, Boone had flown back to the farm in the middle of the night to feed his animals, then made arrangements with his mother's sleepy ranch foreman over his cell phone to have the whole lot of his brood transferred in the morning.

"No," Maude said, raising her hand as if she wanted to touch him, comfort him, but wasn't sure how or where to land her fingers. "There must've been something I could've done. I should've at least told you who I truly was. Who your biological father was."

"What?"

"You heard me." She'd found a resting spot for her comforting hand on his forearm, but he no longer wanted this woman's comfort. Hands fisted at his sides, he ground out, "How could you say that? Clem Wentworth was *everything* to me. Hell, I've spent the past months trying to make my life as meaningful as those of his grandparents, Tallulah and Frank. You're lying."

"Son, I'm so sorry." Tears welled in her eyes. "Clem loved you something fierce. Don't ever doubt that. When I was exiled from the Fairy World, pregnant, alone and broke, Clem was all I had to lean on. It's just that—"

"Stop. I refuse to believe a word of what you're saying."

"You have to. It's the only way we can—"

"Seriously—stop."

His mother was clearly deranged.

Yes . . . Ignore her. Pity her.

His back itched like the devil.

His wings had grown still more in the night.

After returning to Belle's farm and climbing in the window, he'd had a miserable time falling asleep. No position seemed comfortable, especially when the only position he craved was to be held in Belle's arms.

But that—now more than ever—was clearly out of the question.

He was a monster.

"Belle told me how you thought she was out to con me," Maude said, tears still glistening in her eyes.

"She did?" He glanced away from the window's view of the fading red barn and emerald-green pasture to his mother. His mother whom he was going to pretend hadn't just shattered his every belief. She seemed to have aged since the last time he'd seen her. He supposed that lies did that to a person. She'd once been a fading beauty. Now she just came across as tired. "Look," he said, cupping her cheek. "I don't know how much longer I have—you know, as me."

"No, no, no," she said with a few violent shakes of her head. "I don't want to hear this. Right this very minute, Belle's off talking to her ma. Trying to formulate a plan."

"I thought she was in the shower." Boone forced a deep breath. A mental image of Belle's soap-slick curves had made him readjust his boys.

"Which only goes to show that you only *think* you know everything."

"Where does her mother live? Down the road?"

"Try down the continent," Maude said with a snort. "She's in a commune of exiled Fairies in Washington State."

"But how did she get a flight—"

Reaching around him for the coffee pot, Maude said, "You're not the only one around here with wings."

"Are you really the devil?" It was late afternoon when Ewan called out to Boone where he sat at the end of a dock jutting out over the Moody farm pond. The boy carried a plastic sword, and around his shoulders he'd draped a frayed black cape. A Halloween vampire costume that'd seen better days?

Boone got all choked up at the sight of him—this brave, handsome kid. The kid whose mother he'd all but stolen. He'd wanted kids for as long as he could remember. But now, because of these damned wings and whatever monster lurked inside, he'd never have them.

"Well?" the boy asked, raising his chin in a move that reminded Boone so much of Belle that tears sprang to his eyes. What was up with his sudden sentimentality? Was it because he knew his end had to be near? "Are you the devil or not?"

Digger trotted up to join them, tail wagging, tongue lolling.

"Truthfully," Boone said, giving the dog a pat before tossing a pebble into glassy green water, watching concentric circles form, "I don't know. Your uncle seems to think so, but I can't really tell for sure."

"Okay," the boy said, setting his sword on the dock to sit cross-legged beside Boone.

Digger sat, too.

"I cut my finger at school today." Ewan held up his index finger, proudly displaying a yellow smiley-face bandage.

"Ouch."

"Belle's gonna freak. She always does when I get hurt."

"You get hurt a lot?"

"Nah, but you know girls. Always worrying and stuff." He stretched his right leg, kicking at the water with his sneaker toe, then reached into his pocket to pull out a close-shelled box turtle. "This is Toby," he said, holding out the creature for inspection. "I found him on the playground at school. Some of the older kids were throwing rocks at him, but I told 'em to knock it off."

"And they did?" Boone asked, eyebrows raised at this kid's pluck.

"Nah. That's how my finger got cut—running away

249

from them when they started throwing rocks at me. I tripped and fell."

"That sucks," Boone said, his heart going out to the kid. "That's kind of how I feel now—like everyone's throwing rocks at me." Gazing out at the water, Boone added, "Kind of makes me wish a nice kid like you would lift me up and carry me to another pond."

"Yeah." Ewan clamored up only to clomp back down the dock and set his turtle at water's edge.

Digger sprawled out and sighed, closing his eyes for a nap. Boone rubbed him behind his ears. What a great dog. They'd met last night over pie. What an even greater kid. They'd met that morning over Cheerios.

"Man," Ewan said, "I've never seen someone in as much trouble as you. Philbert still thinks I'm a baby, but I saw everything last night. It was like a slasher movie when he tried splitting you in half with that ax."

"Oh?" The kid had replayed it all so matter-of-factly, Boone wasn't sure how to reply.

"He wouldn't've done it, though," Ewan said, rejoining him at the end of the dock. "He can talk mean sometimes, like when Digger's gettin' after a calf, but he doesn't really mean it."

"You sure about that?"

The kid nodded vigorously. "He used to be the Easter Bunny. He couldn't hurt nobody."

"The Easter Bunny, huh?" Boone washed his face with his hands. This was all too much. His wings. The whole Fairy World/Dark World thing. Good God, it was like living in an episode of that TV show Ma was always watching, *Charmed*.

"Belle's a Tooth Fairy. Aunt Lila's been trying to keep up with Belle's route, but she's pretty slow and gets lost a lot. Philbert's been havin' to run the route with her."

As ridiculous as this whole conversation was beginning to sound, Boone just went with it. What else could he do? "So if they're gone," *and I was holding your mother hostage,* "who watches after you?"

"Julep." The boy made a face. "She's a retired leprechaun. Aunt Lila said her son's like crazy rich. He makes a lot of money from wishing wells."

Leprechauns. Wishing wells. Right.

Boone sighed.

"Uh-oh," the boy said, scrambling to his feet and grabbing for his sword. "Belle's home."

"How can you tell?" Boone asked, not all that sure he wanted to know.

"See the glowing rainbow lights coming from her bedroom window?"

Boone made the mistake of looking, and sure enough, it looked as if prism-light was being shot through the second-floor walls.

"Wow," he mumbled under his breath.

"Pretty cool, huh?"

"Yep."

"Come on," the kid said, holding out his hand. "Let's go see her. She's been real sad lately 'cause we don't have enough money, but ever since you've been here, she seems a lot happier."

Taking the trusting boy's hand in his, Boone's heart swelled. "Yeah?" he said, barely able to speak past the lump in his throat over all he'd soon be losing. "Let's go see Belle."

Midway down the slick pond trail leading back to the house, the boy almost lost his footing, but Boone caught him before he fell.

"Thanks," Ewan said. "If I'd've got in that mud, Uncle Phil would've eaten me for dinner."

"No problem," Boone said. "Someday maybe you'll return the favor."

"Mmm," Lila said at dinner that night. "These mashed potatoes are whipped just right. So nice and fluffy and—"

"Lila!" Philbert barked. "I think there's a more important topic on the table than potatoes."

"I don't remember you being such an old fart," Maude said, shooting him a glare.

Philbert fired back, "And I don't remember ever having a fully developed Dark One at my table. As man of this house, I'm responsible for all of you."

"He's my son, Phil." A glass of sweet tea to her lips, Maude added, "Honestly, do you think he's going to attack his own mother right here over Belle's delicious meat loaf?" She beamed Belle's way. "Everything's just delicious, sweetheart. You're going to make a fine wife."

Belle grimaced, toying with her green beans, aching to sneak a peak at Boone, yet scared. He'd been so quiet. What could be going through his head?

After their time on the farm, she didn't want to make some stranger a fine wife—she wanted to be Boone's wife. But that was impossible. Maude knew that, just as she had to know that during all that time they'd spent on the farm, they'd had to do something more with each other than plow fields and weed the garden!

Why was she being so cruel now?

"Since everyone else seems to be sidestepping the issue," Philbert said, buttering a roll as if they were talking about nothing more important than the afternoon farm report, "Belle, I know you ignored my wishes and visited your mother. Why don't you give us the bottom line. What sort of behavior can we expect from this . . ." He coolly eyed Boone who silently ate his meal—meat loaf swimming in hot sauce, gaze locked on his plate. "Well, I'm not sure what to technically label him, but—"

"Boone's a man, Uncle Philbert. A good man. He—"

"He carries a sleeper gene," Philbert said, clanging his fork to his plate. "Do you have any idea what that means? No? Well, I'll tell you. It means his powers are of such an extreme nature that he's had to mature to this age to even possess the mental and physical strength to handle them. Give us the scoop, Belle. Did your mother give you any idea of what he'll soon be capable of?"

Belle had been about to take a bite, but, no longer hungry, she stabbed her fork into her slab of meat. Careful to look anywhere but at Boone, she said, "Okay, seeing that I'm already busted, here's the deal. Mom knew some people who'd escaped from the Underworld. They'd seen entities like Boone. Creatures with wings and a penchant for violence. In an official capacity, they're Bogeymen, charged with frightening children and adults onto straight and narrow paths by means of disturbing dreams. All that," she said with a sad sigh; "that's just his apprenticeship. After that . . ." She steepled her fingers beneath her chin, gazing into the mashed potatoes as opposed to Boone's dear face. "Well . . . after that, no one knows for sure what'll happen. Only that it's not good."

"Okay, then," Lila said with forced good cheer. "Who wants pineapple upside-down cake for dessert?"

"How can you stand being around me?" Boone asked Belle long after Philbert had locked him in for the night, long after Belle had slipped out her own bed-room window and onto the roof to sneak into his room.

They were stretched out together on the bed, and despite the number of times they'd been together, somehow this seemed the most intimate.

The most pure.

Somehow, everything before had just been a test—of what, he wasn't sure. All he knew was that he couldn't fathom a world without her in it. Trouble was, if all she'd reported at dinner were true, he was honor-bound to remove himself from this beautiful woman and her son before he brought them harm. He'd rather kill himself than hurt them with his own hands. Would it come to that?

He had no way of knowing. No one did. Which was why he had to leave now.

Tonight.

"May I kiss you?" he asked, stroking Belle's pale hair back from her forehead, loving the play of moonlight on her porcelain-fine skin.

Eyes big and brimming with tears, she nodded. "I'll be really ticked if you don't."

From somewhere inside him came a smile that all too quickly faded. "What happens if I can't stop kissing you, Princess? I don't want to hurt you."

"You won't," she said. "I love you. And you can't hurt someone you love."

"Yeah, but who said anything about *you* hurting *me*? It works the other way around, remember?"

Those tears began to fall. "Sure," she said, grinning through her pain. "But I know a secret."

"What's that?" he asked, leaning forward to kiss her cheek, the tip of her nose.

"You love me, too."

"And you know that how?" he asked, brushing his lips along her throat.

"Because what I didn't tell Philbert was that if you didn't love me, Mom's friends said you would have already killed me."

That raised the hairs on Boone's forearms. "Y-you're joking, right?"

She shook her head.

"Oh, God," he said, already pushing himself up from the bed. "This has gone too far. If there's even a chance of me hurting you, I'm out of here—now."

"No," she said, hand on his arm. "One other thing I didn't tell all of them down there was that Maude and Philbert were right about bringing us together."

Eyes narrowed, he said, "Why?"

"Well . . ." She trailed her index finger up his forearm, giving him a fresh crop of goose bumps for an entirely different reason. "There's a chance that if we love each other enough, the Light in us might banish the Dark."

"But . . ." He eyed her long and hard. "Go on. There's something else you aren't telling me."

She looked down, licked her lips. "In the, um, same respect, the very act of lovemaking could bring out other tendencies—you know, Dark ones. I've felt it before, Boone. On the farm. Crazy yearnings for . . . well you know." She once again bowed her head, but he slipped his hand beneath her chin, forcing her to meet his gaze.

"You can't imagine how much I want this, Belle. To be with you, in that way, but . . ."

The longer he stared, the warmer his eyes of silvery gray became.

That single word of his—*but*—irrationally enraged

her. "Did anyone ever tell you you're too damned noble, cowboy? Now, where's the fun in that?"

Taking the decision out of his hands, she placed her left hand on his right shoulder, planning to pin him against the bed, but then there was that not-so-little problem of what to do about his wings.

"We can't do this, Belle." He moaned when she kissed his collarbone.

"We *are* doing this, Boone. It's the only way."

He'd risen in the bed, and with palms pressed to his chest, she kissed his pecs, and then a trail down the honed lines of his abs.

Her long hair swung free, whispering against him, every strand kissing him, loving him.

Every inch of her body hummed with greedy hunger.

Vows of chastity be damned.

She no longer cared about her job. It was a stupid job. Being a sniveling do-good Fairy was stupid.

But this . . .

She tugged on his nipple with her teeth.

. . . This was good, dirty fun!

"How's this going to work?" she said, dragging off her T-shirt in anticipation of hammering out the logistics.

"Belle, please, I—"

"Hush," she said, unhooking her bra, loving the widening of his irises as he gazed at her, licking his lips.

Her attention turned lower, to the obvious bulge in his faded jeans.

Good.

Ever the diligent farmer, he was ready to plant his seed.

Needing an appetizer before the main course, she

straddled him, grinding hard. Closing her eyes, tossing her hair back, she raised the corners of her mouth in a womanly smile.

Searching out his mouth, she kissed him hard, loving his shuddering surrender with every hot sweep of their tongues.

Fingers thrust deep into the hair at her temples, he drew her back, staring into her eyes. "Who are you?" he asked. "And what have you done with Belle?"

"Who?"

Abruptly releasing her, thoroughly pissing her off, he edged off the bed.

But she was having none of that.

Fine, if he wanted to do the dirty deed standing up, she had no problem with that. The kinkier the better.

Instantly by his side, nimble fingers on the waistband of his jeans, she made fast work of unlatching the buttons and springing him free. "Ah . . ." she said with a big, hungry grin. "I always took you for the boxer type, but commando works, too.

"Come on," she urged, rubbing the aching tips of her breasts against his chest, pressing his hard length even closer by digging her fingertips into his tight buns. "What're you waiting for? An engraved invitation?" Standing on tiptoes, she once again went for his lips, this time soft, sexy, mewing, "Come on, you big stud . . . do me."

"Do you?" He stopped kissing to raise his eyebrows. "All right," he said, settling his large hands about her slim hips, lifting her out of his way. "That's all I needed to hear."

"Cool," she said with a big, sexy grin. Just in case he hadn't gotten the hint that she was all revved up and ready to go, she twirled a big chunk of her hair.

"I love you," he said, pressing a boring kiss to her forehead. "Never forget I love you." And with that, he buttoned up his jeans, then turned his back on her, flashing her those sexy black wings.

"If you love me," she said, hands at the waist of her own jeans, "then get back over here and show me."

In front of the open window, moonlit curtains writhing in the warm breeze, he said, "I *am* showing you, Belle. Now forget you ever knew me and get on with your life."

Great wings flexed, he blew her a kiss before leaping out the window and flying off into the night.

Chapter Seventeen

"Belle?"

She rolled over in her bed. The voice calling out to her sounded far off, but the annoying shake was all too close.

"Belle? You gotta wake up. Aunt Lila says she lost tonight's schedule and . . ."

Belle grappled with her return to consciousness.

Lila. Filling in for her.

Ewan, shaking her awake.

Boone.

Refusing to kiss her, make love to her, leaving without even a proper goodbye.

"Belle? You okay?"

Her son looked small and alone and worried. Had she done this to him? By keeping him with her, she'd hoped he'd lead a happy life, but, knowing what she did now, maybe he'd have been better off without her. Maybe her own mother had been right in giving her up.

"I love you," he said. "I missed you real bad."

In the thin moonlight streaming into the room, she looked out of herself and into him, at his pale blue eyes and freckles and choppy blond hair.

What was she thinking?

She loved him.

Fiercely.

Which made whatever she was going through all the harder to bear. Was she on the verge of becoming a Dark One? Would she, too, sprout wings? If so, what would happen to her son? Who would see to it that . . .

Refusing to go one step further with that negative line of thought, Belle scooped him into her bed, cradling him in a hug.

"I love you, too," she said, burying her nose in his hair. "And, mmm mmm, you smell good. Like bugs and dirt. How long has it been since you've had a bath?"

He grinned.

"One day?"

He shrugged.

"Two days?"

"I dunno. Maybe."

"Get in the tub," she said.

"But, Belle, it's like one in the morning."

"Oh." She grinned. "Then I guess I'm late for work."

He nodded, scrambling off her lap. "Want me to get your costume?"

"Yes, please."

This sudden normalcy—it was crazy. How could everything seem so right on the surface, when just on the other side of a painfully thin curtain, her whole life was falling apart?

"Here you go," her sweet boy said, reverently laying the pink tulle and satin dream across the foot of her bed.

In what now felt like another lifetime, she hadn't

been able to wait to put on her Fairy costume. Now, all she wanted was to cradle her son close and then find Boone.

Where could he have gone? Back to the farm?

She'd used her wings illegally yesterday to pop in on her mother. After gathering the children's teeth, she'd go there—to Boone's farm. ASAP. She had to know if he was all right. Besides, the animals needed to be fed.

"Belle?" Ewan held out her wings. "You're acting weird."

"I know," she said with a deep sigh.

"This have something to do with Boone leaving?"

"How did you know he was gone?"

"I heard him swooshing his wings and looked out the window, and, like—awesome! There he was. Flying and stuff. Think he'd take me for a ride?"

"I don't know," she said, closing her eyes for just a second, replaying the rush of soaring through the night in his arms. Eyes open, logic firmly in place, she said, "No. It's probably not a good idea."

"Okay." Ewan put on his pouty face. "So when's he coming back?"

"I don't know." Clutching her wings to her chest, she gazed out the window.

"He *is* coming back, though, right?"

"I don't know, sweetie. I just don't know."

"There's been another." Philbert slapped the *Tulsa World* onto the kitchen table and pushed his chair back with a loud scrape against the oak floor.

"Another what?" Maude nibbled the corner of a buttered piece of toast. "Mmm . . . delicious. I get so tired of croissants."

From her end of the table, Lila harrumphed.

"Earthquake," Philbert said. "This one in an arrow-straight line just like the others. It broke a dam. Killed twenty-eight people with flooding. Fourteen more from the quake." He tapped the headline. "Says here the religious right are convinced this is a sign of the second coming. Thousands are lining up along the fault line to pray."

"What's this?" Ewan asked, bounding into the room carrying a large, gift-wrapped box.

Philbert set the paper on the table beside his plate and gestured for the boy to bring the white box with its big red bow to him. "The card says it's for all of us. Where did you find it?"

"On Boone's bed. It was all made and everything, and this box was on top. I was going to ask him if he'd take me flying today."

"He's not there?" Maude asked, toast to her mouth.

"Nope." Ewan tromped to the cabinet for a bowl and the box of Cheerios. Hugging the cereal box, he fetched milk from the fridge, then set all of his loot on the table. "Well?" he asked. "Isn't anyone going to open it? 'Cause if you aren't, then I will."

"Go ahead," Lila said. "It would do us all good to indulge in a nice bit of cheer."

"Hmm . . ." Maude said through her latest bite of toast. "Wonder when he'll be back. I think it'll do us all good to speak more about his condition."

Ewan plucked the red bow from the box, stuck it to the top of his head, then ripped the white paper. "Wonder what it is," he said, giving the box a shake. "It's awfully heavy."

"Go on, Ewan," Philbert said, in no mood for frivolity. "Be done with it."

The boy lifted the lid, then gasped.

"Well?" the two women said in unison.

"Look!" He tipped the open box their way. "It's money. Gobs and gobs of money!"

"Oh, my," Maude said, her complexion paling. "This could only mean one thing."

"What's that?" Lila asked, making careful stacks of the banded hundreds.

"My boy doesn't plan on coming back."

"Ahh, my child. 'Tis so good to finally meet you face to face for a proper, more civilized conversation." After a polite bow, he added, "I'm Darious. King of the Underworld."

Boone looked away from the well-dressed middle-aged man. His black suit fit like it had been custom tailored, his white shirt heavily starched. He wore one of those trendy Tabasco ties, with his dark hair slicked back in a long ponytail.

The place itself was nothing like what Boone had expected the Underworld to be—if indeed this was the famed Underworld. It'd taken two days and three nights to fly by instinct to this place, this elegant chateau perched high in what Boone could only guess were the Himalayas.

Soft classical music flowed from hidden speakers, and fire crackled in a huge stone hearth.

What was this, some kind of sick joke?

"Oh, I assure you," the man said, sipping from a brandy snifter. "'Tis no joke. I've been planning your journey since the day you were fathered by my former right-hand man, Damon. He was big fun. At least till your bitch of a mother stabbed him in his sleep." Darious winked. "He had such a way with the ladies. Well . . . except for that one."

"Great."

Darious smiled. "Yes, it will be great once you realize all that's at stake. This"—he opened his arms wide, taking in the startling panoramic view—"will all be yours to toy with as you please. Earthquakes, floods, tidal waves. Such great fun to see the ants squirm."

"You're sick."

The self-crowned king took another leisurely sip of his brandy. "Hmm . . . I prefer to think of myself as emotionally barren, but I suppose 'sick' could do in a pinch. Drink?" he asked, walking toward an antique mahogany bar lined with crystal decanters and pricey bottles of booze.

Outside tinted windows, sunlight glistened off jagged peaks for as far as the eye could see. The sunlight was blinding on the snow, yet breathtakingly beautiful. A pang shot through Boone. He didn't want to be here alone. He needed Belle here sharing this moment, this place.

"Of course you do," the king said. "After all, as my daughter, she is a true princess in every sense of the word."

"That was just an act she put on to spoof my mother's friends."

"False," he said, adding a few fingers of amber liquid to his glass. "I've seen to it in subtle ways that she's been groomed her whole life for the role. Just as you were. But back to her," he said, all lascivious smile, "she's perfectly suited for the role, don't you think? I mean, really, even if I do say so myself, she's not the sort of girl one stumbles upon every day."

A growl formed deep in Boone's throat. "You've got *me*. Stay away from her."

The man chuckled. "Ah, but I've got my heart set on a matching pair. The two of you together—splendid. The force will be electrifying."

Boone clenched his fists.

"Yes, my child, feel it. The power rushing through you. She felt it the last time you were together, too. Why did you resist? Why, when the joining would've been so easy?"

Laughing, Boone said, "Easy, yeah. Hell, yeah. Right." He headed for the door. "I'm out of here."

The king clapped his hands, replacing the awe-inspiring view with inky black.

Two black-suited thugs approached. They were barrel-chested, with wings much like Boone's only smaller. One man stood at each side of him. All Boone seemed able to focus on was the fact that their suits had slits in the back to accommodate their wings.

"I had so hoped it wouldn't come to this," the man who'd for so long been the greasy voice in his head said. "Dalhart, Drakkon, tend to my child."

"Quit calling me that," Boone raged. "I'm not your child. My father was a wonderful man who—"

"The father to whom you refer, *Clem*, was a pitiful mortal joke. Now, your real father, mmm . . . He was something. Died way too young. He always was one of my favorites. Which is why I've chosen you, as his son, to rule alongside my daughter."

Jaw clenched, muscles in his neck corded, Boone refused to meet the man's stare.

"What's the matter?" Darious asked. "Cat got your tongue?"

Boone sneered, "More like a snake."

The king laughed and laughed. "I'm so relieved to see you have a sense of humor. Life down here can be so dull."

"Where could he be?" Belle stood in the blazing sun, Texas dust swirling at her feet.

A lone tumbleweed crossed the yard, flinging itself against the chicken-coop wall.

She'd searched Boone's farm, from the hay loft to the well house to the pond where she'd fancied them making love, but the place was deserted. Even the animals were gone.

She hated to be gruesome, but not even the animals' bodies remained. Might she hope that was a good sign? Showing that either Boone or someone else had taken them to a safe place where they'd be looked after?

Despite the steady breeze, the farm seemed to have fallen eerily quiet. Belle had tended gardens all her life, and yet weeds had choked this once carefully tended plot to a state of neglect not possible in a mere three days.

Or had it been longer?

Hand to her forehead, Belle couldn't remember.

Everything had become a blur.

Her work.

Her vows.

Her once desperate need for money.

Boone's welcome—and unexpected—package had ensured that all of her family's financial needs would be not just met, but exceeded, for many years to come. Boone had lied—he was still loaded. And where just a few weeks earlier all she could think about was finding money to pay the second and third mortgages and her blackmail payments to Josie, in order to protect her almighty reputation, now all she seemed able to focus on was Boone's lie. How badly it hurt.

His distrust hurt.

His being gone hurt.

What was the point of keeping her reputation untarnished? The only things that mattered were keeping Ewan blissfully unaware of the tenuous state of his world and finding Boone, whose mother still occupied their guest room, having taken to her bed in what Lila described as an apoplectic fit. Count on Lila to choose an over-the-top way of stating the woman was worried sick over the whereabouts of her son.

"So am I, Maude." Belle put her hand to her forehead, shading her itching, burning eyes from blinding midday sun. "So am I."

Boone stood naked, chained to a cavern wall in a drug-induced mental fog.

He could have been there for hours or days.

The only light came from a fading torch on the wall.

The only sounds were far-off screams and a steady drip, drip, drip of water falling from the cavern ceiling some twenty feet over his head.

Shadows and thick smoke made for gruesome company, as did constant fear of what he was becoming.

He closed his eyes and thought of Belle.

Could she really be this prick's daughter?

If so, had that less-than-inspiring speech she'd delivered on the state of his condition truly originated with her mother's friends? Or had she mined her info straight from the bowels of dear old Dad?

If that were true—if . . .

He shook his head. The implications were too much to bear. Then she would've been out to con not only him, but every living creature she'd touched.

No.

He gritted his teeth, working a muscle in his jaw. He didn't believe it. The look in her eyes while talking of his fate, it'd been too filled with shimmering tears.

Boone sighed.

Arched his head back and flexed his great wings.

No one for sure knows what'll happen . . . just that it can't be good.

Swell.

So what were they talking about? Standard-issue demon crap straight out of every Hollywood devil flick ever made? Was he gonna be conning innocent folks into selling their souls, or worse?

Were they talking about the whole eternal-damnation route?

Burning, writhing and all that other hell-and-brimstone fun?

Stomach roiling, Boone violently retched.

Each spasm left him involuntarily yanking harder at his chains until blood oozed down his wrists and elbows and into glistening pools on the rock floor.

How long was His Majesty of Darkness planning on keeping him chained up down here?

Gritting his teeth, he yanked for all he was worth on the chains binding him to the stone wall, but they held.

"Arrrgghh!" he roared.

From the far end of the cavern came a sarcastic

round of applause and laughter. The king, dressed in a broad smile, crisply pressed khakis and a bold tropical-print shirt, clapped again, transforming the dank, dark cavern into an opulent island retreat with gleaming black marble floors and deep-cushioned rattan furniture.

An olive-skinned woman wrapped in an orange sarong, breasts covered by only her long dark hair, reclined on a chaise aimed at the calm sea. Twenty feet from a lanai, gentle surf lapped against powdery white sand. Aquamarine water of a thousand varying shades glistened in the sun.

Another woman strolled into the house from the beach. She wore nothing but a thong bikini bottom. Her long blond hair hung in pigtails drizzling seawater down her pendulous breasts. Her nipples were large and dark—shades of fading hibiscus.

The very air smelled hedonistic.

Of flowers and sex.

As if he were no more than a thirteen-year-old lusting over his first copy of *Hustler*, Boone grew rock hard. He felt ashamed. Completely out of control and shamed, but with his hands still chained to a wall—currently made of lava—he was helpless to even cover himself.

The woman sauntered toward him, her full lips curved into a welcoming smile that told him that if he liked what he saw, he was welcome to all of it and more.

He looked away.

But then another woman strolled through gauzy curtains caressed by the light breeze. And another and another, in every conceivable female flavor. Short, plump blondes. Majestic redheads. Brunettes with legs so long he could wrap them around his waist and—

"Ahh . . ." the king said. "See something that suits your fancy? Or would this be more to your taste?"

Boone looked in the direction the man pointed.

For a moment, glare from the water blocked his view, but then there she was. Belle. Long braids on either side of her breasts, wearing his boxers she'd rolled low on her hips, and that halter she'd made from his favorite T-shirt.

Sweat glistened on her tanned chest, causing the white T-shirt to be transparent.

He hardened to the point that he was in actual physical pain from wanting her, but reminded himself it wasn't her. Just like this place, these other women, every bit of it was controlled by *him*.

"Boone," she said, her legs long and lean and tan in those sexy red boots she called her ruby slippers. "I've been so worried about you, sweetie. How are you? You holding up okay?"

She sauntered to him, pressing her left hand to his chest.

His nostrils flared.

God help him, she even smelled the same. Like sweat and grass and soap.

"I've missed you so," she said. "Why did you run out on me like that? You know . . ." She winked. "Just when things were getting good."

Grinning up at him, she slid her hand down his chest to kneel before him, cupping his balls, taking the rest of him deep into her mouth.

It's not her, Boone cried, willing himself down, to think of anything but her. But the expert sucking was on the verge of making him explode.

"Mmm . . ." she said, gazing up at him with her prettiest smile. The one he remembered from shared meals and chores and kissing. "You like that, don't you?"

God help him, he couldn't breathe.

All he could do was pray for more.

She sucked harder and faster, working his balls.

He fisted his hands, holding his breath in pleasure/pain.

No. This was wrong. This wasn't Belle. This wasn't the woman he loved. He didn't know who, or what, the hell it was, but—

"Oh, for pity's sake," the king said. "You damned halflings. Can't you for once shut off that infernal conscience and just go with the flow?" He clapped his hands again and they were back in the cave.

The women were gone.

More importantly, "Belle" was gone.

Boone's raging erection remained.

"This all could have been so easy." The king sighed. "Oh, well, you wanna do it the hard way, I can oblige."

"I don't know what the hell you want! How can I cooperate when all you ever do is screw with me?"

The king laughed. "It wasn't me trying to screw you just now, pal."

"Get on with it," Boone raged. "What do you want?"

"What do I want?" The king stepped closer, close enough for Boone to smell death on his hot breath. "Simple. I want you to swear loyalty to me."

"And how am I supposed to do that when I don't even know you?"

"Oh, come on, Boone. I've never taken you for the slow type. But if you need a repeat of our formal introduction, here goes." He took a step back to bow. "To some, I'm the Bogeyman. The Dark. The source of all

271

things evil. But I prefer keeping it simple. King of the Underworld will do."

Boone bowed his head and laughed. "This is too much. I thought I'd been around, but—"

"Go ahead, laugh all you want. I want you to be pleased with your decision. Do you think your success in business was all your doing? Or that of your pathetic mortal stepfather? I've been grooming you for years. The Underworld is long overdue for a makeover. We get such bad press down here. The whole death thing. But really, if it weren't for me, just think how overrun Earth would be. Stinking mortals everywhere. They're like rats, really. Or roaches." He shuddered. "Just can't seem to rid the place of them."

Eyes squeezed shut, Boone chanted, "I'm ready to wake up . . . I'm ready to wake up . . ."

"Just say it, Boone. Jump on board the band-wagon, and we can be rid of this tiresome dungeon. So bourgeois."

"I'm going to wake up any minute and all this is going to be gone. I'm going to be home—at my Dallas pent-house—my morning alarm blaring. I'll have hot black coffee, then head for a business meeting. Even better, I'll be back on the farm. Belle will be there—and her son. I'll get her some indoor plumbing. Yeah, she'd like that. A big old whirlpool tub and a flush toilet."

"Mmm . . . sounds cozy."

The king clapped his hands, and they were there.

On the farm.

Only it wasn't.

The house was the same, but bigger. Homey, while at the same time strangely grand.

Boone was reclining in a bubble-filled tub, hands

chained to the adobe wall behind him, when Belle walked in, this time wearing the gold dress he'd first seen her in, her hair piled high and begging to be set free.

He was instantly hard.

The hot water on his wings was insanely erotic.

"Took you long enough to get home," she said. "Ewan's down at the pond, so we've got the whole place to ourselves." The Belle lookalike did a painfully slow striptease, her nipples puckered and perfectly hardened, her smile brilliant and toothy and all for him.

He groaned, again willing away his erection.

"You're not Belle," he said, squeezing his eyes shut tight, willing the vision away. Willing himself away. "This isn't real. None of this is real."

"Bravo," the king said, back on his feet. "You're right. It isn't real. But down here, kiddo, let me give you a glimpse of what's gonna be real if you don't get with the program—and I mean fast." He snapped his fingers.

This time, Boone stood clothed in an impeccably tailored black suit, free from his chains in a horrific scene of about-to-be destruction.

A tornado the likes of which were only seen in nightmares bore down on Belle's family farm, heading in a direct line for the house.

Ewan stood on the front porch transfixed, while around back, Belle cried for him.

"Ewan? Ewan, please! Where are you?"

The boy just stood there, hypnotized by the view.

Boone tried running onto the porch to save him, but this sick bastard calling himself king had frozen his feet to the ground. "Stop this!" he cried out to the freak intent on destroying all of their lives. "What have they ever done to you? Belle is *not* your daughter. She's a good woman. Ewan's a complete innocent."

The monster funnel cloud bore down on them all, roaring like a thousand freight trains, smashing everything in its path with sharp, wind-driven teeth.

Maniacally laughing, the king called above the roar, "I live for this! Ain't it grand?"

Boone grabbed him by the lapels of his fancy suit, giving him a hard shake. "Stop this! Or else—"

"Oh?" Darious chuckled. "Now *you're* making threats? I don't think so." He pointed his finger toward the house, engulfing the porch in flames so hot Boone felt them clear across the yard.

Worse yet, he was loving the heat. It'd made him instantly, exquisitely hard.

"Okay," Boone said, getting the picture that he was way outclassed. "Let them live—and I mean *all* of them. Ewan, Belle, my mom, Lila—even Philbert."

The tornado bore closer.

The flames leapt higher and hotter.

"Mmm . . ." the suit said, "I always did enjoy a nice bonfire."

"Damn you, make it stop!"

"And you'll agree to become my apprentice? Willingly doing my bidding for all time?"

"As long as they remain safe . . . yes."

With a snap of the king's fingers, the fire was out.

The sky was blue.

A robin happily twittered on the front-porch rail, and Ewan, laughing, chased Digger around the yard.

Boone hunched over, bracing his knees. "Thank God."

"God had nothing to do with this one."

"Go to hell," Boone said, strolling across the lawn to the woman and child he loved.

"As you wish." One more clap, and they were both in what any sane person would consider hell—and this time, it wasn't a beach.

Chapter Eighteen

"Belle, what are you doing?" Lila paused beside the kitchen table, mouth open wide enough for flies to buzz in.

Belle looked down at her bowl of early-morning cereal, at the fat drops of hot sauce staining the milk. "Something about it tasted off," she said, making a face. "Maybe the milk's about to go bad." She took a spoonful of cereal, sprinkled on still more lethal red drops, then ate the rest of the bowl, ignoring Lila's stare.

"Did Ewan get off to school allright?" her aunt asked, finally taking a seat.

"Um-hmm." Belle sprinkled more drops on the tips of her fingers, noisily sucking the delicacy. "He almost didn't make the bus, but somehow I've got a little more spring in my step this morning, so I just carried him the rest of the way there."

Lila raised her eyebrows. "What are you, um, planning on doing with the rest of your day?"

"I think I should look for Boone some more, don't you?"

"You know where he is, Belle. It's a place you don't want to be."

"Oh, come on. You don't really believe all that stuff Philbert's been spouting about the big, bad Underworld, do you?"

Lila toyed with the hot-sauce bottle, but Belle snatched it from her.

There wasn't much left.

Town was a good twenty minutes away, and somehow she figured that once her next craving hit, she wasn't going to be in the mood for a car ride.

Her aunt pushed her chair back from the table and stood.

"Where you going?" Belle asked.

"To get your uncle."

Belle rolled her eyes.

Holding the cereal bowl to her lips, she slurped the rest of the milk, then licked the last bit of hot sauce clinging to the sides of the bowl.

She stood, set the bowl in the sink, put the milk back in the fridge, then took the back stairs to her room—what precious little remained of the hot sauce in hand.

In the cozy, buttercream-yellow room, she strolled past her wrought-iron bed and antique oak dresser to yank open the closet door.

The room seemed inordinately bright, so there was no need to turn on the closet light.

Besides, she knew just where she was heading.

Ordinarily when she put her wings on, she wore her uniform, but she figured in this case, the pair of Boone's boxers she'd had on when he'd taken her from the farm and a T-shirt would do just fine.

After setting her hot sauce safely on a high shelf, she

reached for her gossamer silver wings that fit much like a backpack.

In seconds, she'd strapped them on.

Standing in the dark closet, wincing from the over-abundance of light, she closed her eyes and raised her arms, willing herself to Boone.

Wherever he may be, oh, spirits of light and air, please help me find him by taking me directly there.

A low buzzing swarmed in her ears and mind until blinding rainbows of light transported her to another place. Hopefully, a better place where she would be reunited with the man she loved.

Boone's skin burned like a thousand stinging bees.

His arms ached like molten lead.

The only thing making the pain bearable was the knowledge that his sacrifice had made Belle and Ewan safe.

He'd tread water in this slushy ice pit for years.

Logically, he should've been long since dead, but he was slowly coming to the realization that nothing in this place was logical.

Heat was what he most craved, hence the punishing cold.

"How's your spa treatment going?" the king asked from a black leather sofa across the blue-tinted ice cavern. On either side of him, two blondes dressed in black leather bikinis cozied to his chest. They both held lollipops, licking them suggestively.

To his far right a fire roared, tempting him far more than the half-naked blondes.

"Go to hell," Boone spat.

The king almost busted a gut laughing. "Oh, Boone, stop. You're such a funny guy."

279

The once-dim cavern erupted with a burst of rainbow-hued light.

Boone winced, looking away.

"Ah, I wondered how long it would take." The king checked his flashy gold watch. "Apparently not long."

"Who's that?" the taller of the two blondes asked, eyeing Belle as she emerged from an ever-growing iridescent bubble.

Boone's heart raced.

Was it really her?

Or was this just another of *his* tricks?

"Rest assured, my child, it's really her. That's been my plan all along, you know. To make the two of you into a gruesome twosome, raining terror across the land."

The blonde with the biggest boobs giggled.

The king kissed her. "Mmm . . . good flavor. Jalapeño?" She nodded.

"Boone!" Belle cried, running to his hole in the cavern floor. She tried reaching out to him, but her sneakers found no purchase on the slick ice. She fell, only to squirrel herself spread-eagled, reaching out her hands. "Grab on to me. I'll pull you out."

"No!" he said. "Get away from me—fast as you can. It's a trick. All of this."

A powerful keening wind began, hurling icy bullets at their exposed skin. The additional pain mattered little to Boone, for, having made his deals, he was already mired soul-deep in despair, but for Belle, there was still time.

Hope.

"Belle!" he cried above the crazy storm. "Listen to me! Leave while you still can!" The driving ice blinded him, making it that much harder to stay afloat.

Boone knew they were mere feet apart, yet he couldn't see her, only feel her. Her goodness. Her Light.

"No!" he heard her shout. "If we both believe in the Light hard enough, we can fight him, Boone! We *will* win!"

"Please, Belle, save yourself! Go home to Ewan! He needs you!"

"We need *you*!" Not thinking, just doing, Belle lurched forward, knowing his watery grave must be near. If she could just get to him, there was still hope. Always hope.

And then, whoosh!—her feet fell out from under her and bone-deep cold the likes of which she'd never known seeped into her skin. She panicked, floundering, taking in more water than air.

Boone. She had to save Boone.

But then he was there, saving her, wrapping his arms around her in banded-steel warmth.

"Belle . . . Belle . . ." he said, kissing her forehead while keeping them both afloat by kicking his feet.

Her teeth chattered so hard she couldn't speak, but she could pray.

Wrapping her arms around this man she'd somehow grown to love, she tucked her head beneath his, beseeching with all her heart . . . *Wherever safety may be, oh, spirits of light and air, please help us find it by taking us directly there.*

Warmth.

The two lay with limbs tangled on the bed on Boone's great-grandparents' farm. Sunshine, sweet and pure and healing, washed them in shimmering strokes.

Belle closed her eyes and thanked the Light.

Yes. She'd prayed for safety, and her wings had transported them to the one place she'd never felt more complete. Did Boone feel the same?

Judging by the glow in his silvery-gray eyes—yes. A thousand times, yes!

"Thank you," he said, cupping her face in his hands. "You did it. You believed in the world's goodness, and you were—"

"Boone, look!" she said, happy tears stinging her eyes as she ran her hands along the smooth contours of his back. "Your wings. They're gone."

He sagged with relief, and she eased him down on the bed. "You can't imagine," he said, eyes closed, lips curved into a relieved smile, "how damned good this feels. I haven't rested on my back since—"

"Shh." She silenced him with a butterfly-soft kiss. "It's all right. It's over. We never have to think about any of that again."

"I love you," he said.

"I love you, too."

"Think Ewan would want an ex-Dark One for a dad?"

Tearing all over again, she nodded. Kissing him wet and deep.

Pausing for air, sweeping fallen hair from her face to tuck it behind her ears, Boone asked, "Think you could not only stand to marry an ex-Dark One, but marry him wearing that dress you tried on?"

"You mean your great-grandmother's wedding dress? You saw?"

"Strictly by accident," he said, not looking the least bit sorry. "I was on my way to the outhouse. Caught sight of you through the window. I knew the decent thing to do would be to look away, but—"

"But . . ." Belle kissed him again, this time long and leisurely while straddling his hips, loving the feel of his hard against her soft. "You never have been known for decency."

"Hey, now," he fought back, tickling beneath her arms. "I'm as decent as they come."

"Oh yeah?" she said with a teasing grin. "Prove it."

Wielding one of his most potent bad-boy grins, he said, "Now that's a challenge if I ever heard one. Take off that wet T-shirt, woman."

Pouting, she said, "I thought that was your job?"

"Oh? And just how am I supposed to do that job with you sitting on top of me?"

"Excellent point." She grinned, tugging off the wet top, glad she'd been in such a hurry to get to him that she hadn't bothered putting on a bra.

The sudden cool puckered her nipples.

Ever the gentleman, Boone covered them with his palms. "Don't want those beauties catching their death of cold."

She arched her head back and groaned when, beneath his teasing hands, her nipples grew still harder as her breasts swelled, aching in anticipation of the moment they'd both waited for such a long time to come.

Scooting just out of his reach to sit on his thighs, she latched her fingers through the belt loops of his jeans. Without saying a word, she opened the top button, then scooted farther back so she could press her warm lips to the cool, tanned skin of his belly.

A tremor rippled through him.

A faint moan spilled from his lips.

The knowledge that her little kiss had had such a big effect empowered her to reach for the zipper and tug downward. With each agonizingly slow pull she paused to press more hot kisses to his cool flesh.

He wore no boxers or briefs beneath those jeans.

Because he liked going commando?

Or because she'd taken them all while they'd lived out here on the farm?

Her long, still-damp hair sweeping his belly, she figured that either way it didn't much matter. She reaped the benefits!

At last she heard his swift intake of breath as the sides of her hands brushed the silken, swollen length of him.

"Sorry," she said, sending an anything-but-sorry smile his way. "Didn't mean to disturb you."

"The hell you didn't." His breath was ragged when she pressed her lips to the spot her fingers had just been. "If I didn't know better," he halfheartedly complained, "I'd say your whole life is about disturbing me."

"That bad?" she asked innocently, sliding still farther down on his legs so she could pull his jeans past his hips and beyond to set him springing free. Once she'd dragged his wet jeans over his feet to sling them to the floor, she crawled back up the length of him, closing her hand around the part standing at attention.

"No," he finally said. "Hell, no, that's not bad. At the moment, being disturbed is a very good thing."

"I'm glad. Wouldn't want you feeling the slightest discomfort."

"Liar." Wearing that Texas-size grin she'd come to love, he rolled out from under her and right off the bed. Standing, magnificently naked, he asked, "How about taking a turn at your own game, Princess?"

She shrugged, then adopted her best Bugoslavian accent. "You muzt remember, commoner, I am royalty.

I cannot be tit-ill-ated by mere mortal pleazures."

"Oh, now there's a challenge if I've ever heard one. Them's fightin' words, Princess." He knelt before her, eye level with her chest.

She tensed, anticipating the heady torture of him finally taking one of her still-hard nipples into his mouth, but he didn't. Instead, bracing his hands on either side of her, he wrapped a lasso of heat around her neck with slow, moist kisses that made it hard for her to sit upright.

She slipped her arms about his neck, intent on bringing his lips to hers, but not only did he not give in to her silent request, he reprimanded her. "Shame on you. I would have thought a princess of your stature would have grown accustomed to being serviced."

"Oh, you're bad," she said, arching her head in naughty pleasure when his kisses fell lower to the base of her throat, then lower, lower, until his hot breath tickled her begging breasts.

He looked up. "And I'm about to get so much worse."

Always true to his word, Boone did just that, settling his lips, then his teeth, around one aching nipple while he covered her other heavy breast with his hand.

His gentle sucking was sweet torture, liquid warmth. Her hands at the back of his head, she pressed him closer, closer, yet no matter how good all of this felt, she wanted much more, much lower.

He released one breast to give equal sucking favor to her other, yet his hands stayed put on the mattress. She felt the radiant heat from his wrists on her hips and thighs.

"Suitably distracted yet?" he asked. His voice was all boyish charm, but the wicked handsome curve of his lips promised only manly favors.

285

Unable to find words to describe the myriad of distractions he'd introduced to her greedy body, she could only nod.

"Good. Now lean back."

Her eyes widened. "Excuse me?"

"Do it." He winked. "I promise you'll like the results."

Knowing she would, she followed his command, eager to claim her reward for being good.

Lying with her hair spilling about her cheeks and shoulders and her back pressed against the damp, quilt-covered mattress, she closed her eyes, giving in to the dizzying feel of someone else taking charge. For countless years, she'd cared for everyone around her, but now, selfishly, rightly, it was her turn to receive pleasure rather than give.

She groaned at the feel of her lover's large, callused hands sliding up her thighs and hips, then down to the waistband of her still-damp boxers—the boxers that'd grown hot and even wetter between her legs. He slid them down and off, pairing them with his jeans on the floor, edging her sideways on the bed.

How long had it been since she was willfully naked before anyone other than herself in a mirror? And that earlier fallen-towel incident in the kitchen didn't count!

With this, she was officially on her way to breaking her most sacred Tooth Fairy vow, yet she no longer cared. Yes, she would miss the job, but not nearly as much as she would have missed never having known this wonderful man's touch.

She swallowed hard when he lifted first one foot and then the other up onto the antique bed's side rails, his smiling self in between.

The position was wicked, centering her every thought

and breath on the fact that all her throbbing secrets were now the focus of Boone's attention. Hands on her inner thighs, he opened her wide, leaning in. Strong, sure hands kneaded her hips while his mouth kissed the near-virgin plains of her inner thighs.

It all felt so good, yet she wanted so much more.

She wanted him closer.

Loving *all* of her.

Slowly he complied, bringing his hands lower and mouth higher. With his thumbs, he rubbed tantalizing circles atop her hipbones, while with his tongue he explored the vee just below.

Still it wasn't enough.

Not nearly enough.

She slowly bucked against him, trying to convey her wishes.

He got the hint and moved lower, deeper, parting her, then setting up a rhythm with his tongue and fingers that took her in a white-hot flash to wonders she'd only dreamt of knowing.

"Oh, God," she moaned again and again with each heightened wave of pleasure.

"Nope, just me," he teased.

She grinned, shook her head from side to side.

"Open your eyes," he said.

And though she didn't want to face him for fear she'd wake and the dream would end, she did as he asked, to be rewarded by his intense silvery stare.

In the heartbeat their gazes locked, he lowered her feet and swung her hips, shifting her farther back on the bed before entering her.

There was none of the groping there'd been with her first lover, but a single bold, confident stroke that took her very breath away.

She wanted to close her eyes again, to privately savor the pleasure once again building and spreading within her, but he held tight with his stare, challenging her to share herself wholly and completely with no one ever again but him.

He gripped her shoulders, giving him the leverage to plunge still deeper.

"I want to kiss you," he said. So he did, over and deeper again.

But it still wasn't enough.

Never enough.

Carefully keeping them coupled, he lifted her toward him, then eased to a standing position. Her arms wrapped about his neck, her legs circling his hips, she kissed him again, reveling in the sensation of flight. For there, held in his arms with nothing but air and the certainty of his grip, her soul had been given wings.

Before, she thought she'd found happiness in his physical wings, but this, knowing that from here on he'd be safely hers for all eternity, was so very much better.

Time slowed, then stopped, abandoning them in a euphoric state of suspended animation.

The only sounds were the pounding of their hearts and the contrasting slow and easy rhythm Boone worked inside her. He covered her mouth with his, asked her tongue to dance, then took her on a dreamy Texas waltz.

Together, they found release, and together, both sweaty and hot, they laughed, kissed, petted and loved. Their breathing slowed, and they kissed some more.

"Thank you," he said. "This was well worth the wait."

Kissing his cheek, nose and eyebrows, she said, "I

love you. I love everything about you, from your—"

"Oh, enough!" The king clapped, and they were returned to the icy cavern, plunged back into the killing pool. "Hell's bells," he said with a dramatic eye roll, "why couldn't they just end it with a shared smoke and tequila?"

The blondes were seated beside him, and the one with bigger boobs started back up with her giggling.

"W-what happened?" Belle asked, shivering and clinging to Boone, helping him kick to keep them both afloat.

"It was a trick," Boone said. "Mind games. You're not real. N-none of this was real." His teeth chattered, too.

"Yes, Boone. It was. I love you. I loved loving you. We escaped him once, and that just proves our love is strong enough that we can do it again."

"So touching," the king called out. "Blech. All this sweet talk is giving me wretched indigestion." Sloughing off the two blondes, he leaned forward, resting his elbows on his knees. "Here's the deal," he said. "I let you two escape to get the one thing I want worse than either of you—your child. My grandchild."

Belle's eyes widened, and she retreated deeper into Boone's hold.

The king—her father—rolled his eyes. "Oh, yes, cling to each other, kiddies. For now that my seed is planted, I have need for only one of you, and even that's temporary."

He clapped, and Belle was instantly out of the water, dressed in a pink satin robe and fuzzy slippers. She reclined on a pink velvet chaise—a chaise locked in a golden cage.

"That's better," he said, wicked eyes gleaming his

pleasure. "Wouldn't want the little mommy catching her death of cold."

"Boone!" Belle cried, instantly up from the ridiculous chair, tripping over the ridiculously long ties to her robe to fall against cold metal bars. "Boone, fight him. Will yourself away!"

Her lover's teeth chattered so bad he couldn't speak, just looked at her with an agony that ate at her soul.

Closing her eyes, forcing her breathing to slow, Belle repeated over and over her magic spell for flight. She'd used it hundreds of times per night for hundreds upon thousands of nights, substituting different children's names, but now she only used Boone's.

Wherever safety may be, oh, spirits of light and air, please help Boone find it by taking him directly there.

The king cleared his throat. "Pardon me for interrupting still one more touching scene, but Belle, my dear, you seem to have forgotten one very important thing."

Ignoring his cruel taunt, she chanted the flight spell over and over again.

She had to get Boone safely home.

Back to Maude, who would need him in her last days.

She had to get him back to Ewan, who needed a kind and loving father far more than a mother too cowardly to publicly claim him.

Locking her gaze on Boone's dear silvery eyes, she chanted the spell yet again, never believing for one second that if she didn't wish hard enough it wouldn't work.

Laughing, the king said, "Oh, dear," to his buxom companions. "She seems to have forgotten that neither of them are going anywhere without her silly wings."

He leaned in to the taller of the two blondes for a lick of her sucker. "Mmm . . . Tabasco?"

Her pepper-red lips delivered a playful pout. "How do you always guess?"

He preened. "Just a special knack." Easing back against deep leather cushions, planting an arm around each woman, he said, "So, girls, care to place a wager on how long it'll take our dear friend Boone to drown?"

Chapter Nineteen

"Aunt Lila?" Ewan asked, looking up from the kitchen table where he was doing his math homework to check out the green clouds hugging the earth.

"Yes?" She stood at the kitchen window holding a potato in one hand and the peeler in the other. She was frowning, and Aunt Lila *never* frowned.

"Where do you think Belle is? And Boone? Shouldn't they be getting home before this storm?"

"Yes," she said, peeling furiously. "But just because we think they ought to come home doesn't mean they will."

Thunder boomed, shaking the house hard enough to rattle the ice in Ewan's grape Kool-Aid.

He pushed back his chair and went to stand at the back-door window. "Not very nice of them not to at least call," he said in a quiet voice.

"Nope," Lila said, lips pressed tight while she kept right on peeling.

"Think we're gonna have a tornado?"

"Honestly, child." She slammed down the peeler and

tossed the potato in the sink. "Don't you ever do anything but ask questions?"

"Sorry," he said, bowing his head.

"No, I'm the sorry one. Come here," she said, pulling him in for a hug. "Let me show you a trick my sixth-grade teacher showed us once when we were scared of a storm."

Arm around his shoulder, she took him to the big double window in the living room, then pressed his hand to the glass. It felt cold, and fog formed around his fingers.

"Nope," she said.

"To what?"

"No tornado today. All that steam around your fingers tells us so."

He scrunched his forehead and looked up at her. Sometimes Aunt Lila said some pretty goofy stuff. Was this one of those times? "That true?"

Grinning, she shrugged. "Beats me, but it got me out of the kitchen, and you out of doing homework. Let's say we take some of that money Boone left and buy everyone pizza and ice cream for dinner."

"Yeah!"

"Well?" she said, ruffling his hair. "Don't just stand there, go get your shoes on, and we'll skedaddle."

"Whoa," Uncle Philbert said when Ewan slammed into him, racing through the dining room for the front stairs. Last he remembered, that was where he'd left his shoes. "What's your hurry?"

"Lila said we're havin' pizza and ice cream for supper. I gotta get my shoes."

Philbert frowned.

Man, Ewan hated it when grown-ups frowned.

"Sorry," his uncle said. "But you two aren't going anywhere in this weather. I got a bad feeling."

"Oh, you've always got a bad feeling 'bout some-thing or other," Maude said, hands on her hips as she trudged down the stairs. "Let the poor kid have some pizza. Lord knows, he's had precious little fun around here the past few days."

"Oh, and you think anything about us helplessly sit-ting around here waiting to see if Belle and Boone are returned from the Underworld is fun?"

"Hush!" Lila said from the base of the stairs.

"The Underworld?" Ewan asked. "What's that?"

"Now look what you did," Lila said.

Maude clomped in her high heels the rest of the way down the stairs, then hit Philbert over the head with her big purple purse.

"Ouch," he said, rubbing his head. "That hurt."

"Good," Maude said. "Do you think it doesn't hurt that boy, knowing his momma might at this very—"

"She's not really my mom," Ewan said. "Wish she was, but—"

"What else you been keepin' from this boy, Phil?"

"None of your business, Maude."

Boone's mom gave Ewan a real sad sort of look be-fore turning back to Uncle Philbert. "Anyway, all I was saying is that we're all a tad bit on edge, what with this sitting around and waiting. Maybe what we ought to be doing is taking action."

Lightning struck close to the house.

Thunder boomed.

Rain fell so hard, Ewan could hardly see across the yard to the barn.

"In this weather," Philbert said, "just what is it you plan on doing?"

"You know," Maude said. "And it sure doesn't have a darned thing to do with the rain."

"Oh, no." Lila was instantly in between them. "You're not talking about strapping on my wings, are you?"

"What else would you have us do? Somebody's got to go after those two, and it may as well be me," Maude said.

"No," Philbert said, turning his back on the women to head for his recliner and TV remote. "No, let's just wait here. Sooner or later, we'll have to get some sort of sign."

"Sign for what?" Maude asked.

Philbert flicked on the TV. News was on. From the looks of it, awful news.

Ewan edged closer to the TV, as did Lila and Maude.

"Scientists worldwide say they've never seen anything like it," some newswoman said, standing in front of an awesomely deep ditch. "And after this latest batch of quakes in Arkansas, the line now stretches all the way into Oklahoma. Members of the U.S. Geological Survey have already descended upon the small town of Oakville, and residents living in line with the fault are being encouraged by local law enforcement to evacuate their homes."

"Is that sign enough for you?" Philbert said, flicking off the TV.

Maude stumbled back to land her big behind on the sofa.

"That's our town they just showed," Ewan said to no one in particular.

"What're we going to do?" Lila asked. "We have to tell someone. For years, the Fairy World has peacefully co-existed with the Underworld, but now . . ."

"Oh?" Philbert laughed. "And just who do you propose we tell, Lila? The president? You think he's going to tell the King of the Underworld that he'd better behave or he's sending in the marines?"

"Quit being so mean!" Ewan cried to his uncle, who before all this mess started had never said one hateful thing in his whole life. "I'm sick and tired of everyone always being so sad. Why can't we just find Belle and Boone and bring them home?"

"Come here, Ewan," Maude said, patting the sofa cushion beside her. "I wanna tell you a story."

Though Ewan usually tried to stay away from Boone's mom because she wore an awful lot of perfume that sometimes made his nose itch, he figured just this once he'd be able to tough it out.

"Okay," she said. "Have you ever heard folks talk about going to heaven or hell when they die?"

Duh. He nodded.

"Well, where we're concerned—Fairies, that is—all you need know is there's a good place and a bad. We call them the Light and the Dark."

"Maude, I—" Philbert pushed himself up from his chair.

"Oh, hush, and sit back down," Maude said. "Don't you think you've kept this boy in the dark long enough?" To Ewan she said, "You do know you're livin' with a bunch of Fairies, right?"

He nodded.

"Good, at least that'll give us a nice jumping-off point. Okay." She took a deep breath. "The Earth was given as a gift to two brothers and a sister. 'Cept for Darious, their real names I can't even begin to pronounce, so let's just think of them in terms of Light and Dark. Darious is Dark."

"O-okay."

"Well, anyway, one brother was assigned to rule over

the Upperworld, and the other brother got the Underworld. Right off the bat, you can imagine that caused quite a fuss, so ever since then, the two have had more than a few turf wars. You know what that means?"

"Sort of. That's like when the big kids on our school playground make us little kids get away from the swings."

Double lightning bolts singed the big maple out front.

Aunt Lila, nervous, fluttered a glance that way.

"That's right," Maude said as if nothing had happened. "So anyway—"

"Wait," Ewan interjected. "What'd the sister get?"

"Ahh . . . She got the best parts of all. The In Between." Maude tickled Ewan's belly, and he scrunched up laughing. "That's kind of like the cream in the middle of a Twinkie, which has always been one of Boone's favorite foods."

"Really?" Ewan asked, eyes wide. "Belle, too."

"Wonderful," Maude said. "That's a good sign—that they both like some of the same things." She tweaked his nose. "And I'll bet that includes loving you."

Sensing that even though she might be stinky, she was very nice, Ewan leaned closer. Maude was soft and warm, and like a grandma, wrapped her arm around him, making him feel, at least for the moment, safe.

"So anyway," Maude said, softly stroking his hair. "You know what angels are, right?"

"They protect us."

"Yep. You're right again. Only us Fairies call them Guardians. Well, once there got to be so many folks in the Upperworld that the big brother and his helpers, the Guardians, couldn't keep everything straight, he made the Fairies. Now we're in charge of fun stuff. Nothing really important, but we sure make life a whole lot happier for mortals, who are kind of like our cherished pets."

"Maude," Philbert said, back out of his chair and looking out the window at the churning wall of angry gray-green clouds. "What does any of this have to do with our current situation?"

"If you'd just hush up, I'll get around to it. Now, Ewan, where was I?"

"Fairies doin' fun stuff."

"Right. Okay, then. Since the brother who got stuck with the Underworld is never happy—remember? His name is Darious?"

Ewan nodded.

"He doesn't much cotton to anyone else bein' happy, either. Now, every once in a while, just to mess with his big brother, he takes a Guardian, or Fairy, and has 'em do something wrong. Now, in their minds and hearts, the Fairies or Guardians think they're bad, but really, it's the Underworld King making them do it."

"Like when I feed all my meat loaf to Digger?"

"Sorry, sweetie," she said, patting his back, "but that's just plain orneriness you've got to work through. I'm talking *major* wrongs."

"Oh."

"Bottom line, though they don't know it—at least not Boone—Belle and Boone are pretty powerful Fairies, and the Underworld King likes nothing better than to take the most powerful Fairies and mess with 'em."

"Like how?"

Maude got a scared look in her eyes. "I'm not sure.

All I know is, the folks we love might be in some mighty big trouble, so—"

"So what we need to do is pray they come home safe," Lila said. "The end."

Ewan's aunt crossed the room to put her hands over his ears, but he still heard when she said, "What are you trying to do, scare the poor boy half to death? You will *not* tell him about one of us wishing ourselves down into the belly of that awful place. I won't have him traumatized any more than he already—"

At the same time as another bolt of lightning struck, thunder shook the house's bones.

Digger came running through his doggy door.

Uncle Phil gave the dog a dirty look, like he was gonna get mud all over the floor, but before he could start yelling, someone knocked on the front door.

"Philbert! Lila! Y'all in there?"

Aunt Lila and Uncle Philbert shared a look, then Philbert walked over to let in Sheriff Walters.

Digger walked over to sniff the sheriff's muddy feet.

Ewan cringed. Boy, was Philbert fixin' to yell.

"What're y'all doin' just sittin' around?" the scruffy-bearded, round little sheriff said. "Haven't you heard any news? We've got to get y'all out of here. That crack in the earth is headin' straight for this—whoa!"

The house started moving. All Lila's knick-knacks were jumping around as if some great big dog had picked up their house with his teeth and was giving it a shake.

Ewan tried getting to his aunt and uncle, but parts of the ceiling fell down, dividing the room.

He tried getting to Maude, but the sofa had fallen through a huge hole in the floor.

Digger was whining and crying.

Ewan went over to him, trying to keep him safe, but then the dog fell through the hole.

Digger's crying was awful. Even worse was his sudden silence a moment later.

Was he dead?

The sheriff ran out the front door, hollering for Ewan to follow, but Ewan was frozen with fear.

Digger? Where are you? Are you dead? Lila? Maude? Uncle Phil?

Ewan tried hard not to cry, but he wasn't sure if he could hold off much longer. What was happening? Was this the end of the world? Was everyone he loved dead?

He thought about what Maude had been telling him. About the two brothers being in a fight.

He thought about Aunt Lila covering his ears when Maude had been about to tell him one of the grownups was planning on using Lila's wings to wish themselves to the Underworld.

Hell—that was where Belle and Boone were.

If he went to get them, would they know how to fix all of this? Could they make everything right?

Taking the stairs two at a time, Ewan figured there was only one way to find out, and it started with getting Aunt Lila's wings.

Belle's stomach knotted as she gripped the cage bars so hard her knuckles turned white.

Keep swimming, she willed to the man she loved. *You can do it, you know you can do it . . .*

"Oh, look," the king said—Belle refused to think of this monster as her father. "She's crying. Isn't that sweet?"

"Can't we just hold him under?" one of the blondes asked, unwrapping a new sucker. "This is getting boring."

"Patience," he said. "You must learn the fine art of watching mortals suffer, Denise. It's like learning to appreciate fine wine."

The other blonde laughed. "I like cheap wine and even cheaper thrills."

The girls high-fived each other over their boss.

Belle's soft cries turned to sobs. "Boone!" she screamed. "Don't you go under!"

"See?" the king said with a satisfied smile. "This party's livening up already."

"Boone, please," Belle begged. "Please don't give up."

Fingertips on her temples, she said over and over the spell that allowed her to fly anywhere on the planet on the fare of her slightest whim. In this case, though, their captor had been right. Without her wings, her spell was useless.

She looked up. "Boone! Your wings! Fly, Boone! Fly!"

"She's a little short on gray matter," the blonde with the sucker said. "Can't she see his wings are frozen to his back?"

Sure enough, they were.

And on that note, all hope was lost.

Chapter Twenty

The house shook so badly, Ewan had to press his hands to the walls just to shuffle down the upstairs hall.

Crash!

When he got in front of Belle's room, part of the ceiling caved in.

Rain plunged through the hole, mixing with fallen plaster and dust, making the wood floor feel like the muddy pond trail.

He'd slipped there that afternoon with Boone, and Boone had saved him from gobs of trouble. Uncle Philbert hated it when Ewan got mud all over the house. He'd have been grounded for sure.

"I'm gonna return the favor, Boone," Ewan said now. "I'm not gonna let you down."

Ewan's teeth chattered, while at the same time he felt hot and queasy, but still he kept on.

If I can just get to Lila's wings . . .

He'd seen Belle use her wings lots of times. It didn't seem hard. All you had to do was believe.

Finally he was there, just a few feet from Lila's door, but just as he slid his way through, part of her ceiling caved in, blocking the way to the special closet where she kept her wings.

What he wanted to do was sit down and cry, but if he was gonna save Belle and their new friend, Boone, Ewan knew he had to keep going.

Imagining himself out in the yard playing king of the mountain, he began to climb over the pile of timber and shingles. When nails clawed through his jeans, gashing his legs, he didn't care about that, either.

With Digger and the rest of his family gone, he had to save Belle and Boone.

Saving them was all that mattered.

Belle had made a great substitute mom to him, but he'd always wanted more.

A *real* mom and dad.

Sure, he thought, tossing aside a big board, then wiping cold rain from his eyes, he hardly knew Boone, but something about just being with him told Ewan he'd make a great dad if only he'd marry Belle. Maybe then Boone and Belle would adopt him.

But how were they going to do that if they died?

More determined than ever, Ewan kept climbing, then finally he could see it—Lila's closet door. But only half of it was showing—the top half. The bottom half was covered with more wood and shingles and stuff.

Crash!

A tree branch punched through the window, blocking the top half of the door, too.

Ewan tried staying strong, but his arms and legs were bleeding and he was tired.

Really, really tired.

Collapsing right there on the floor, he tried swallowing his tears of fright and frustration, but, like the obstacles in his path, the tears just kept coming.

Everyone he loved was dead.

Digger. Aunt Lila and Uncle Philbert. Even Boone's mom. Ewan was sorry he'd thought her perfume smelled bad. If he could smell it again right now, he'd promise to think it smelled pretty. Only he knew by the heavy feeling in his heart that all the promises in the world weren't going to bring her back, just like he'd failed in his mission to bring Belle and Boone back.

Besides, even if he did save them, look what they'd come home to.

There was no more home.

Ewan didn't think it was possible, but the house shook even harder.

Rain poured through the holes in the roof even harder, and then it felt like the whole floor was falling out from under him—probably because it was.

Bam!

After a terrifying fall that'd happened so fast, he wouldn't have believed it if he weren't now sitting on a pile of shingles in the kitchen.

Ewan's heart beat so hard, he was afraid it might explode out of his chest.

How was he going to get back upstairs?

How was he going to save Belle and Boone?

Crying, shaking, bleeding, he pushed himself up.

If he had to claw his way through Lila's closet door, he would.

The big house shuddered again, puking more of the upstairs down.

Ewan threw his hands over his head, protecting himself from the plaster rain, when out of the gloomy green darkness he saw them: Lila's wings! He wouldn't have to climb back upstairs after all. The upstairs had come to him!

Brushing more muck from his face and eyes, he grabbed the wings and strapped them on.

Okay, he needed a rhyming spell.

Hands on his forehead, he willed the stuff from his head, just like when he was taking a really hard math test.

"Come on," he said. "What does Belle say whenever she flies?"

More stuff fell around him, but Ewan climbed to the top of the pile where nothing more could fall on him but rain.

The storm pounded him, wiping the dust and muck and blood clean, wiping his mind clean so he could think.

"Oh, great and mighty—no . . ." Fingers squeezing his forehead, he tried again. Okay, Belle always started the rhyme a certain way, then added in the names of the kids she was going to buy the teeth from. But how did it go?

However . . . Whenever . . . It definitely started with a *w*.

Wherever!

Okay, he had the first word, the rest should be easy. Closing his eyes and scrunching up his face from concentrating so hard, he said, "Wherever Belle and Boone may be, oh, spirits of light and air, please help me find them by taking me directly there."

He did it!

He'd remembered every bit of it.

For a second he felt as happy as when the vet had

saved Digger after he'd been hit by a car. But then Ewan realized, what did he have to be happy about? It wasn't like he was actually going anywhere. And this time, Digger hadn't been saved.

In his mind, Ewan said the rhyme again and again until finally a shimmering rainbow bubble swallowed him, and then he was teeny tiny and floating, floating until—poof!

The bubble popped and he was stepping out onto the other side—wherever that was!

"Boone!"

Ewan turned to see Belle stuck in a cage. She was screaming for Boone to keep swimming.

The whole room was blue ice. And there was Boone, looking like he was about to drown in a watery pit with big chunks of ice in it. What was this awful place?

"Welcome," some dude dressed in a black suit said to him. He'd been sitting on a black sofa with two girls, but he stood up and slowly walked toward Ewan holding out his hand like he wanted Ewan to shake it. "I've been expecting you. I must say you're a persistent little fella." The dude in the suit raised his chin and smiled. "Chip off the old block, eh?"

"I'm not little," Ewan said, raising his chin.

"Ewan!" Belle cried. "Get away from him! Run as fast as you can!"

The way Ewan's heart was pounding in his chest, he figured Belle was probably right. He should run, but he'd come too far to even think about giving up now.

Belle was back to screaming at Boone, and then him, and with all that noise, Ewan had a hard time thinking straight.

Who was this guy? And why was he keeping Belle in

a cage and trying to drown Boone? What had they ever done to him?

"They were happy," Suit Dude said, like he was wearing headphones into Ewan's mind. "If there's one thing I can't stand, it's happy." The man shuddered. "Just thinking about it gives me indigestion. So," he said, hand on Ewan's back, guiding him toward the sofa and two almost naked girls. "What can I do for you?"

"Let Belle and Boone go."

"Mmm . . . you're a scrappy little thing. I like that."

"I already told you I'm not little."

"So you did." The man clapped his hands, and where the black sofa and the girls had been there appeared a supercool video-game room and a table loaded with pizza and cans of Pepsi and great bowls filled with candy bars and popcorn.

At one end of the room there was even a big movie screen, and on it played the action flick he'd begged Philbert to take him to see.

"Wow," Ewan said, slowly heading that way.

"Ewan!" he vaguely heard Belle cry. "Sweetie, don't go near any of that! It's a trap! This man is tricky! Nothing here is as it seems!"

"Cool!" Ewan cried, slipping off Lila's wings and dropping them on the ice floor. "You've got every single Xbox game and Playstation 2 and Game Cube and—" He grabbed a handful of popcorn in one hand and a slice of cheese pizza in the other.

Man, Maude told him Belle and Boone were in a place like hell, but this place seemed more like heaven to him.

"That's right," the dude said. "This *is* heaven, Ewan. Little—I'm sorry, *big* boy heaven. All for you."

"*Ewan! Nooooo!*"

Ewan heard Belle, but as if she were shouting from far off. And anyway, what would it hurt just to play a few quick games?

"*Ewan, please, sweetie! I love you! Please don't go any farther!*"

Ewan took a bite of pizza and slowly chewed.

Man, he'd had a rough day.

Much worse than that time he'd gotten grounded for dumping Lila's sardines in the pond to see if they'd come back to life. And anyway, he didn't even see why she ate them, seeing how they were nasty and . . . he took another bite of pizza.

Mmm . . . really good.

That whole thing with the sardines hadn't been his fault. Nothing was his fault. He was a good kid. The greatest.

"*Ewan!*" Belle cried, her voice farther and farther away. "*Get Lila's wings! Say the spell! Save yourself, right now!*"

Save himself? From what? This was a pretty awesome setup. The best. Almost too good to be true.

Too good to be true . . .

Ewan looked over at Belle. She was screaming and crying and shaking the bars of her cage.

And there was Boone, shivering and almost as blue as the cave's ice walls.

But wait a minute. Screaming? Shivering? Why, when there was a nice, crackling fire and all this fun stuff to do and eat?

"*Ewan, please!*" Belle crumpled to her knees.

Man, she was crying as hard as he'd cried back at the house.

Back at the house . . .

309

So what was he doing here?

He set his food on the edge of the table, pressing his fingers to his forehead.

Think, Ewan, think.

"Why think?" the dude said. "There will be plenty of time for that later. Right now, why don't you just enjoy yourself? Take a load off." He smiled real big—creepy big. "Chill."

"I don't know . . ." Ewan glanced back over at Belle and Boone. They didn't look so hot. "Why don't you let them go first? Then I could have some fun."

"Sure," the man said. "You grab your pizza and pick a game, and I'll set them free."

"You will?" Ewan raised his eyebrows.

"Of course I will."

Ewan ran off to play, when *bam*. He was in a cage, too, and all the fun stuff was gone. There was nothing but an ice floor and the popcorn that'd spilled from his hand.

"Not." The dude—*crazy* dude—laughed so hard he snorted.

Ewan felt like crying. Kind of like what Belle was doing, but he couldn't cry when he was so freakin' mad! This guy had tricked him. Made him forget all about saving his friends.

"I hate you!" Ewan spat. "Let Belle and Boone go. They're really nice people, and I'm just some dumb kid who couldn't even remember I came here to save them."

"Go on," the man said.

"So just keep me and let them go. I'm not even Belle's real kid, but just some orphan she picked up on some church pew. I'm not important, but Belle's the

Tooth Fairy. Lots of kids need her, not just me. And Belle needs Boone. I think she loves him. So anyway, just keep me, and I promise to work real hard and do whatever you tell me to and—"

"Stop it, Ewan!" Belle cried. "You *are* my son! I only said you weren't so I could keep my job! Please, sweetheart, reach through those bars and use Lila's wings! I love you—use those wings to wish yourself somewhere safe!"

You are *my son!*

Was it true? Could it really be true? How many times had he wished and hoped? But why hadn't she told him? He was good at keeping secrets. After all, he hadn't told anyone about her being a Fairy. Didn't she love him enough to trust him?

"No," Crazy Dude said in a kind tone. "She didn't trust you. In fact, all this time she's been ashamed of you. That's why she never told you the truth."

"That's not true," Belle said, crying all the harder. "Keeping you a secret was horribly wrong, Ewan, but I only did it to save you—so that we could all be together. Philbert and Lila were both retired. We had to have the money from my job to live. I didn't want you to grow up like me, sweetie—without any mom. This way, I was always there for you. I love you, baby. Please don't ever doubt how much I love you."

"Really?" Ewan had tried awfully hard not to cry, but seeing Belle like that, sad because to keep her job as Tooth Fairy she'd had to lie to him . . . well, instead of being mad at her, it kind of made him proud. Like he'd helped her on an important mission. And hey, if he was truly her son, that meant he was part Fairy, too! And one day he might even be an Easter Bunny like Uncle Phil!

311

Suit Dude laughed. "Oh, no, my child. Do you honestly think this bad woman who's hidden so much from you would ever allow you to be a *real* Fairy? Now, if you chose to stay with me, then—"

"Enough, Darious!" a woman's voice commanded from somewhere over Ewan's head.

Blinding white light shot from the cave's ceiling, filling the once-gloomy room with glowing heat.

Like magic, Boone rose from the pool.

Belle's cage bars dissolved.

Belle ran to Boone, taking off her robe to wrap around him where he lay shivering on the cavern's ice floor.

Ewan's cage disappeared, too, so he ran over to Belle, cowering beside her, helping her keep Boone warm.

Beside Crazy Dude another light struck with a high-pitched humming noise, and then the noise stopped, and a beautiful woman stood beside him. She had long red hair, was barefoot and wore faded jeans and a sky-blue T-shirt that said *Peace Out*.

Staring the man up and down, arms crossed, she shook her head. "The whole family has really had it with you. And after this stunt, you can just forget being invited to Fantasia's birthday."

"So. I didn't want to go anyway."

"Good. 'Cause you're not." Tucking her hair behind her ears, she eyed the trio shivering on the ice. With but one nod, Light circled them and the shivering stopped. "Rules being rules," she said, "I've had to stand by and watch you play dirty pool, but no more. A grown woman sacrificing herself is one thing, but a child sacrificing himself to save his mother? Game over."

"But you heard the kid. Until just now, she's been such a horrid mother she didn't even bother telling him she was his mom."

"And why is that?" the woman asked. "Because of more stupid rules."

"Yes, but—"

She held her hand up palm out. "Talk to the hand 'cause the heart isn't listening. We're out of here."

"But, Feliciatoria, wait—"

Too late.

The four of them were already gone.

Damn.

Darious clapped his hands and his black couch reappeared, sans the girls.

Oooh, how he hated family. Always lousing up his life just when it was getting good.

"It's beautiful . . ." The three of them were back on Belle's family farm, only it wasn't the farm as she'd known it, but better.

The grass was greener—plush, like carpet. Acres and acres of sweet-smelling flowerbeds were painted in purples and yellows and pinks. There were fountains—too many to count. And the house itself had been extensively remodeled with a fresh regal-white paint job and Aunt Lila's antebellum columns and fainting porch.

Only now, Belle's dear aunt wasn't fainting, but dashing down the steps. Ewan's hound dog Digger and Philbert and Maude were right behind her.

Leaning closer into Boone, tucking a protective arm around Ewan, Belle had to wonder if this was all a dream, or another of *his* tricks?

"There's my boy," Maude said, crushing Boone in a

hug. He was once again dressed in his jeans—the ones that made Belle's cheeks blaze upon remembering where they'd been left. Belle was back in her boxers and T-shirt. Too weird.

"Guess what, Aunt Lila." Ewan said. "Guess what."

The sight of her brave son excitedly jumping up and down removed the questions from Belle's heart and filled it with pride.

"Belle's not just Belle anymore, but my mom."

"Well, sweetheart," Lila said, "that's the best thing I've heard all day."

Ewan turned to Belle, looking up at her with such love that she hated herself all over again for not telling him sooner. "I can call you that—*Mom*—can't I?"

Too choked-up to speak, Belle nodded, hugging him close. "I love you," she said, kissing the top of his head. "I don't deserve you. I'm so, so sorry."

"Mom," he said in the condescending tone only kids can. "Stop crying, and look at this place. It was gone. And I mean like wiped off the planet *gone*. Digger died. And Lila and Phil and Maude and the sheriff—they were gone, too. You gotta be happy. We've got our house back, and all our family, and now I've even got a real mom."

You always have, baby. You always have.

Belle nodded, only now gathering the courage to look at her aunt to whom she'd also lied for so many years. "Hi, Lila. I've missed you."

"Lordy, girl, I've missed you, too." Without a single look of disappointment or condemnation over the fact that for the second time in the Moody family history, one of them was going to be stripped of her wings, Lila pulled her close.

Belle melted in her arms.

All of this—it was amazing.

The house.

The love.

Almost too good to be real, but it was. But then, making love with Boone had felt real, and look where that had landed them.

All of a sudden, even in the midst of joyous hugging and tears, Belle couldn't shake the feeling that everything wasn't quite right, but she supposed such a feeling was only natural after all they'd been through. Being rescued from the Underworld by one of the Immortals wasn't something that happened every day.

It stood to reason she'd still be a little shaken up.

Long after everyone had gotten their fill of hugging, and Digger had settled in for a nap on one of the new lawn chairs out back, and the news of her being Ewan's real mother was openly and shamelessly rejoiced over, as was her recent engagement to Boone, Lila fixed a delicious lunch in her newly remodeled kitchen.

Chicken salad and fresh sliced peaches. Homemade sugar cookies, and even ice cream for dessert that Uncle Philbert and Boone took turns handcranking by the swimming pool.

The swimming pool!

There'd never been one of those before.

Still shaking her head at the transformation her house and family had undergone, Belle went inside to make a fresh batch of iced tea when she got a shock to find the red-haired Immortal seated on the marble-topped counter, swinging her bare feet.

"Hi," she said.

"Um . . . hi." Belle wasn't sure if she was supposed to

bow, or avert her eyes, or what, so she did both—just in case.

"No, no, no," the woman said, hopping off the counter to tug Belle upright. "See? This is what I hate about my job. No one seems to get the fact that I'm just regular folks. Anyway," she said, snatching a potato chip out of an open bag Ewan had left on the new kitchen table, "I'm sensing, like, a huge amount of doubt from you. Wanna talk?"

Belle put her hands over her mouth.

No way was this really happening.

Talking with the King of the Underworld that morning, then an Immortal that afternoon.

Her legs turned to rubber, and a hot flash made her palms sweat and her head spin.

The Immortal eyed her funnily, then slipped her arm about Belle's waist, guiding her to the posh new white-and-gold living room. "Maybe you ought to sit down."

Belle nodded, heeding the woman's advice.

"First off," the woman said, sitting cross-legged beside her on the gold brocade sofa, reaching for Belle's right hand and giving it a squeeze, "I'm sorry my brother put you and your family through all of that. He has issues. Dad's looking into a good clinic to ship him to."

"Oh."

"Second—"

"Everything all right in—" Plate in hand, Boone sauntered into the room, Digger hot on his heels, doggy eyes hopeful for a handout. "Oh, hey, I didn't know you had comp—" Boone's silvery eyes widened. "It's you . . ."

"Feeling better?" the Immortal asked.

Stumbling into the nearest chair, he nodded.

"Maybe it's a good thing the two of you are together for this," she said. "Boone, I was just about to tell Belle, that you two will have to be especially diligent in teaching this child of yours the ways of the Light as opposed to the Dark. Through no fault of your own, the two of you have a considerable amount of Darkness flowing through you. Your child will have even more, which is why my brother has taken such an interest in your union. Together you become a powerful force, for either Light or Dark. The choice is ultimately yours, as it will be for your child, but"—she laughed— "let's just say that, like my brother, I'm not above a little bribery to win you over to my side."

"I have a question," Boone asked, plate on his lap, hand absentmindedly rubbing behind Digger's ears.

"Shoot," the woman said with a brilliant smile.

"What about these?" With his free hand, he pointed to his wings.

Her smile faded. "I'm afraid that, like your Darkness, they're a part of you. The fact that they are still there means a part of your soul still wars with your decision." She looked down, then back up. "I don't mean to meddle in your business, but do you think there's a chance that part of you *enjoyed* being Dark?"

He sighed, raked his fingers through his hair.

Belle's heart cried out to him. They'd already been through so much. Why this? Why now? Why couldn't he embrace the Light within himself? Within her?

"Well," the woman said, "you two seem like you have a lot to talk about, so I'm outta here. Peace out," she said with a big grin before gliding in a ball of light right through the front door—the *closed* front door.

317

After a few pregnant moments, the silence of which was almost too much to bear, Belle said, "Talk to me, Boone. What're you thinking?"

He laughed, but it wasn't a happy laugh, but one teaming with irony and pain.

A splash sounded out back in the pool, followed by Ewan's happy shriek.

Digger clambered to his feet, charging out his kitchen doggy door.

Boone's gaze followed the dog's path before he sadly turned to her. "Do you have any idea how many lies I've told you?"

Swallowing hard, she shook her head.

"Because I thought you were out to con me, I told you I was broke. And that my mother was dying. You know, maybe to gain sympathy points in case part of you was *human*." He laughed. "Funny, though, how it turns out neither of us were human—especially me."

"So she's okay, then? Your mom?"

He nodded.

"That's good." Water under the bridge. What did any of what happened between them on the farm matter now that they were together on a so much deeper level?

Who cared how they'd gotten there? It only mattered that they stayed.

Rising from the sofa, Belle went to him, fell on her knees in front of him. Grasping his big hands in her small ones, she said, "Make love to me. Please."

"With these wings—I . . . how? It's too dangerous. You have your family to think of. I love you too much to risk the Dark rising in you."

Eyes welling with tears, heart actually physically aching, she said, "After the miracle we've just experienced, Boone, you of all people should know that where there's a will there's a way."

Casting her a cautious smile, he squeezed her hands and said, "Show me that way, Belle. *Please*, show me that way."

Chapter Twenty-one

This time, there was no fevered groping to take off their clothes, only a slow and easy building of momentum, of dreams, until Boone stood proud and naked braced against Belle's bedroom wall, sheathed inside her, her legs wrapped around his waist, her arms around his neck, her heart around his soul.

He loved this woman with a purity he hadn't known existed. Wanted her with fire he hadn't known could burn so hot.

He was scared to death of losing her.

Downright terrified of keeping her.

He kissed her long and deep and hard, and she kissed him back, tasting of sugar cookies.

"I love you," she said, hand cupping his stubbled cheek. He should've shaved for her. But then, hell, if a part of him couldn't even shed this damned Darkness for her, for her son, the son he'd like to be his, then what good was a shave?

"I love you," he said, "but—"

Fingers to his lips, she silenced him, and he let her.

There'd be time enough for talk later.

Right now, he just wanted to feel.

The hot, sweet slickness of her shelter, her warmth.

In and out he thrust, whispering dozens of good-byes, or maybe hellos. He wasn't sure. Couldn't be sure. All he could do was love her, cherish her, grip his fingers into her soft, sweet bottom, plunging deeper, kissing her deeper, showing her with his tongue what his heart couldn't find words to say.

She mewed, bit his shoulder. "Yes. Oh my gosh, yes."

He thrust still harder, feeling the power of her, of their union, from his toes to the tips of his damned wings.

Yes, dammit, he wanted to embrace the Light. For if being with her like this was considered Dark, he was a dead man walking.

He couldn't be with her and not have her.

Her mews intensified, and she bit him harder to keep from crying out her pleasure.

He felt his end approach, and it seized him with hot/cold chills. It was building and building and he was falling and falling. There was no more denying it.

He *was* Dark.

Desperate.

These damnable wings pulsing with pleasure were his proof. His shame.

There was no saving him.

He could only save her.

Ewan.

And so with one last, shimmering thrust, he exploded inside her, then started the long mental journey to leave them both.

"You've been awfully quiet tonight," Belle said, cozying up to Boone in the back row of their new home theater. Ewan was in his glory in the front row with a big bucket of popcorn on one side and Digger on the other. He'd wanted to invite a friend, but in light of Boone's wings, inviting anyone over outside of family was out of the question.

After a long, boisterous family dinner, Lila had gone to her room to watch her shows on her new flat-screen TV. Philbert and Lila launched WW III over a game of Scrabble.

Taking Belle's hand, lacing their fingers, then kissing her inner wrist, Boone said, "My mood's nothing personal. Guess I'm just tired."

She grinned. "That's too bad. I had my heart set on a repeat of this afternoon's performance." It might be selfish, but she needed something to get her mind off of her impending meeting with the Fairy Council.

That afternoon, as was his duty as head of their household, Philbert had notified the Council of her change in status. Effective immediately, she had been stripped of all of her Tooth Fairy duties. All that was left to do was make her formal return of her uniform and wings. But she'd take care of that tomorrow.

She could tell that Philbert had been sick over turning her in, but she'd understood, and harbored no ill will. Being with Boone, openly rejoicing in the miracle of her son—those were her decisions.

Her new life.

Just thinking about the exciting new future the three of them would share made her all tingly inside, as did thinking about once again being in Boone's arms. "Well?" she asked. "Wanna sneak off to the barn for some smooching?"

He smiled, but the emotion didn't reach his eyes. *You're still worried about your wings, aren't you?* She wanted to ask the question but was afraid of his answer. It stood to reason that, just as she had set her mind on tidying up the still unraveled pieces of her old life, so had Boone. Yes, having a husband for herself and a father for Ewan who sported a large set of wings was going to pose the occasional problem, but it was nothing she couldn't work around. She only prayed that, with time, Boone would feel the same.

Midway through the movie, she yawned, and after they said good night to Ewan, Boone walked Belle to her bedroom door. "Every bone in my body wants to go in there with you," he said.

Her arms circling his waist, she said, "I want you to come, but I suppose that after this afternoon's transgression we ought to behave until the wedding, huh?"

"You still want to marry me?" He swept the hair back from her forehead. "What about your job?"

She looked down. "I'll miss it, but, geesh, even if I hadn't just broken my every vow, I'd just signed a new ten-year contract. Are you really prepared to wait that long?"

His answer was a kiss that left her weak and dizzy in every part of her but her heart. That beat strong and true for the man she'd always dreamt of finding but never thought she actually would.

"I love you," she said, standing on her tiptoes for one last kiss before bed. "Good night."

Goodbye.

Hands shoved into his pocket, Boone took a deep breath, then forced himself to turn his back and heart on the only woman he'd ever loved.

* * *

Hours later, long after all in the house had stilled, Boone crept out the front door.

He hated this.

Skulking off in the middle of the night—not even saying goodbye to his own mother. But what else could he do? No way was he subjecting any more of the people he loved to this Dark side of himself, so if leaving them protected them, it was obviously the only thing he could do.

Down the porch steps, midway across the lawn, he turned around for one last look.

Digger came loping up, nudging his head under Boone's palm for a rub. Tears flooding his eyes, Boone gave the dog what he wanted, wishing he could just for once get what he wanted. Peace. A little contentment.

"I love you," he whispered to the dog. To the occupants inside the house. He took one last deep breath, then prepared for flight.

"Going somewhere?" asked a voice out of the darkness—this time a human voice. Philbert.

"Yeah," Boone said. "I was just heading back to my farm to grab a few clothes, then—"

"We have clothing stores here in town."

"Sure, but I, ah, need to check on my livestock."

"Maude said you had all your livestock brought to her house days ago."

Boone looked at his feet. "As I'm sure you full well know, Mr. Moody, I'm leaving to protect your niece and nephew. You. Hell, I'd think that you more than anyone would be glad to see me go."

"Is that what you think of me? That just because of what happened your first night here, I'd want to see Belle and Ewan heartbroken?"

Boone laughed sharply. "You were the one who greeted me with an ax aimed at my chest."

"And you know full well why."

"Right. Because I'm a freakin' Bogeyman. I'm a danger not only to myself, but to everyone I'm around. That's why I'm leaving. All of you—especially Belle and Ewan—will be a damn sight better off without me."

"Don't you think you ought to let Belle and Ewan decide that for themselves?"

"What I think is that you ought to mind your own business."

"*They* are my business. Now, come along inside. There's a lot more I'd like to talk to you about, and it'll go down easier with more of that fried chicken and chocolate cake we had for supper."

"Mom?"

Belle lurched awake, warm sun streaming through her bedroom window. Even better was the sight of her son's big blue eyes.

Mmm . . . how I love being called Mom.

"Good morning, handsome," she said, dragging him squirming and squealing over for big, wet kisses on his cheeks and chin. Once he stopped giggling, she asked, "Did I oversleep again?"

"Nah, you don't have a job anymore, remember?"

"Ugh." She fell back against her pillow. "Thanks for reminding me. But you still have to get ready for school, so what're you doing bugging me when you're supposed to be brushing your gorgeous teeth?" She gave him another kiss topped off with a tickle.

Just talking about teeth in light of knowing she was turning in her wings today was a bummer, but seeing how every other aspect of her life was sheer perfection, she was determined not to let her wing-stripping ceremony get her down.

"It's Saturday," he said. "And anyways, all I came in here to ask is where's Boone? I was gonna ask him to show me some more dives in the pool, but I can't find him anywhere."

"He's not still in bed?"

"Nope."

"And he's not downstairs eating breakfast with his mom or reading the paper?"

Ewan rolled his eyes.

"What?"

"I'm almost nine, Mom. I'm not stupid."

"Did I say you were?" Kissing and tickling her son all over again, certain Boone was just out for a walk—no doubt still worrying about his wings—Belle indulged in a few more minutes' wrestling with her son, then shooed him out to look some more for Boone while she got ready for her big day.

Standing in her closet, she nibbled the inside of her lower lip.

What did one wear to a public hanging?

And—ew! What was a bottle of hot sauce doing in there?

"Mom!" Ewan called from the top of the stairs.

"What, sweetie? I'm trying to get dressed."

Heavy sneakers on, he clomped into her room.

"What's the matter now?" she asked, settling for the black dress she'd worn to a neighbor's funeral last spring, then flicking off the closet light.

She tossed the hot sauce in the trash.

"*Nobody's* here," Ewan said. "Digger's outside, but everyone else . . . it's like they all just vanished."

Goose bumps marched up Belle's forearms.

Please, no.

Not again.

Not after they'd already been through so much.

Forcing herself to take a deep breath, trying to be logical, Belle convinced herself they couldn't have all just disappeared without good reason. "You know what?" she said with an oversized grin. "I bet they all went for a walk down by the pond. They're probably trying to spot your turtle."

"I checked. And Maude and Lila are too afraid of getting ticks to even walk off the porch, let alone go down to the pond."

"True," Belle said with a wry grin, sitting on the foot of the bed. "All right then. I bet they all went shopping. Probably Boone offered to go along. To help lift heavy stuff."

Ewan scrunched his adorable face. "Geez, Mom, how's Boone supposed to walk into the grocery store with no shirt on and wings?"

Her heart sank. "Good point."

Ewan hurled himself backward onto the bed beside her. "Where did they all go?"

On her feet, headed for the bedroom door, Belle said, "Did you check for a note?"

"No." He stood, too.

"Well, there you go. I'm sure they at least left a note."

Together they headed downstairs to the kitchen to check out the fridge doors that served as the household bulletin board.

"Hmm . . ." Belle said when there was nothing but a shopping list and Ewan's school permission slip for an upcoming trip to the Tulsa Zoo.

"Told you," Ewan said.

Belle slid her fingers through her hair.

What did this mean?

On legs gone wobbly, she backed herself into a kitchen chair. Had yesterday been nothing more than a dream? Was she still in the Underworld, gradually losing everyone she held dear?

"Come here," she said, tugging Ewan by the hem of his Spider-Man PJ's T-shirt to get him into her arms. "I'm sure they'll all be back real soon. And when they are, we'll feel silly for worrying."

Wriggling out of her arms, fixing her with a stare far too serious for a boy his age, he said, "Tell me the truth, Mom. D-did . . . *he* . . . take them?"

"No," she said, pulling him back, burying her face in his hair. *Boone, where are you? Why aren't you here? Today, of all days, I need you. I love you.* "No, sweetie, none of us will ever go anywhere near that awful place again."

"You sure?"

"Yep." *Liar.*

Despite being a nervous wreck, Belle managed to get Ewan to eat some cereal and orange slices. Then she dragged herself upstairs for a shower. The whole while she listened intently or looked out any available window for signs of her family's return.

Since her wings were no longer active, a Fairy Council assistant was coming to the house to transport her at noon.

Though Ewan hadn't been invited, there was no way she was leaving him home alone. When the assistant arrived, Belle insisted her son also be transported to the meeting. There was still no sign of Boone or the others.

"Thank you," she said to the wide-eyed receptionist

upon their arrival. The slight blonde curtsied, then turned down one of the endless corridors at the World Fairy Council's New York City headquarters.

"Man," Ewan said, eyes even wider than usual. "This place is huge." The chamber they stood in—on the top floor of one of the world's tallest buildings—had at least a fifty-foot glass ceiling, lined with equally tall walls of windows peering out on the world and sky and sea.

With its white leather and chrome furniture and thick, pale blue carpet, merely standing in the space felt akin to flight—not Fairy flight, but Dark flight.

The kind she'd done with Boone.

"No kidding," Belle said, switching her heavy uniform to her other arm, wishing she could get her mind off of worry for Boone and the others to focus on the matter at hand.

Her first time in this room had been a happy one.

She'd been waiting to be given her uniform and wings.

Gosh, how she'd loved being a Tooth Fairy. Loved knowing she brought joy to so many children. Loved to be doing her part to make the world a happier place.

All things considered, though, she loved Ewan more.

She loved Boone more, and if giving up her career guaranteed a lifetime with them, it would be worth it.

If only Boone were here with her.

She so badly needed his reassurance and support.

But just as she knew how deeply she loved him, she also knew he wouldn't miss this meeting unless it was unavoidable. She just prayed his urgency wasn't of the life-or-death variety they'd only just weathered.

"Ms. Moody," a tall, slim man said from between towering mirrored twin doors. His skin was so pale, he looked more like an undertaker than a Fairy. "The Council will see you now."

She gulped.

Turning to Ewan, she said, "Looks like they have some pretty good magazines. Think you'll be all right out here for just a little bit?"

"I'd rather go with you, Mom. Tell them how good you are at your job."

"I know, baby," she said, wrapping him in a hug, inadvertently burying his little head in pink tulle and sequins. "But this is one time I should be on my own. Yeah, I'm sad about losing my wings, but I deserve to. I told a lot of lies to an awful lot of good people—especially you." She kissed the top of his head. "I love you."

"I love you, too, Mom."

Mom. There was that wonderful word again. The word that gave her strength when the man she needed to lean on was nowhere to be found.

"Ms. Moody," the undertaker said, "the Council has a very full agenda this afternoon."

"Of course." She gave Ewan one last hug before smoothing her hair, then walking through the doors that would strip her of the only identity she'd ever known.

Wiping tears from her eyes, she reassured herself that after the misery of this meeting she'd be forging whole new identities of wife and mother.

"Greetings," said a voice from behind a gauzy blue curtain through which shadows could be seen, but not individual faces. Council members were chosen at random from the Fairy World. Any Fairy in good standing with the current Council was eligible to serve—but not lowlifes like her.

"H-hello," Belle said, mouth dry.

This room, like the reception area, was mostly windows save for the curtain behind which the Council sat.

"Do you have anything to say on your behalf before we begin?"

"Um . . ." There was so much she'd like to say, but did she have the nerve?

Nibbling her lower lip, she thought back to all Boone and her had been through. About how hard she'd struggled over the past decade to keep her family in food, clothing and shelter. About the night she'd first met Boone when she'd convinced all those hoity-toity socialites that she was a far-off glamorous princess instead of a simple country girl.

Did she have the nerve?

In the immortal words of the princess, *Puh-leeze*.

Clinging to the uniform she'd worked so hard to earn, Belle raised her chin. "You know, as a matter of fact, I do have quite a bit to say—starting with the question of why do Tooth Fairies have to be celibate? I mean, I know all about the purity thing, but think about it. For nearly a decade, I've been proof that it doesn't make a hill of beans difference when it comes to being a good Tooth Fairy. Yes, I made a mistake and got pregnant, but the son I ended up with is a miracle—not a mistake. I so deeply believed this that I even paid Tooth Fairy candidate Josie Landers blackmail money to keep quiet about the weekend Ewan was conceived." Belle took a deep, shuddering breath. "I love my job, and I'm sorry I lied to keep it, but you know what? I'd do it again. And I wish my own mother had been as brave. She hung her head in shame. Gave me up to be raised by Fairy relations who you all deemed suitable, but the fact of the matter is . . ."

She paused to wipe tears with the backs of her hands. "The fact is, I needed my mom. I needed her, and all of you and your stupid rules took her away. How many others are out there, unable to stand up to your impossibly high standards? And for that matter, why do Tooth Fairies have to be women? Why does the Easter Bunny always have to be a man? I realize it's too late for me, but for everyone else out there living two lives just to conform to your wishes, please, please," she begged, hugging her uniform, "please give these archaic rules a second look."

"Is that all?" a muffled masculine voice asked.

Unable to speak through her grief, she nodded.

"Very well, then. After a brief deliberation, we'll return."

Deliberation?

Wait a minute.

Hadn't the verdict already been decided?

She was guilty. They all knew it. Why make her stand here another minute more when she should be out looking for Boone and everyone else?

Belle set her uniform on a table at the front of the room, then went to stand in front of the wall of windows. Staring out at the big wide world, dying inside from the enormity of her upcoming search, Belle finally heard the Council's curtain swish.

While the condemned couldn't see those they pleaded their case to, they at least had the right to see who handed out their sentence.

"Ms. Moody," the undertaker said. "The Council is ready to deliver your verdict."

Squeezing her eyes shut on yet another batch of tears, Belle fought for air.

She had to keep it together just a short while longer; then she could be on her way to finding her loved ones and starting her new life.

After a deep, halting breath, she found the courage to slowly turn around.

. . . And be shocked!

Philbert? Maude? Both were seated at the head of the ten-member Council. But how? How had she not known?

And if they were here . . .

Her heart raced at the implication that Boone and Lila might be here, too.

"Ms. Moody," Philbert said.

"Yes?" Though his formality was disarming, it made so much clear. His insistence upon immediately turning her in. His holding an ax over both her and Boone. He was the head of the Fairy Council. If he'd shown one bit of favoritism toward her, the entire fate of the Fairy World could have been jeopardized.

Yet Lila had covered for her all those nights.

Why hadn't he said anything about that?

Or maybe he had?

With an inward groan, she thought, *Yep, I'm toast*.

Sitting ramrod straight, dressed in a flowing white robe, Philbert said, "We very much appreciate your candor with your earlier comments. According to Fairy Law, by all rights, your lies should strip you of your wings, along with your standing in the Fairy Kingdom."

Heart thundering, Belle nodded.

"However, your job performance record is one of the finest ever. This puts us all in the rather awkward position of agreeing with you that your having had a child had no bearing whatsoever on your ability to perform your Tooth Fairy services. Furthermore, we're left wondering if perhaps part of the reason for your out-standing performance is the fact that you *do* have a child. And therefore understand how important it is to make children happy and comfortable in this increasingly uncertain world." He rummaged through a pile of documents, signed three, then said, "Therefore, Ms. Moody, it is the unanimous decision of this Council that, effective immediately, you shall be reinstated in your former position with all titles and privileges formally held."

"B-but . . ." Belle brought her hands to her mouth. No way. "But I'm getting married."

"We are all aware of that fact," her uncle said, his grim demeanor considerably lightened by a wink.

He slammed a diamond-studded silver gavel, then said, "I hereby pronounce this case adjourned. There will be a fifteen-minute recess before our next hearing."

One by one, the Council members descended from their dais, either shaking her hand and congratulating her on reversing centuries-old archaic Fairy Law, or, as in the case of Philbert and Maude, to enfold her in happy hugs.

One by one, they all left the room, and then one very short male and one very tall, very handsome man entered.

Ewan and Boone.

Both smiling.

Boone wore a dark suit. The breadth of his shoulders and chest stole what little remained of her oxygen. Aside from the first night they'd met, she'd never seen him in anything but jeans and a T-shirt, and then no shirt because of his wings.

His wings . . .

"Boone? Your wings. They're—"

"Gone," Ewan interjected. "But that's old news. Hey, Mom, now that you've still got your wings, can I sometimes use 'em to get to the beach?"

"No," she said, laughing through her tears, hugging both her son and the man she felt like slugging for scaring her so badly.

After shooing Ewan back into the reception area to sit with Lila, who'd apparently also come along for the ride without bothering to tell her, Belle, blessedly alone with Boone, lovingly pummeled his chest. "You scared me half to death. Why didn't you tell me you'd be here?"

"Probably because I didn't know until your uncle informed me."

"And that means?" She grinned up at him, cupping her hand to his clean-shaven cheek.

"Long story short, last night I was about to chuck it all—us. Life. The wings scared me. Bad. The fact that they meant there was still a Dark side of me. A part that could turn on you or Ewan, or even the baby at any time." He cradled his hand to her belly. "You are still—"

"Yes. I mean, I assume so. So, who or what do I have to thank for putting some sense into you?"

"Your uncle. I was sneaking out of the house last night when he busted me."

"So? What did he say that my love for you couldn't?" Tears sprang to her eyes at the thought that he really had been on the verge of leaving her forever.

"Oh, Princess," he said, pulling her close, kissing the top of her head. "It was never a matter of me not loving you, but of loving you so damned much, the thought of one day hurting you—and Ewan—wasn't an option. You two represent the fruition of my every dream. You're the total package—right down to Digger, the perfect dog. But as much as I wanted to be part of all that, I couldn't take a chance of destroying you. I was leaving to protect you."

"No more leaving," she said, arms around his waist, loving him to a degree that made her dizzy from the thrill.

"Gotcha."

"Yes, you do."

"You know how happy Ma's gonna be to have royalty in the family?"

Belle reddened. "Boone? Oh my gosh, what're we going to do? I mean, if I show up in Clairemonte Falls as your wife without my Bugoslavian accent, then everyone's going to know—"

"You're right," he said, abruptly releasing her to head for the door. "The wedding's off."

"Are you serious?" she asked, chasing after him.

"No," he said when she spun him around by his sleeve. "And I can't believe you would for a second think I wouldn't marry you to protect my mother's reputation—especially when, just like you said, she started this whole thing."

"But—"

He silenced her with a kiss. A wondrous kiss that curled her toes and rocked her soul. "Are you always going to argue this much, Princess? 'Cause if so, then maybe I should find a more agreeable woman who—"

"Do you need a spanking?"

"Mmm . . ." He shot her the lazy grin that'd claimed her so many days ago back on the farm. "Spank me, Princess. Spank me."

Feigning boredom instead of being turned on right there in the Fairy Council's chamber, Belle rolled her eyes. "Figures you'd like it."

"You might, too," he said, giving her a light smack on her behind before scooping her uniform up with one hand and guiding her out of the room with the other.

She sighed contentedly. "Is this what I have to look forward to for the next seventy or so years?"

He winked. "If you're lucky."

Kissing Frogs
Laura Marie Altom

Biologist Lucy Gordon has one chance in a million to capture her every dream. It all depends upon her discovering a new species of frog. Then one day, by a miraculous twist of fate, that frog finds her. Consumed with joy, she kisses the little bugger smack dab on his lips.

Poof! As magically as he'd appeared, he is gone. In his place is a wholly naked, wholly medieval bad-boy prince who claims she's saved him from an amphibian eternity. When the gorgeous prince returns her kiss and her soul melts, her choice between frog and prince becomes less clear. With the power to transform Wolfe back into a wart-covered creature, Lucy has to choose her own happily ever after: fame, money, and respect? Or love?

KATE ANGELL
DRIVE ME CRAZY

Cade Nyland doesn't think that anything good can come of the new dent in his classic black Sting Ray, even if it does happen at the hands of a sexy young woman. He is determined to win his twelfth road rally race of the year.

TZ Blake only enters Chugger Charlie's tight butt competition to win enough money to keep her auto repair shop open. What she ends up with is a position as navigator in a rally race. All she has to do is pretend she knows where she is going. All factors indicate that the unlikely duo is in for a bumpy ride . . . and each eagerly anticipates the jostling that will bring them closer together.